Praise for CBA Bestselling Author Lori Copeland

"As always, Lori Copeland manages to find something new and fresh to bring to her 'love and laughter' western romances. The wild ostriches, the cast of delightful, endearing characters and the added mystery all lend themselves to making *Bridal Lace and Buckskin* a delight!"
—*Romantic Times BOOKreviews*

"Copeland produces a wacky jumble of humorous characters beset by serious circumstances. Joy wins in the end."
—*Romantic Times BOOKreviews* on
A Case of Crooked Letters

"A riveting adventure in page-turning mystery and laugh-out-loud humor. Lori Copeland at her best!"
—Karen Kingsbury, bestselling author of the
Redemption series on *A Case of Bad Taste*

"The characters in *A Case of Bad Taste* are both fun and frustrating, mischievous and maddening.
As Maude says, 'Life's a hoot!'"
—Bestselling author Brandilyn Collins

"Filled with emotion, danger and humor,
Ruth is sure to warm your heart."
—*Romantic Times BOOKreviews*

LORI COPELAND

Refreshed version of
BRIDAL LACE AND BUCKSKIN,
newly revised by author

Steeple
Hill®

Published by Steeple Hill Books™

STEEPLE HILL BOOKS

Steeple
Hill®

ISBN-13: 978-0-373-78572-8
ISBN-10:   0-373-78572-0

YELLOW ROSE BRIDE

This is the revised text of a work first published as
BRIDAL LACE & BUCKSKIN by Ivy Books in 1996.

Copyright © 1996 as BRIDAL LACE AND BUCKSKIN
by Lori Copeland

Copyright © 2006 as YELLOW ROSE BRIDE
by Copeland, Inc.

www.SteepleHill.com

Printed in U.S.A.

To Cheryl Hodde, Brenda Minton and Barbara Warren:
gal pals who keep me laughing through the
ups and downs of publishing.

Dear Reader,

Often an author gets the privilege to revise older novels—to go back and say all the things she meant to say but didn't. *Yellow Rose Bride* is such a book. Originally published in 1996 in the secular market as *Bridal Lace and Buckskin*, Vonnie and Adam's story quickly became a favorite with readers.

In 1998, I moved to the Christian market, where I now publish exclusively, but my older work lives on. I was asked to rewrite *Buckskin* for the Christian market, a God-given opportunity to portray the characters and their values in a new light. I hope you'll enjoy the story—laugh and cry with a couple destined to be together both here and in eternity.

Warmly,

Prologue

Louisiana/Texas Border, 1865

A beleaguered set of riders topped a rise. Shoulders rounded and heads bobbing with fatigue, the weary band rode slowly toward home.

Heat rose from the rutted surface in shimmering mirages; the horses' heavy hooves left puffs of dry dust in the air. The backs and underarms of the men's uniforms showed dark sweat pouring from bodies so thin that bones poked through their pale skin.

The soldiers were young, mere boys. War had aged them far beyond their years, stripped their faces of innocence, toughened their hearts and attitudes. Fatigue and bitterness marked their features now; their eyes darted warily to every bush and ditch.

Could it have been only three short years since they had ridden away from their families, filled with idealism, confident of victory?

"Let the Yanks come!" they'd shouted. The South would give them what-for and send them packing, tails tucked in shame.

With fear in their hearts and prayers on their lips, mothers had watched their sons ride into battle.

Fathers had stood by, grim faced, throats working against painful knots that choked the very life from their hearts. A man didn't cry, but he hurt. Hurt real bad.

Reaching the crossroad, the soldiers paused to shake hands.

Removing his hat, the oldest, El Johnson, spoke first, his voice dry and void of emotion. "Guess this is where we split up." Horses shied, tails switching flies.

The men nodded briefly before reining their horses in opposite directions.

They had ridden only a few yards before El turned to shout over his shoulder. "No need to let this ruin our lives. War is war. A man ought not be judged for doing what he's called to do."

Now they were forced to relive the past few hours. There wasn't a one who would say they had intended it to happen. Coming up on that family—

Nerves frayed, tempers short. The war was over, but apparently the family hadn't heard the news.

Each rider searched his conscience for some explanation, a straw to grasp to alleviate his own guilt. Had he believed his life to be at stake? Was that why it happened?

There was no way of knowing now whether the family meant them harm. But if the farmer hadn't pulled his rifle…if El hadn't panicked and fired first…

If.

If.

It had all happened so fast. One minute they were warily eyeing each other, the next, violence erupted.

Brutal, unflinching violence.

Shots rang out. Screams filled the air.

Why? God, why?

Heat wrapped around the men like a wet blanket, stifling and oppressive. The air smelled of sweat and blood. Time had stood still.

Afterward, the riders stared transfixed at the lifeless bodies slumped on the blood-soaked ground, horrified by the unexpected brutality. The old man, his wife, two sons and a daughter stared sightlessly up at them.

No matter how many times the men had witnessed death, it made them sick to their stomachs. How did such injustice happen? They weren't bent on vengeance. They were going home.

Home!

The war was over—there wasn't going to be any more killing in the name of glory.

The tangible smell of death had hung thick in the air. Teague Taylor finally spoke, his voice a harsh whisper. "Let's get out of here."

The men had stood paralyzed, hats in hand, tears rolling from the corners of their eyes as they viewed the carnage. Franz began to recite The Lord's Prayer in a hushed, heavy

German accent. P.K. suddenly bolted toward the bushes to be sick.

Finally, Teague spoke. "We can't just leave them here. We have to bury them."

They studied the young girl, maybe three, four years old, a rag doll still clutched tightly to the front of her bloody dress.

"Somebody's *got* to bury them. It's not fittin' to leave them here like this," Teague demanded.

P.K. and Franz quietly moved toward their horses for shovels.

As the sound of steel bit into earth, El said that he was going to search the wagon for valuables.

The others stayed back, trying to distance themselves.

Jumping down from the wagon a while later, El grinned, holding up a black velvet pouch for inspection. "Look at this."

Teague eyed the sack warily. His filthy uniform was ragged, his shoes worn through at the soles and toes. "What is it?"

"Jewels. Priceless jewels." El lowered his voice. "Rubies, sapphires, diamonds—there's a king's ransom here!"

The boy turned away. "Put it back. We can't take it. It's not ours."

"Are you crazy? And leave it for someone else?" El's eyes darted to Franz and P.K., then back to Teague. Thrusting the pouch into the boy's clenched fist, he growled, "Look, I'm not proud of what happened, either, but it happened. Keep your mouth shut—I'm going to search the bodies."

Teague watched as El rolled the farmer's lifeless form onto its back and searched the coveralls. Removing a gold pocket watch, he tossed it to Teague.

Teague stared at the ill-gotten gain, fighting back a wave of sickness.

When he looked up again, P.K. had stopped short to lean on his shovel, his eyes fastened on Teague. His gaze hardened. Disgust was evident in his strained features.

Teague swallowed. He wanted to shout that it wasn't his pouch or watch, that El had forced it on him, but his horror at what he had seen stilled his tongue. Words failed him. Loathing burned hot in P.K.'s eyes as he spun on his heel and walked off.

As the last spadeful of dirt covered the graves, P.K. Baldwin averted his eyes. A muscle worked tightly in his jaw, and condemnation burned brightly in his eyes.

The soldiers stood motionless, staring at the five fresh graves. They turned and walked back to the horses.

As El passed Teague, he grinned. "Keep your mouth shut."

Teague winced. "Those jewels have blood on them!"

El's features hardened. "Don't be a *fool*. You've got a family to think of. We all do."

Swinging into his saddle, El motioned the small party to move out.

Teague stared at the pouch, bile rising to his throat. Spiraling out of the saddle, he stumbled to the bushes and lost the little bit of food they'd scavenged that day.

Chapter One

❧

Amarillo, Texas
1898—33 years later

The most memorable event in Vonnie Taylor's life took place in rural Amarillo in the late summer of '98 when Adam Baldwin predictably announced his engagement to Beth Baylor.

"I do declare that Adam Baldwin is the best-looking man in Potter County." Hildy Mae Addison's eyes were riveted to the gorgeous sight. "Just looking at him makes my heart flutter like a butterfly's wings!"

"Hildy Mae!" Mora Dawson slapped a hand across her mouth. "You should be ashamed of yourself."

"For what?" The young woman giggled. "I know a good-looking man when I see one."

"Very *good* looks," Carolyn Henderson concluded.

Vonnie edged away, eyeing the tray of cherry tarts, attempting a show of enthusiasm she didn't feel. "My, doesn't the pastry look wonderful?"

Mora sighed. "I wonder if Beth knows how lucky she is."

Carolyn nodded. "She knows. And even if she didn't, she'd say she did."

Giggles broke out. Beth was known to go to any lengths to keep peace. At times she could be insanely agreeable. Yet, everyone knew the Baldwin/Baylor marriage was arranged by the senior Baldwin. *Remember that, Vonnie. Arranged…* but Adam had consented.

"Ladies," Vonnie cautioned. "Beth is a lovely person."

The murmurs readily concurred that Beth was the nicest person anyone could hope to meet. And the luckiest. When the eldest Baldwin son's engagement to Beth Baylor was announced, the town's eligible female population had groaned with envy.

Vonnie casually bit into flaky crust, feigning indifference to the conversation though her insides churned like a waterwheel. *And now, the nicest person in Potter County would marry the best-looking man in Texas.*

How utterly ideal.

The girls nodded when Janie Bennett and her fiancé, Edward Lassitor, strolled by.

"Evening, Jane, Edward."

"Evening, Hildy." Jane flashed friendly smiles at the women. "Mora, Carolyn, Vonnie."

Simultaneous pleasantries prevailed.

"Janie's so nice," Carolyn said as the couple walked on.

"I can scarcely wait to see her gown. Vonnie, you can't keep us in suspense any longer! What's it like?"

"Ah, but you'll have to wait until the wedding." Vonnie tried for a teasing tone, doing her best not to allow her true feelings to show. Beth might be the nicest girl in the county, but few wouldn't agree that Vonnie Taylor was the prettiest. Coal-black hair, amethyst-colored eyes, dimples men found irresistible. Half Cherokee, half white. Yet no one ever spoke of Vonnie's mixed heritage. Not even P.K. Baldwin.

"You're not serious! You're honestly going to make us wait until the wedding?" Mora and Carolyn chorused.

Hildy's generous lips formed a pout. "You're cruel!"

Her words held no malice. Vonnie knew she wasn't just pretty fluff. Brides came from as far away as the West Coast to purchase one of her exquisite gowns. At the tender age of twelve, she had shown an astonishing ability with needle and thread. By fifteen, anyone who saw her work marveled that she was so gifted. She could craft a simple piece of lace into a work of art.

"I'll bet the gown's frighteningly expensive," Mora guessed.

Carolyn sniffed. "Edward can afford it."

"Edward won't be paying for it. Tool Bennett is paying for everything," Mora confided in a hushed whisper.

"Who said?"

"I overheard Mrs. Bennett telling Martha Gibbings at the church social last week. The wedding is costing a fortune, but Tool won't hear of anything less than the very best for his only daughter."

"Oh dear," Hildy's voice dipped to a reverent whisper. "Will you look at those eyes? Have you ever seen such a deep blue! There's not a man here who could hold a candle to him." To Vonnie's consternation Adam Baldwin was once again the focus of attention.

"He's so handsome he makes my teeth ache," Hildy confessed. "And he's engaged." She brightened. "To our Beth—though I'm absolutely blue with envy."

Vonnie had to agree she was blue, emotionally. Adam, in dark gray trousers, frock coat and burgundy vest, was the best-looking man—not just in Potter County, but the world. But then she was partial to this particular Baldwin. Painfully so.

She picked up a silver tray of bizcotela and brightly offered it around. "Cookies, anyone?"

"I've heard he's quite the gentleman," Carolyn said as she thoughtfully selected a sweet. "Beth said he hung wash for her when she was feeling poorly last week."

"He didn't!"

"He did! Beth said so herself." Carolyn bent closer. "But she made me promise absolute secrecy, so don't breathe a word of it to anyone."

Three heads bobbed. Three pair of covetous eyes returned to Adam's sculpted features. He was deep in conversation with the governor.

"I tell you, son," the governor blustered, "the railroad coming in is the best thing that's ever happened to us!"

"Oh," Hildy murmured. "He sees us." She flashed a grin. "Personally? I'd take any one of the Baldwin brothers."

Carolyn giggled. "To where, darlin'?"

"Who cares?" Mora and Carolyn parroted in unison. Vonnie shook her head.

The four men bore a striking resemblance; it was impossible to say who was the most attractive. They had dark brown, wavy hair, the irresistible Baldwin sky-blue eyes, and skin tanned to nut brown by the hot Texas sun.

Adam, Andrew, Joey, Pat. The brothers were the crème de la crème of Potter County, easily at home in buckskin or expensive Boston tweed.

"Why, Carolyn, what would James say if he heard you drooling over the Baldwin brothers?" Hildy chided.

Carolyn's cheeks pinked and she daintily lifted her cup to her mouth. "James and I are only friends."

"Of course, you are." Vonnie finally entered the good-natured conversation, encouraged by the change in subject.

Hildy suddenly froze, her mouth formed around a cookie. "He's walking this way."

The women's eyes focused on Adam effortlessly weaving his way across the crowded room. His gaze lightly skimmed Vonnie as he approached the four women. "Ladies?"

Carolyn blushed cherry-red. "Mr. Baldwin."

He cocked his head. "Something wrong?"

"Oh, my stars, no," Hildy said. She glanced at Vonnie.

"No?" He smiled, showing even, white teeth beneath a dark tan. "Then I trust you're having a good time?"

"Oh, wonderful," Hildy said.

"Everything's so nice," Carolyn murmured.

"The food's delicious," Mora assured him.

He nodded. "I'm glad you're enjoying yourselves." His eyes returned to Vonnie. Offering his left arm, he smiled. "Would you do me the honor of having a glass of punch?"

Vonnie's breath caught when his eyes skimmed her with easy familiarity. She swallowed. "Of course."

Mora, Hildy and Carolyn stood aside as Adam escorted her to the refreshment center.

Sipping from a cup, Vonnie met Adam's eyes in silent challenge. Eyes the color of a Montana sky stared into hers. Indeed, Adam Baldwin could make a woman's head spin.

"You look lovely tonight."

"Thank you. We were commenting that Beth is positively radiant."

His eyes flicked briefly to his fiancée, who was chatting with Carolyn's father, the honorable Judge Clive Henderson. "Beth is a beautiful woman."

His voice set off the same familiar rush of emotion deep inside Vonnie. The resonant baritone left her feeling slightly giddy. Seven years had failed to change anything.

"You're very fortunate. Beth will make a wonderful mate."

"Yes, so I'm told."

"Have you set a date?"

"Not yet."

The woodsy spice of his cologne circled her. Beneath crystal chandeliers, where dappled prisms of light swirled among the smiling couples, she'd never felt more miserable.

Discreetly stepping closer, Adam whispered softly against her ear. "Why are you here?"

"You need to ask?"

Faking a blissful smile, Vonnie gripped the cup tightly. Her dress of yellow silk trimmed with black lace ruffles whispered delicately against the coarse fabric of his dark gray trousers.

His voice held a slight edge now. "Do you plan to make a scene?"

She peered up at him, her eyes wide as if the mere thought of making a scene was scandalous. "Me? Heavens, no. Why would I make a scene?"

"Strong hunch," he said, tight-lipped.

"I wouldn't miss this for the world. We're a close-knit community. If any member of the church failed to show up at an event of this magnitude, the neighbors would talk."

A muscle tightened in his jaw.

She smiled, skimming the room.

"My mother seems to be enjoying herself. She's eaten at least six petits fours." Vonnie focused on the fragile-looking woman sitting inside the veranda doorway. Cammy Taylor, a quiet, unassuming lady, sipped punch, giving polite interest to Vera Clark's endless chatter. Vera appeared to take Cammy's nodding courtesy for rapt attention, but Vonnie knew better. Her mother wasn't interested in Vera's gout. She came tonight to spite P.K. Baldwin.

Adam's warm breath fanned her ear, and for a giddy moment the room tilted. "I notice your father isn't worried about proprieties."

"Father?" She laughed. "A team of wild horses couldn't have brought him here."

Coolness shadowed Adam's eyes.

She tilted a violet glance up at him and clarified, though it wasn't necessary. "I believe his exact words were, 'I'd sooner be in a room of rattlers.'"

Chiseled lips parted to reveal a row of perfectly matched teeth as he accepted the lethal thrust. "You'll be sure to give Teague my best."

"He'll be thrilled."

Lifting a dark brow, Adam appeared to be waiting for the other shoe to drop. When she didn't respond, he said quietly, "There's bound to be more you have to say."

"Yes. I hope you both will be very happy."

She set the cup aside and quickly walked away. Ignoring the shocked expressions on her friends' faces, Vonnie swept by them and disappeared onto the veranda. Adam covered the awkward moment by casually threading his way through the crowd, following her.

Acknowledging the various greetings, he trailed close on Vonnie's heels, pulling the veranda double doors closed behind him for privacy.

"All right," he accused. "Say what you came here to say."

"You *really* want to hear it?"

"Vonnie, don't make a scene," he warned.

Whirling, her eyes locked with his in a spirited challenge. "Over you? Don't make me laugh."

"What are you really doing here tonight?"

Her brow lifted with mockery. "Who would have a better reason to be here?"

"You're going to be difficult about this, aren't you? I hope we can handle this in a civil manner."

She wrapped her arms around her waist and stepped to a low wall covered in dying bougainvillea. "I'm not sure I can be civil."

Propping a boot on the flowered garden ledge, he stood silent. Finally he said, "You're looking good."

Moving another step away, she surveyed the brilliant sky. The stars looked so close she was sure she could reach up and touch them. She could remember only one other night when they'd been so bright, so perfect.

"You're not obligated to say that."

He looked away impatiently. "I wasn't saying it because I thought I had to say it."

"Then, thank you." Her voice was even more unsteady than she'd feared.

Silence stretched between them.

"Why did you come?" he repeated. Grasping her by the shoulders, he shook her gently. "What did you expect?"

What did she expect? Resentment flooded her. What did she expect? Tears burned her eyes and she blinked.

Turning away, he said, "Stop looking at me that way."

She closed her eyes to keep from seeing him at all.

His voice held quiet desperation now. "I don't know what you expected." He struggled for the right words. "You didn't think it would just go away, did you?"

"I don't know what I thought, but I didn't expect you to marry Beth." She heard the hurt in her voice.

For the briefest of moments she thought she saw compassion in his eyes. But then it was gone. She steeled herself against the feelings roiling inside. "Congratulations. With the Baylors' land and your family's wealth, the Baldwins will control a sizable chunk of Potter County."

"I'm not marrying Beth to spite you."

"Then why are you marrying her?" Vonnie held her breath as she waited for the answer. *If you say you love her, I'll die.*

"You know why I'm marrying her." He refused to meet her eyes.

She averted her gaze. Yes, she knew—his father had arranged the union. P.K. had always wanted the Baylor land.

Lord, how can I bear this? I love him beyond words. How can I let him go to another woman—even to Beth, who would make him a devoted wife? Calm me, Lord, help me be strong, and help me veil how this is tearing me apart.

This time he was the one who looked away. "What does love have to do with it?"

"Are you saying you're not in love with her?"

His voice turned harsh again. "I'm marrying Beth, understand?"

Oh, she understood. She understood only too well. He was like his father: headstrong and brash. She shivered, drawing the tulle-and-lace scarf closer over her shoulders. She suddenly felt chilled to the bone, though the night was hot. Hadn't she known it would come to this? Hadn't she told herself a million times it would end this way? He would never tell Beth. Nor would she. Ever.

"I assume you want my cooperation?"

He avoided her eyes. "Yes."

She vowed she wouldn't cry. She wouldn't give him that satisfaction. Tears were already spilling from the corners of her eyes. "I'm supposed to keep quiet? Never tell Beth we were married?"

"It was just a ceremony. Annulled as soon as we came to our senses. We never had a chance to be married—not in the Biblical sense."

Just a ceremony. She swallowed against the painful knot suddenly impeding the back of her throat.

"There's no use in Beth ever knowing. It would hurt her pointlessly."

"I'd want to know," she said, turning back to confront him.

"Well, you're not Beth."

"No," she said. "I'm not Beth. Silly me, I was only your wife."

"Briefly," he reminded.

"Too long," she said, knowing it was a lie.

Stepping off the veranda, she disappeared into the darkness.

"Lord, I know I don't have a right to him. He was never really mine. We were too young, but I love him."

Tears blurred her sight. Her steps faltered and she searched the sky. God was there; He was beside her no matter how foolish her actions, yet she didn't believe in her heart that He could help her face this. It was too hurtful, too unthinkable, yet so true—Adam belonged to another.

Chapter Two

✤

It was impetuous…daring…stupid, they'd decided in the dawn of reality.

Propping his booted foot against the windowsill, Adam tipped his chair back and focused on the rain pattering against the study window. They had been so young. Young and crazy.

Steepling his fingers to his forehead, he relived the summer of '91. What a pair they'd been. Innocence mixed with the foolish cup of youth.

It had started with puppy love that steadily blossomed from the time Adam had first seen pretty little Vonnie Taylor at the First Freewill Church's annual Fourth of July picnic. Add a summer night and a full moon and you had trouble. He'd grown from a barefoot show-off into a seventeen-year-old man. Vonnie Taylor had sprouted from an impish tease into a fifteen-year-old woman, who, with the glance of an eye, could reduce him to a bashful kid.

Add the forbidden—neither was supposed to speak to the other—and you had the seeds of a budding rebellion.

In those days neither one of them understood the bitter feud that raged between the two families. They knew there was bad blood between P.K. Baldwin and Teague Taylor, but at nine and seven, they didn't attempt to understand the origin of the dispute. The hatred between P.K. and Teague had happened long before Adam and Vonnie were born.

Adam was piling potato salad on his plate that hot July afternoon. Vonnie had sidled up beside him, dressed in a lavender calico dress and matching bonnet. She'd sipped a cup of cool lemonade, tilted a dangerous look up at him and read him his future. "I am going to marry you someday, Adam Baldwin. We're going to be man and wife. Forever."

He'd about dumped his plate of food in Flossy Norman's lap.

"You don't even know what that means," he accused, feeling a red blush crawl up his neck. He didn't either…exactly. Forever. He didn't think so.

Tilting her chin haughtily, she glared at him in challenge. "Do too."

From that moment on, Vonnie Taylor hadn't been far from his thoughts.

Adam slid further down in the chair, a smile forming at the corners of his mouth when he recalled the sassy little girl she'd been. They'd been too naive, and too caught up in teasing each other, to care that P.K. Baldwin had forbidden his boys to associate with the Taylor girl. Consequently, the Baldwin brothers went out of their way to plague her. And she returned it in kind.

Every Sunday Adam and Andrew stared a hole through Vonnie the whole time they sat across the aisle from her in the First Freewill Church.

The diminutive black-haired charmer stared right back—singling out the eldest, Adam, to unleash her flirtations upon. He'd poke out his tongue, cross his eyes, push up his nose in preposterous faces in hopes of making her laugh out loud. But she'd look right back at him over her hymnbook and never crack a smile. Though he'd do his best to stare her down, she wouldn't budge an inch.

The years passed and the Sunday-morning glances became less hostile. Liquid, clear-blue eyes searched sleepy lavender ones with mild curiosity. Shy Sunday-morning smiles replaced silly faces, and his efforts to attract her attention grew more bold.

He tied Beth Baylor's braid to the church pew.

He silently, but no less earnestly, rolled his eyes while emphatically mouthing Ilda Freeman's soprano solos along with her.

At fourteen, he responded to the preacher's request for hymn suggestions by shooting his hand into the air and waving it for attention. He'd requested that they sing "Gladly, the Cross-eyed Bear."

Vonnie had refused to look at him as the congregation dutifully turned to page thirty-six in their hymnals and sang "Gladly, The Cross I Bear."

Adolescence evolved into mid teens. Young, lithe bodies filled out. His narrow shoulders broadened, legs lengthened, muscles grew hard, and the peach fuzz on his jaw became a real beard that confronted him daily. Her oval face matured into a puzzle of tilted violet eyes, pert nose and narrow chin. Her quick, thin body softened and rounded. The silent interest between the oldest Baldwin boy and the Taylor girl flourished.

By his seventeenth birthday he'd developed a full-blown case of puppy love for her. That was the summer they'd started sneaking away to Liken's Pond. Things were starting to get out of hand. They both knew they were courting danger, but that made their secret meetings even more fascinating.

The pond, one of the few that survived the hot summers, was tucked behind scraggly creosote bushes that lined the bank. A few yards out, yuccas pointed white flowers toward the clear blue sky, their green spiny leaves contrasting with the sandy soil. Piñon and cypress trees crept close to shade the banks after noon. Juniper trees mingled with mesquite bush. But where Adam and Vonnie sought privacy, the sycamore shaded them in the summer, and floated its leaves like boats on the water in the fall. It was a special place, a place of wonder.

It was Saturday. Chores were done. A shimmering sun beat down on the scorched earth. The fragrance of grass baking in the heat-saturated air.

The pond was a good two miles from George Liken's house. Only an occasional, wandering Hereford intruded upon their privacy.

Treading water, they faced each other, arms looped over shoulders, savoring the stolen moments. If P.K. or Teague ever got wind of the secret meetings, their budding relationship would stop.

"What did you tell your father?"

"Told him I'd be with Tate Morgan shoeing a horse. He'll say I was if anyone asks. What about you?"

"Doing needlepoint with the new neighbor, Nettie Donaldson. I asked God for forgiveness."

Even now, years later, Adam could smell the sweetness of her skin, still see the silken curtain of her hair floating in the water—

"Am I interrupting, son?"

Adam brought the chair legs to the floor with a thump, sat up straight and forced himself to focus on his father, who stood framed in the doorway. Still a commanding figure, at fifty-two, his snow-white hair was the only external evidence that time was passing. But Adam knew his father's health had not been good of late.

"No, come in, Dad."

P.K. entered the study, carrying a foul-looking herbal tonic. He caught Adam's glance at the glass and shrugged. "Rain has my knee acting up."

Sinking into the oversize leather wingback chair, he stretched his legs out in front of him, balancing the glass on his thigh.

"Nice party last night."

Laying a stack of papers aside, Adam reached for the grain report he'd been reading earlier.

"Yes, Alma knows how to throw a party."

"Mmm-hmm," P.K. mused. "Don't know what we'd do without Alma. Fine woman. Beth have a good time?"

"Seemed to."

"Now there's a woman you can be proud of, son. Beth's an excellent choice for a wife. Comes from good stock. None finer than Leighton and Gillian Baylor. You'll be starting a family right away?"

Adam shook his head, negative.

"Have you discussed kids?" P.K. asked. "You're not getting any younger."

Adam focused on the grain report. "What's age got to do with it? I know many a man that's fathered a child late in life."

"Oh, I don't know. Two young people in love—I'd have thought the subject might have come up. Thought maybe new ways had changed the idea of not discussing it until after the marriage, but apparently it hasn't." P.K. sipped his tonic. "You want children, don't you? None of us is getting any younger, you know—"

"Actually, Dad, I haven't thought about it." Children were the last thing on his mind. He had to get through the wedding first.

"I wouldn't put it off too long," P.K. said. "Time passes quickly."

"I know, Dad. You want grandchildren."

"I do, and I'm not apologizing for it. Should have a houseful by now."

Adam quieted his irritation. What was this talk of love and grandkids? P.K. Baldwin didn't have a sentimental bone in his body. He tossed the grain report onto the desk. "I guess we're pretending this isn't an arranged marriage. If Beth didn't bring a dowry of five hundred acres of prime land you wouldn't be so eager to have her become a Baldwin."

P.K. lifted his glass, staring at the murky liquid. "That's a little cold, isn't it?"

"But true." Adam's tone hardened. "The town's abuzz with the Baylors' daughter marrying into the family."

"She'll make you a good wife."

"And the Baylors' land doesn't hurt a thing. That right?"

P.K.'s features remained as bland as Alma's bread pudding. "Son. It's only land, and we have all we need. I'm thinking of your future happiness."

Alma bustled in, bearing a tray with cups and a silver pot of fresh coffee. The Hispanic woman was more than a housekeeper—she was a vital part of the Baldwin family. She had single-handedly raised Andrew, Pat and Joey after Ceilia Baldwin's death when Adam was ten.

"I thought you gentlemen might enjoy coffee."

"None for me, thanks," P.K. said as Alma set the tray on the corner of the desk.

"Then you would like one of the nice cinnamon rolls I just took out of the oven, *sí?*"

Adam smiled. "Just coffee, Alma."

She bent to pat his lean cheek. "You should eat. You will need all your strength to make many *niños* for your father, no?" Picking up the silver pot, she smiled at P.K. "Señor Baldwin?"

P.K. toasted her with his glass. "I'm drinking my pain tonic."

She sent a cautious look at him before shuffling out on slippered feet.

When the door closed behind her, P.K. pushed himself up and stepped to the window. Tugging the curtain aside, he focused on the rain rolling off the roof of the hacienda and splashing onto the rock veranda.

Adam bent over another report, but he didn't see it. He heard the rain drumming on the roof, but his mind had returned to that hot summer day seven years earlier.

"Adam, this is crazy!" Vonnie giggled as they raced through the small grove of trees, hand in hand. The orange sky was in the midst of another spectacular sunset.

Flinging his arms wide, Adam let out a joyous whoop, causing her to break into laughter. She tried to clamp her hand over his mouth, but their feet tangled and they toppled to the ground, laughing. Between short, raspy breaths, they hugged each other so tightly he thought their ribs would crack.

He could hardly believe it! He'd convinced Vonnie to marry him!

Sitting up, he looked deeply into her eyes. "I love you, Vonnie Taylor."

He could see in her eyes that she believed him, to the very depths of her soul.

"You know we're going to be in trouble when they find out."

"Trouble" wouldn't cover it. His father would horsewhip him. "They can tie me to the stake and burn me alive," he vowed. "We're going to do it."

"But how do we even know the judge will travel this road—"

His hand covered her mouth, stifling her protests.

"I overheard the men talking at the feed store, yesterday," he whispered. "They said a judge from Lubbock was coming through here today. All we have to do is watch for him, Vonnie. He'll ride through here."

"But it's late…"

"Come on." He pulled her to her feet.

It was nearly dark when a dust-covered Jenny Lind buggy, with patched roof and floral curtains for privacy, rolled down the road. Vonnie and Adam studied it and the lanky driver from the shadows.

"Do you think it's him?"

"It's got to be."

The tall, thin man in the dusty black frock coat and stovepipe hat gingerly stepped down from the buggy and gathered some pieces of wood. In a few minutes he had a campfire going and a skillet on the fire, into which he forked thick slices of bacon.

Adam and Vonnie approached the campsite. "Judge?"

Startled, the man frowned up at them.

"What do you want?"

Drawing a deep breath, Adam cleared his throat. "Sorry to interrupt your supper, sir, but me and my lady here…we want to get married."

Straightening, the man studied a trembling Vonnie. "Married?"

"Yes, sir."

Adam was holding her hand so tightly she protested with a soft whimper.

The old man's pale eyes swept Vonnie. "You got your folks' permission?"

"Don't need it, sir. We're old enough to make up our own minds."

The man's eyes centered on him.

"You are the judge, aren't you? We heard you were coming."

The man nodded slowly, his attention drifting back to Vonnie.

"You can marry us?"

"If you got a dollar for the license—"

"I got a dollar," Adam said, digging into his pocket and producing a silver coin.

The coin Adam dropped into the judge's narrow hand disappeared into the pocket of the shiny suit jacket.

"Got a ring?"

"No, sir," Adam said.

The judge eyed Vonnie. "You sure you want to do this, young lady?"

"I'm sure," she said.

Adam slipped his arm around her and drew her closer to his side.

The judge dusted his coat and straightened it, then settled his hat more firmly on his head, tugging it down low on his forehead. Adam could barely see his eyes now.

"Do you love this…woman?"

"I do," Adam said.

"You'll take care of her come sickness or other troubles?"

"I will."

"No matter what happens, you'll stay with her?"

"I will," he vowed. "We both believe in the gospel, sir. I'll take care of her."

"Young lady, do you love this man?"

"I do," she whispered.

"You'll take care of him in the good and bad times?"

"I will."

"No matter what life hands you, you'll stick with him?"

"I will."

"Then I pronounce you man and wife. Kiss your bride."

Adam's arm tightened around her; his lips brushed hers. "I love you," he whispered against her mouth.

"I love you, too."

The judge bent to turn his bacon before it burned. "Where you heading now, young people?"

"We're staying with friends tonight," Adam said.

"Then what?"

"Not sure." At the time, he didn't want to think about tomorrow and what would surely happen.

"Planning on walking, are you?"

"We got horses, by the trees."

"Uh-huh. Well, my blessin's to you both."

"Thanks, Judge. Thanks a lot." He looked at his bride. "Thanks a whole lot!"

"Have you spoken to Beth about the building plans?" P.K.'s voice broke into Adam's thoughts.

Getting up, he moved to the file cabinet. "No, but I'll get around to it."

"Get around to it? Son, it takes time to build a house. We'll need to get the men started as soon as possible. You'll want to move your bride in shortly after the honeymoon, won't you?"

"I'll talk to Beth, Dad."

P.K. had raised his sons with an iron hand. No give, no take. His way or no way. Adam knew the land had been a hard taskmaster. Building a ranch the size of Cabeza del Lobo—Wolf's Head—out of the desert had been grueling, demanding more than most men could give. Many had folded up and left, selling out to the highest bidder, often P.K. His father had stuck it out, made his mark on the land. He'd done it without a wife's support, while raising four boys with a housekeeper's help. Adam respected him for that. They'd butted heads over a lot of things, but how to run the ranch wasn't one of them. P.K.'s cattle and horse instincts were still indisputable.

The Baldwin ranch was a sprawling establishment with patios and flowering gardens surrounding spacious adobe buildings. P.K. owned four sitios of land, 73,240 acres, but he controlled more than a million acres. At the peak of his prosperity, the ranch supported 50,000 Hereford-graded cattle, 15,000 horses, and 6,000 mules. Some thirty Mexican and Opata Indian families lived on the ranch, harvesting hay, vegetables and fruit, in addition to overseeing the livestock. The Baldwin water supply was plentiful; five springs, creeks that flowed in the spring and fall, and an underground river easily tapped by wells.

Forty acres situated to the south of the main hacienda were reserved for Adam and his wife. Pat, Joey and Andrew had been allotted similar parcels with adjoining property lines.

P.K. had made sure that when his sons married, they had ample room to raise his grandchildren.

Adam knew that the prosperous appearances were deceiving. The past few years Cabeza Del Lobo had fallen on hard times, which was why P.K. was pushing for this marriage with Beth. Adam was expected to step up and do his duty for the good of the family. He sighed. Beth deserved a better man than he. She deserved to marry a man who loved her.

His thoughts turned to Vonnie and the feud between their fathers. Even now, when their children were grown, P.K. and Teague Taylor hated each other more than ever. Sometimes he caught P.K. staring at Vonnie—resenting her heritage? He was never sure. He had never openly spoken about the half Cherokee/half white blood that ran through Teague's adopted daughter's veins. He'd known that Teague loved his child with great intensity and whatever lay between the two men, P.K. had never stepped over the line and used racial inequality to further inflame the rift.

Letting the curtain drop back into place, P.K. returned to the chair. "Noticed you drank punch with the Taylor girl last night."

"Mmm," Adam responded absently.

"Was that necessary?"

Filing a folder away, Adam closed the drawer. "Only being polite, Dad."

P.K. grunted. "Noticed her useless father didn't bother to show up."

"Did you really expect him to?"

"I expect nothing out of Teague Taylor." P.K. took a swig of tonic.

The dispute between the two families had gone on for so long Adam had lost sympathy for either side. The act that had sparked his father's ire was never forgiven.

"Better leave that woman alone. She'll get you in trouble," P.K. muttered.

Adam glanced up. "Who?"

"The Taylor girl."

"Her name's Vonnie, and she's hardly a girl anymore."

"Vonnie," P.K. repeated. "I don't care what her name is—you leave her alone." He was muttering. "I've seen her type. Sashaying around—turning men's heads with those strange-looking eyes. You leave her alone. And you tell Andrew, Pat and Joey to do the same. There isn't a Taylor worth their salt."

Adam couldn't remember how many times they'd had this conversation. It was getting old. "Why tell me? I'm engaged, remember?"

"Engaged or not, you keep your eyes to yourself." P.K. frowned. "There was a time I worried about you and the Taylor girl."

Adam glanced up.

"Don't think I didn't see the way you two looked at each other when you were younger. I'm not blind. Many a Sunday I considered throwing a bucket of water on you to cool you off. You were just lucky Alma convinced me that it was childish fancies. For a time, I was starting to wonder."

Adam bent low over the desk. "I didn't look at Vonnie Taylor any certain way."

"Don't tell me you didn't. I'll tell you now what I told you then. You stay away from the Taylors. All of them."

"Personally, I think you overreact when it comes to the Taylors."

"You don't know a thing about it. The Taylors are trash!"

"How can you say that? The Flying Feather is a respected ranch."

"The Flying Feather, ha! Teague wouldn't have a red cent if he hadn't loaned his last dollar to the owner of a traveling sideshow and had to take that pair of ostriches as payment."

"Maybe, but he took a pair of birds and built it into a sound business."

P.K. scoffed. "Until Teague got stuck with those birds he was dirt-poor. The community felt sorry for Cammy Taylor having a baby girl she'd brought home to raise and Teague so broke he couldn't afford monthly staples. Man didn't have a lick of sense. If he had a dollar and someone gave him a hard-luck tale he'd hand it over. If it hadn't been for neighbor's charity, his family would have gone hungry many a day."

Today the Taylor spread was the third largest in the community and thriving. A bitter pill for P.K. to swallow.

His father stared out the window, speaking absently, as if he had forgotten Adam was in the room. "Teague always acted like he was so holy and righteous. Butter wouldn't melt in his mouth he was so self-righteous. Well, in my book, it's a sin to let your family do without, especially when you could have done something about it."

Adam pushed to his feet, his voice bordering on impatience. "For the life of me, I cannot understand what happened between you and Teague Taylor that made you such bitter enemies."

P.K. looked over his shoulder, back ramrod straight, as if he had just now remembered Adam's presence. His features darkened. "It's between me and Teague."

"So you've said for as long as I can remember. What you've failed to say is why the hatred runs so deep. All this talk of murder, jewels. None of it makes sense. If you expect me to hate the Taylors as much as you do, you need to give me a reason. A solid reason."

"My word is my reason. That's all you need."

And it's all he'd get; Adam knew that only too well.

Turning from the window, P.K. downed the last of his tonic. "You won't forget to talk to Beth about the house plans?"

"I'll speak to her tonight."

"Good. I'll tell Manny to start on your furniture. I thought cherry would be nice. Nice, big pieces—maybe done up in Aztec fabric in reds, blues and yellows. What do you think? Something colorful?"

Adam felt the familiar surge of resentment. P.K. controlled his son's life down to the furniture he would sit on.

"Beth and I haven't set a date, Dad."

With a gesture, he brushed the detail aside. "It'll take a while to get the furniture built. No use waiting until the last minute. What do you think? Aztec fabric?"

Adam shrugged. "Talk to Beth."

Moving back to the window, P.K. gazed out. Adam could see the pride glistening in his eyes. Cabeza Del Lobo had been built by sweat and hard work. No one had ever given P.K. Baldwin anything. He had taken ten acres and carved out an empire. He would die if he lost the place in payment of a bad note.

Teague Taylor had taken two birds and lucked out.

Adam studied his father from beneath lowered lashes. He

stood at the window, his lean body more bent than Adam remembered, shifting his weight on one leg. He suddenly found himself wondering what *had* taken place between Teague and P.K. to cause such bitter animosity?

He'd heard things like, the man's foolish. He wasn't worth his salt. Traitor to his own kind. But never a concrete motive for such resentment.

When he married Vonnie he'd been too young to approach P.K., to demand a reason for the dispute.

Now, all of a sudden, he wanted to know.

Chapter Three

❧

The night Adam married Vonnie Taylor he knew she was all he'd ever wanted from life. She'd looked so pretty in the flickering flames of the judge's campfire; he had thanked God over and over that she had taken vows to be his for the rest of their lives.

They'd ridden away together. Mr. and Mrs. Adam Baldwin. Just saying the words in his mind had thrilled him. An hour later they'd reached the boardinghouse that sat at the edge of a crossroads. The border town had a store, a church, a one-room school, a stable, three bars. Not much.

The aged lady, wearing a long gown and nightcap, who answered their knock was put out by their late arrival. They had to shout to make her understand they wanted a room for the night.

"You want what? Supper's over!"

"We don't need supper. We need a place to stay," Adam shouted. "A room."

"A broom! What do you want with a broom?"

"A place to sleep," Vonnie offered, pantomiming sleeping by tilting her head and folding her hands against her cheek.

"We just got married!" Adam said.

She frowned. "Buried!"

Finally the old woman understood, directing them to a tiny but cozy room on the second floor of the two-story clapboard structure. Vonnie had climbed the stairs in silence. Once inside the room she had stood with her back to the door, looking as frightened as someone who suddenly had found herself on the edge of a cliff—and looking incredibly young, as well. He didn't feel all that old or wise at the moment.

He had gently turned her to face him, drawing her into his arms. He'd kissed her, but for once she didn't respond. Instead, she seemed reluctant...uncertain.

"What's wrong? Tell me."

"Oh, Adam. We're really married?" Her slender body shook with emotion.

"That's right, we're married. Forever." He held her tighter, liking the thought. Forever.

She shook her head. "What have we done? Oh, Adam, we're in bad trouble."

He suddenly realized the enormity of their actions. He swallowed, wishing he could reassure her, but he didn't feel very sure himself. "It's all right, darlin'. We'll go tell our parents right now."

"We can't tell your father! P.K. will rip my hide right off and render me in hot oil. Oh, my stars! What are we going to do?" She broke free of his embrace, wringing her hands.

"It'll be all right. I…I love you. Everything will work out. P.K. and Teague will be mad—"

"Mad? Adam, mad? They'll be *furious*."

She bit her lower lip so hard he thought she'd bite it clean through. He tried to console her but she resisted.

"We're married. There's nothing they can do."

"Adam, I'm scared. Daddy will have the marriage annulled."

"I won't let him." He tried to take her into his arms, but she pushed him away. She suddenly seemed distant, not at all like the sweet angel he'd married.

"No, Adam. We've made a terrible mistake."

"Calm down." Panic rose in his throat. She stood against the door, trembling, her eyes shining with tears.

"They can never know," she said.

Her eyes had met his and he would have done anything to erase the fear and remorse he saw. "Stop acting like this. You're making me crazy."

"They can never know," she repeated. "We'll pretend it never happened."

The meaning of her words had gradually sunk in. Adam frowned. "Pretend we didn't get married?"

"It's the only answer. No one has to know, Adam, except us. Daddy can't know—he'd be so disappointed in me."

"We love each other."

"We're too young to love each other," she said. "Daddy will have your hide. I'm too young to get married. So are you."

Disbelief had settled over Adam. "You're more worried about what your father will think than how I feel?"

She shook her head wildly. "I'm worried about you, Adam. I mean it—Daddy will be wild with rage."

"I agree he doesn't like the Baldwins…"

"He hates the Baldwins—your father hates the Taylors."

"We both knew that when we got married." His voice had started to rise. What was she doing? Fear coursed through him. "Why didn't that bother you before we got married?"

She had blinked up at him, tears soaking her lashes. Burying her face in her hands, she'd cried harder.

He glared at her. "Is that your answer? To bawl?"

"I can't face Daddy and tell him I married you. I can't."

Adam heaved a sigh of pure frustration. "You're such a daddy's girl you'd forfeit my love for his pride?"

Nodding, she sobbed harder.

Something had snapped inside of him. Furious that she would leave him now—now when they had risked everything to be together. He refused to look at her.

"You can stop crying. I'm taking you home." He didn't try to keep the contempt from his voice.

"I'm…so…sorry."

Turning on his heel, he had left the room. Sorry? She wouldn't have a chance to humiliate a Baldwin a second time.

Shortly after that, P.K. was thrown from his horse during roundup and trampled. His leg was badly injured, and he required complete bed rest. It had been weeks before he was able to ride again. During that time, Adam had been forced to take charge. In a sense it had been a good thing. Long hours and hard work had kept his mind off Vonnie.

From that time on, Vonnie went out of her way to avoid him. Even in church, she sat as far away from him as she could and disappeared as soon as the last amen was uttered. He finally stopped going to services, because seeing her only fueled his anger.

Before he knew it, nearly two years had passed. Vonnie had perfected her talent for sewing and soon was the most sought after seamstress for her remarkable gowns.

One hot night, he found himself alone with her at a church function. By then there was nothing to say about the past, about the one night that was etched permanently into their memory. Like the Baldwins and Taylors, they pointedly ignored each other.

It was as if the marriage had never taken place.

Adam leaned his head back against the chair, recalling the brief ceremony. He'd managed to get her home without being seen and the next morning he had talked to Judge Clive Henderson, who had given him a tongue-lashing, the memory of which still stung. After he'd calmed down, Clive had agreed to arrange for the annulment and promised to take the secret to his grave. So far he had kept his promise.

The room was quiet except for the buzzing of a bluebottle fly. Adam focused on the question he had tried hard to ignore. Why *did* he have such a difficult time forgetting that firelight wedding ceremony and the pride and love he'd felt in his bride? He had another wedding in his future. This one would take place in a church where there would be guests and flowers and a proper preacher. Beth would make a beautiful bride, and later, she would keep a fine home, make a loving mother and a caring wife. So why was he still thinking about the one woman he couldn't forget?

Chapter Four

❦

"Another one?"

"Another one," Vonnie said, watching Garrett Beasley ring up five spools of white satin thread. "And I'm going to need sixteen more yards of Duchesse lace, Mr. Beasley."

"I'll order it right away." His pot-bellied clerk's eyes twinkled. "Getting it here, now that's another thing."

"Do you think—"

"I'll send the order out first thing tomorrow morning. You know I will."

Vonnie smiled. Mr. Beasley had a real talent for making customers feel special.

"There you go, little lady," he said, adding the thread to her purchases. "Heard you're making the Wilson gown?"

"Yes, when it's finished I'll bring it by and let you see it."

Rumors about the gown had been in all the newspapers.

Hammond Wilson, a prominent Phoenix millionaire, doted on his eldest daughter, Emily, and had commissioned Vonnie to make the point de Flandre gown for a handsome sum. The pure white lace with graceful, rhythmic patterns of leaves, flowers and scrolls was widely regarded as the most beautiful of the pillow laces. The accompanying Flemish Duchesse bridal veil was certain to become a Wilson heirloom treasure.

"Business must be booming," he said. "Had a man stop by earlier in the week asking about you. Seems they've heard about your bridal gowns way up there in New York."

"Business is good." Almost too good, she added to herself, thinking about the bolts of cream satin stacked on her cutting table.

"Sounds like the Bennett wedding is going to be quite a shindig." He transferred a bolt of tulle to the cutting table. "Twenty more yards, you say?"

"Mmm, better make it twenty-five, just to be sure."

"Twenty-five it is."

While he measured and cut the silk net, Vonnie browsed. Outside, the sun was beaching the horizon. Most of the stores were closing, while the bars and bawdy houses were just starting their business day.

Beasley's was one of the first delicatessens in the town. The idea that you could buy ready-to-eat products and dry goods at the same time was a real hit with the customers.

Closing her eyes, she sniffed the tantalizing mix of cured hams, loose spices and fresh pies. Freshly ground coffee and hot cinnamon buns.

The countertops brimmed with a colorful array of foods.

Glass cases full of cakes, pickles in trays, and a big tub of sweet creamery butter added character to Beasley's Grocery. Sitting beside buckets of salt herring and salt mackerel were barrels of crackers, cookies, nuts and other dried condiments. There were big bushels of apples and a crock of mincemeat. Bunches of long bolognas and fat cheeses wrapped in netting dangled from the ceiling. The store was charmingly chaotic.

"Yep, seems like everybody's decided to get married at the same time. Looks like Adam and Beth will be next," Beasley continued as he cut the fabric.

"Looks that way."

"Fine young men, those Baldwin boys. Fine young men."

Vonnie picked up an ornately carved music box and carefully wound the little key at the back. A boy and girl in a swing turned slowly to the strains of "I'll Take You Home Again, Kathleen."

"Yes, Beth and Adam make a handsome couple," Beasley rattled on as he wrote the price of each item on the back of a bag and totaled it. "Reckon P.K.'s hopes are high on having his first grandchild by this time next year—"

"I'll also need six packages of seed pearls, Mr. Beasley."

If he thought anything about her interruption, it didn't show.

"White or ivory?"

"The white, I think."

He tore a long sheet of brown wrapping paper off the roll he kept under the counter. "How're your folks doing? Saw Cammy the other day."

"Good, thank you."

"And the birds?"

"We have a new batch of babies."

"Is that a fact? My goodness, those birds must be interesting to raise."

"They are indeed."

The community knew how proud Teague Taylor was of his ostriches. Little did Teague know that when he got the pair of adult, pure North African ostriches, he had hit the jackpot. When he'd come home dragging the two birds behind him, rumor had it Cammy was miffed over having another pair of mouths to feed but had quickly changed her mind. The birds developed into a profitable business, with over a hundred birds now at the Flying Feather. The feathers and meat provided the Taylors with a comfortable income.

The store owner peered over his glasses at Vonnie. "What's that your father calls the chicks?"

"Waddlebabies." Vonnie laughed, thinking of the newly hatched ostriches. They were curious things, playful as week-old kittens. When they walked across their pens, it was clear why Teague had pinned them with the nickname.

"Waddlebabies. That Teague. He's quite a character. Always has been." He tied the string on the package of material. "That about do you for today?" He wrapped the buttons in a second bundle.

"That should do it. Thank you so much."

Anxious to be on her way, Vonnie paid for her purchases. She'd gotten a late start today, and Mr. Beasley had stayed open later than usual to accommodate her.

Twilight was gathering when she stepped onto the plank sidewalk.

The heavy scent of cattle fouled the air tonight. Cattle. Cabeza Del Lobo.

Adam Baldwin.

Why did her thoughts always stray to Adam?

Franz Schuyler slowly made his way down the sidewalk, his stool hooked over one arm and his long-handled lighter held like a scepter. He lit the gas lanterns, one by one, until the dusty street resembled a brick-paved city avenue.

Lamplight had always been a delight for Vonnie. Franz was like some wizened elf who quietly went about his work without fuss or bother. With a touch of a wand, the town's gas lanterns sprang to life.

"Evening, Franz," Vonnie called.

The old man had always been a favorite town character. Of Dutch and German descent, his parents had cursed him with a strange little body. Squat and decidedly rotund, he reminded Vonnie of Santa Claus pictured in the books Cammy had ordered from back East. His snow-white hair and twinkling blue eyes made her want to sit on his lap and recite her Christmas list. Wouldn't that have raised a few eyebrows!

The lamplighter glanced up and waved. "Shopping again?" He made his way down the street toward her, carefully trimming and lighting each of the lanterns. The sun had disappeared now. The mellow lantern light gave the street a golden glow.

"My, my," he said, standing back to admire her. "Has anyone told you that you get prettier every day?"

Vonnie's smile was one of deep affection for the man

who, she was sure, was not as old as he appeared to be. "No, but it's sweet of you to say so."

"It's true."

"You say that to all the girls."

"Not to all of them," he denied. "Only the prettiest ones."

They shared a comfortable laugh, then turned toward the north as a cool breeze suddenly sprang up.

"Nice weather today," he commented.

"Yes, it's been so hot." At times the sun seemed cruel. "How's Audrey?"

Sadness touched Franz's eyes, and he slowly shook his head. "Not good, little one, not so good."

"I'm sorry." Vonnie rested her hand on his sleeve.

Audrey Schuyler was dying, slowly but surely. Everyone knew it. With a quiet dignity she bore the knowledge that she hadn't many days left. Audrey and Cammy Taylor had been friends since childhood. Vonnie couldn't remember a year when the Schuylers hadn't been at the Taylor house for Thanksgiving and Christmas. Audrey's special cherry-rum fruitcake was a treat they all looked forward to sharing on Christmas Eve.

But the fruitcake wouldn't be there this year. For the past few months, Audrey had steadily lost ground, and Cammy Taylor refused to accept her friend's terminal illness. She still clung to the belief that a miracle would occur and Audrey would be spared.

"But," Franz sighed, his smile returning, though it was a bit dim. "Any day you wake up is a good day, isn't it?" He touched the packages she held. "Guess you're making another beautiful wedding dress?"

"Yes. Janie Bennett's. She's getting married next month."

"Ah, yes." Franz nodded. "I saw the young lovers at the party the other night. Edward appears smitten to the gills."

"He is. Hopelessly so."

Setting his stool and stepping up, he touched the wand to the lamp above her head and smiled wistfully. "Ah, to be that young again."

Yes. To be young and foolish again.

"Franz," she said, "if Audrey feels up to it, why don't you come for supper Wednesday night? Mother would love it. She's been wanting to bake a blackberry cobbler, and what's a blackberry cobbler without you around to eat it?"

Franz chuckled. "Well, I don't know what would stop us. A man can hardly pass up an offer like that. I'll tell Audrey. She'll feel better just thinking about it."

"Wonderful. We'll expect you Wednesday."

"Wednesday, we'll look forward to it."

She accompanied him as he carefully made his way down the sidewalk. His wife's lingering illness had taken its toll on him. Where he had once stood straight and proud, he now was slightly stooped and worn. Her heart ached. What would Franz do without Audrey? They were so close, married young, and had no children. They had no one but each other.

"Oh, and Vonnie?" Franz called over his shoulder.

"Yes?"

"Tell Cammy to put enough sugar in the cobbler this time." He flashed a grin over his shoulder that reminded Vonnie of a younger, happier man. "Last one was right-down sour."

Shaking her head at his good-natured teasing, she waved and laid her packages on the seat of her waiting buggy. She had to hurry. Cammy would be fussing, and Teague would be upset if she wasn't home before dark.

The light breeze faded quickly. A stillness lay over the countryside by the time she got home.

She glanced toward the ostrich pens as she left her buggy for the stable hand, Roel, to unhitch.

"Mother?" Vonnie called out, dumping her packages on the mahogany deacon's bench in the foyer.

The Taylor house was a large, two-story cedar, built by Vonnie's grandfather, Reginald Edimious Taylor, and his sons. The Italianate Victorian house, with its slightly pitched roof, square towers and round-arched windows, represented more than a home: it was a tribute to the Taylor men's ingenuity and quality craftsmanship, which had earned them a living in those days.

"In the kitchen!"

The click of nails on hardwood floors signaled that Suki, the family mutt, was approaching to extend her usual greeting. Leaping high in the air, she demanded Vonnie's attention.

"Down, Suki...yes, I'm happy to see you, too." She rubbed the dog's ears, then gave her an affectionate pat. "Come on. Let's go find Mother."

The aroma of frying meat filled the air, and Vonnie followed it to the kitchen at the back of the house. The spacious cooking and eating area was her favorite room in the house. Fourteen windows kept the room light and cheery all year round, and she never tired of the panoramic view. Cammy Taylor was at the stove, dishing up thick slices of ham.

Cammy, a small, frail-looking woman with the figure of a young girl, looked up. Her laugh was a tinkle, her eyes bright as a bird's, and she was never certain of anything, she'd tell anyone—except that she'd loved Teague Taylor since she was a girl of fourteen.

"I was afraid you wouldn't make it home before dark."

"You know Brigette. She can smell the barn a mile away. She was high-stepping by the time we reached the lane. Daddy not in yet?"

"No, I've called him twice, but he's still out at the pens."

Vonnie hung her bonnet on a peg and went to the hutch to get the everyday china. "Mmm, smells good in here."

"Daddy wanted ham tonight—and rhubarb pie."

"I saw Franz earlier." Vonnie gathered silverware to set the table.

"You did? Did he say how Audrey is today?"

"Not good, I'm afraid."

"Well, after supper I'll have your daddy carry a big piece of pie over to her. She loves rhubarb. Always did, even as a child."

Folding napkins, Vonnie placed one beside each plate.

"I invited them for supper Wednesday night."

"Wonderful. The fresh air will do Audrey good. She stays closed up in that house too much." Dumping collard greens into a bowl, Cammy carried them to the table. "That daddy of yours—Vonnie, go tell him his supper's getting cold."

The words had no sooner left her mouth when the back door opened, and Teague Taylor came in, stomping his feet. Her daddy had always reminded Vonnie of P.K. Baldwin. They were from the same hardy stock: whipcord thin, skin leatherlike from the sun, hair a steel-gray, eyes that squinted permanently into the future.

"Well, well," he said, glancing at Cammy, then at Vonnie. "If it isn't the two prettiest little gals in Potter County."

"Oh, go on with you," Cammy said, waving a long fork in his direction.

Vonnie was amazed that after thirty-five years, Teague Taylor could still make her mother blush. She smiled, enjoying her parents' spirited antics. Her mother and dad had an enviable relationship, an affectionate and teasing kind of love that made her long for a marriage like theirs. They'd adopted her young, an infant, but she'd never thought of her birth mother. Cammy was her only mother.

Cammy carried a bowl of potatoes to the table, brushing past Teague on the way and bumping him pointedly with her hip.

With a sweep of his arms, Teague scooped his wife off her feet and held her to his chest in a bone-crushing hug. Protesting laughingly, she swatted at him, demanding to be put down.

Teague and Cammy had that rare relationship, able to weather any crisis that came their way. Theirs was a marriage of respect and mutual trust. A marriage based on love for each other and love of God. Teague and Cammy lived their belief, except for Teague's unrelenting hatred for P.K. Baldwin. If Vonnie could find a man who would make her half as happy as Teague made Cammy, she'd marry him on the spot.

But then, that's exactly what she had done, wasn't it?

Kissing her soundly, Teague set Cammy back on her feet, then hugged Vonnie.

"How you doing, Puddin'?"

"Good, Dad. How about you?"

"If I felt any better, you'd have to tie me down!" He pumped a wash pan full of water, splashed his face and reached for a towel. "Order that lace you wanted?"

"I did. And the buttons. Mr. Beasley's ordering more Duchesse for me. Should be here in plenty of time to finish the Wilson dress."

"Duchesse, huh? I suppose that's something all womanified and frilly?"

"Something like that." She grinned. Womanified. "How are the birds?"

"Looking good, ladies. Real good."

Cammy slid a pan of biscuits from the oven. "Harold Jenson stopped by this afternoon. Said there was a man in Phoenix interested in buying a pair."

"He wants adults?"

"Harold thought he did—and Lewis Tanner stopped by again. He wants that fifty acres, Teague. He's offering to pay top price for it."

Teague grunted. "I'll bet he does."

"Honestly, you ought to consider his offer. We don't need the land."

"We sure don't *need* Lewis's dirty money. The Good Book says we're to avoid the appearance of evil, that includes taking money earned in ways God wouldn't approve. Besides, you know he hates the birds. He'd like nothing better than to see us sell out to someone who'll run cattle."

"You'll do what you want, but I think the offer's worth considering."

Teague switched the subject. "That's the third person this month wanting birds. If I keep selling at this rate I won't have enough roosters for my own flock." He rubbed a bar of soap to a high lather and scrubbed his elbows.

"Daddy, I saw Franz when I was in town."

Teague kept scrubbing. "Did you?"

"He sends his best. He and Audrey are coming for supper Wednesday night."

Teague rinsed his arms. "Well, your momma will enjoy the company. Hand me a towel there, will you, Puddin'?"

Vonnie stepped to the hutch to get a hand cloth. "Franz said to tell you to put enough sugar in the cobbler this time, Mom."

"You tell Franz Schuyler that I'm baking the cobbler, not him."

Handing the towel to her father, Vonnie grinned. "You tell him yourself."

"Don't think that I won't."

Drying off, Teague met her gaze. "Heard you danced with Adam the other night."

Vonnie winced. "Mother."

"Oh, don't get all flustered. I remarked to your daddy that it was a shame there was such bad blood between him and P.K. Adam's a fine man. Not only handsome, but responsible and levelheaded. A woman could do worse."

Teague tweaked Vonnie under the chin as he moved to the table. "You stay away from the Baldwins. If I catch you anywhere near one of P.K.'s boys, I'll tan your hide."

The teasing tone was gone. "I mean it, Vonnie. P.K. Baldwin may go to church and believe in the Almighty, but he's not my idea of a Christian. I don't want my girl taking up with a nonbeliever—"

Vonnie interrupted. "Adam believes!"

"Nevertheless, you're not to go around him. Besides, he's about to be married."

Vonnie busied herself with cups and saucers. No use trying to convince him that Adam was a Christian. Teague Taylor held to strict beliefs. He wasn't a man who took his faith lightly. "You don't have to remind me that he's marrying Beth," she couldn't help adding.

"That's Leighton Baylor's problem, not mine." He glanced at his wife. "What smells so good?"

"Ham…rhubarb pie," Cammy announced.

"Rhubarb? You little sweetheart!" He pecked her on the cheek as he walked by. "If we weren't already married, I'd marry you again." He eyed the heaping plate of meat. "I could eat a horse."

"Sit down, I'm taking up the gravy right now. Vonnie, honey, hand me a—" Cammy suddenly paused, frowning. "Teague? What's wrong?"

Teague's face had suddenly turned white as a sheet, his mouth tight with pain.

"Daddy?" Vonnie looked up as she was about to place a fork on the table.

Shaking his head as if he didn't understand himself, his left hand drifted to his chest, his fingers curling into his shirt. A puzzled look came into his eyes, then surprise.

"Teague?"

"Daddy?" Vonnie reached out to steady him as anguish marked her father's face. His gaze met hers, his eyes suddenly full of love. A cold wave of panic swept her.

His mouth opened, but no words came out. Then his legs buckled, and he slumped to the floor, both hands against his chest.

Screaming, Cammy dropped the platter of meat. Ham scattered across the floor, mingling with the shattered china.

"God help us! Teague!" Sinking to her knees, Cammy cradled her husband's lifeless form in her arms. "No, no, no," she whispered over and over. "You can't do this—you can't do this—you can't leave me—don't leave me, Teague—"

Kneeling beside her father, Vonnie reached for his hand, hoping to find a pulse. There was none.

In the blink of an eye, Teague Taylor had left this earth.

Chapter Five

❧

Mourners began arriving for the funeral mid-morning. Buggies filled the yard of the Flying Feather Ranch; the kitchen table groaned beneath the weight of food brought by thoughtful friends and concerned neighbors. Cammy had withdrawn into herself. Vonnie was concerned about her mother.

Drying her eyes, she watched the guests' arrival from the parlor front window. She'd retreated here to escape the soft words of sympathy that were beginning to grate on her nerves. Everyone was well-meaning, but nothing could soften the pain of the loss that cut so deeply through her. Cammy hadn't come out of her room yet today. Vonnie was even more worried about how she was going to get her through the funeral. Her mother and father had been so close.

"Vonnie?"

She turned from the window. "Yes, Mrs. Lincoln."

"The preacher's here. Dear, Cammy hasn't come down yet. Should someone go see about her?"

Moving from the window, Vonnie dabbed at her moist eyes with a handkerchief. "I'll go. Tell Pastor Higgins I'll be with him in a few minutes. Has everyone had coffee?"

"Everyone's fine. You see to your mother. Is she doing all right?"

"Not so well, Mrs. Lincoln. She and Daddy were—"

"I know, dear." Eugenia Lincoln and Cammy had been neighbors for years. Mrs. Lincoln had lost her own husband five years earlier. "It will take time, but one day she'll begin to take up her life again. Oh, the pain will still be there, but it will lessen. One day she'll begin to remember the good things about her life with Teague."

"Thank you, Mrs. Lincoln." Vonnie smiled, dabbing at her eyes. "She'll need your friendship."

"She'll have it." Eugenia said, patting Vonnie's arm.

A moment later, Vonnie knocked lightly on her mother's door. When there was no response, she opened the door gently.

"Mother?"

The shades were drawn down tight. It took a moment for Vonnie's eyes to adjust, then she saw her mother half-reclining on a fainting couch in the corner.

"Mother, the service will begin in half an hour."

Cammy hadn't dressed yet. Her hair hung in a tangled mat over her shoulders. She looked as if she had aged twenty years in the past twenty-four hours.

"Pastor Higgins is here, and all our neighbors and friends. You should come downstairs."

"I can't…I can't go through this."

Vonnie knelt beside the couch, her fingers gently reaching to stroke her mother's trembling hand.

"You must, Momma. They've been so good to come, to offer their help and sympathy."

Cammy turned lifeless eyes on her. "What good will words do? Teague is gone. Nothing will ever be the same again."

"I know you feel that way now, Momma, but you can't hide up here for the rest of your life. As painful as this is, we have to face it, together."

"I can't be with those people. Not now—please, leave me be." Vonnie's patience was stretched to the breaking point.

"Momma, Daddy wouldn't want you to behave like this. He'd want you to be strong, to trust God. You know Daddy trusted without question. He'd expect us to do the same."

Cammy covered her eyes with her hand and held a sodden handkerchief to her trembling lips. "He shouldn't have left me."

"He didn't have a choice. He didn't want to die, Momma!" She took Cammy's hand, holding tightly. "God will give us the strength needed."

Cammy began to sob, and Vonnie was sorry she'd been sharp with her. She had spent most of her life with Teague Taylor, and part of her was gone. She had every right to grieve. Vonnie had been a gift from God. Cammy believed she would never have a child. Then one afternoon she had stumbled across a dying woman. A dying woman who had given her a child. Her parents had doted on her. The three had become nearly inseparable. Vonnie understood that her mother would grieve deeply, but this retreating to her room, to inside herself, distressed her.

"I'll help you get dressed. What about the blue? Daddy loved the blue dress on you."

Vonnie began to search through the armoire for the new dress she'd made her mother in the spring. "I sewed it special for Easter, remember? And Daddy commented on how nice you looked in it."

"Vonnie—"

"Try, Momma. The burial is in thirty minutes. You've got to be there." She took a deep breath, fighting back tears. "For me."

Resigned, Cammy got up, visibly weak from not eating. She managed to get dressed and brush her hair into a semblance of order. She leaned heavily on Vonnie's arm as they descended the stairs. Mrs. Lincoln was in the foyer and saw them first.

"Cammy," she murmured, stepping forward to meet them. "Teague would say you look like a bluebonnet in the summer."

"Oh, Eugenia." Cammy broke down, walking into her friend's arms.

Vonnie let Mrs. Lincoln take charge of her mother, watching them go into the large parlor together. Murmurs of condolences floated out to her as Vonnie retreated outside.

The sun was shining, a light breeze. She lifted her eyes to the heavens and whispered, "You're going to have to help us get through this. I know Daddy's there with You, but this is so hard for us." A peace filled her and for a moment she imagined that she felt Teague's firm hand on her shoulder, urging her on.

Moving toward the family cemetery, which Teague had prepared in a grove of birch trees about a hundred yards from the house, she gathered her fortitude around her like a shroud. Teague's parents were buried here. They'd lived with Cammy and Teague until their deaths, when Vonnie was three. And Great-Aunt Alice and Uncle Sill were here. Vonnie pushed open the gate, pausing momentarily as the gaping hole in the ground where her father would be laid to rest jarred her senses. The ranch hands had been busy this morning.

Tears sprang to her eyes. She sagged against the gate as the enormity of the past twenty-four hours hit her.

She clung to the weathered boards, her lips moving in silent prayer. Now, as never before, she realized the comfort of being a child of God. How could anyone go through life without the love and strength that only He could give?

She remained at the grave site, grieving alone. When she started back to the house, the funeral party was already spilling out onto the lawn, parting to stand aside as six pall-bearers carried the freshly planed pine casket toward the cemetery. Cammy, still firmly in Mrs. Lincoln's control, followed her husband's body, a linen handkerchief to her eyes. Vonnie watched the strangely quiet procession make its way across the wide lawn.

Ed Hogan had come. Teague had bought feed from him for years. The Newton sisters were there because they were simply good neighbors. Cammy had taken a kettle of chicken soup to the sisters when one had come down with pneumonia last year. Teague had gone with her and cut a cord of firewood when he noticed their supply was running low.

There was Pastor Higgins, and his wife Pearl, and Franz and frail Audrey. Hildy Addison, Mora and Carolyn were there having arrived last night to be with her.

And then there were the Baldwins. They'd come as a matter of courtesy rather than friendship. It would have looked impolite if they'd been missing, since most of the town had seen fit to pay their condolences.

The five men stood well back from the group now circling the casket. Andrew, two years younger than Adam, had disliked Teague intensely. Vonnie knew he'd had a crush on her since school, but he'd detested her father. They'd been in the same class throughout their childhood. He and Adam had even fought over her once when they thought P.K. wasn't looking.

Her eyes slipped to the woman who was standing beside Adam. *She* should be standing by him, not Beth. He should be by *her* side, to console her, to hold her, to love her…. Her thoughts stopped short. Beth was one of the nicest women around—kind, even tempered. Vonnie couldn't find it in her heart to resent Beth's place beside Adam.

"Dear friends," Pastor Higgins began as the assemblage gathered closer to the open grave.

Vonnie moved to one side of Cammy as Mrs. Lincoln closed in on the other. Cammy clung to Vonnie's arm like a lost child.

"We are gathered here today to say goodbye to a loyal friend, a loving husband and father, a good neighbor—"

Andrew Baldwin held his hat in both hands, his eyes lowered. He studied his feet and the casket, but Vonnie could feel his frequent glances.

"—and we know that one day we will see our friend again and we will then rejoice together. Let us pray. Our Father…"

Bowing her head, Vonnie watched Adam standing beside Beth through brimming eyes. P.K., Andrew, Pat and Joey stood nearby. P.K., like her father, was a pillar of the community. The men had more in common than just being neighbors. They were two of a kind, the breed of man who had carved a place for families in this vast land, who proved that perseverance and providence, yoked by sweat and ingenuity, could build a good life.

Alike in spirit, they were alike in appearance as well— tall, rangy, broad shouldered, faces weathered, near the same age.

She studied Adam, her eyes blurred with pain and tears, praying to block out the sight of the man she loved. The warm sun brought out the blond highlights in his brown hair. If she had been taking inventory, she could have noted that he'd not bothered to get a haircut in several weeks. His hair had a tendency to curl when he let it grow, and now it was waving against the collar of a blue shirt that matched his eyes.

Suddenly the memory of the boy she'd loved sprang up. At seventeen, Adam had been larger than most of the boys his age. He'd done the work of a grown man since he had been thirteen. Everyone knew that he and his brothers would one day inherit Cabeza Del Lobo.

The other boys accepted that. Each had his own duties. Andrew was in charge of the hired hands, while the others worked the horses and cattle. Vonnie had heard her father comment to Cammy that P.K. was staying closer to the house more and more these days. Stiffening of the joints, he'd said, made the days long for P.K. Whatever the differences between the two men, her father's notice of Adam's father had been genuine.

It would be natural, she'd thought, for the two men who were responsible for Amarillo turning into a thriving community to be friends, or at least business partners. But such was not the case. P.K. and Teague rarely looked in the same direction when forced to be in the same place at the same time, much less socialized.

Yet, she'd found no real reason for such hatred. Differences maybe, but Teague had tolerated differences with everyone *but* P.K.

"Amen."

Pastor Higgins motioned Vonnie forward, and she carefully took a handful of dirt and sprinkled it on her father's coffin.

Oh, Daddy. What are we going to do without you?

The moment was so emotional she felt her defenses crumbling. Holding on to her mother's arm, she helped Cammy sprinkle dirt on the casket.

"I'll be stopping by in a day or two," Pastor Higgins murmured as he grasped their hands a moment later. "My prayers are with you. Should you need anything, don't hesitate to send for me."

Vonnie blinked back tears. "Thank you, Pastor. It was a lovely service."

Suddenly she wished everyone was gone. She wanted to be alone, to cry and grieve with her mother.

One by one the mourners passed by, the women hugging first her mother then her, the men shuffling by uttering a few barely audible words.

Everyone had expressed their remorse when P.K. approached. For a moment he didn't say anything, just looked down at the ground. Eventually, he cleared his throat and met Vonnie's eyes.

He opened his mouth to speak, but words failed him. Reaching for Cammy's hand, he squeezed it briefly before moving on.

"I'm sorry, Vonnie," Andrew said, taking her hand in his.

"It was kind of you to come, Andrew."

"Vonnie," Pat said. He seemed uncertain of what he should say when it was his turn.

"Thank you for coming, Pat."

"You're welcome, ma'am… I'm real sorry for you and your mother."

Ma'am. The address made her sound so old.

Joey nodded and followed his brothers out the cemetery gate.

And then it was Adam's turn. Beth clung to his side, holding his arm protectively. Taking Vonnie's hand, he held it for a moment. The show of respect made her pain even more evident. "I'm sorry, Vonnie."

She swallowed, overwhelmed with the impulse to lean

against his broad chest and sob her heart out. She had realized her foolishness long ago. She should have respected their vows, stood up to Teague, but she hadn't. Now she had lost Adam forever.

"Thank you," she managed.

His thumb moved lightly across her knuckles. He'd held her hand this way, his thumb brushing back and forth, the night they stood before an ill-prepared judge and were married.

For a moment she swayed lightly against him, overcome by emotion. Her forehead rested against his chest, her eyes closed. She felt his need to put his arms around her, to hold her, but he didn't. What had been between them was over. The love they'd once shared was nothing but a nice memory.

When Adam had begun courting Beth, Vonnie knew P.K. was pleased. Beth was the kind of woman P.K. appreciated, one who was agreeable. Nothing ever upset her. She was flexible; she adjusted. Whatever Adam wanted, Beth was willing to accommodate. She would be the ideal wife, and her father owned land P.K. had wanted for years.

When it was apparent she'd lingered too long, Vonnie straightened, color flooding her cheeks. How could she have weakened like that, leaning on Adam and making a spectacle of herself? Beth would think her shamelessly forward.

Always thoughtful and good-hearted, Beth was the first to the bedside of a sick person, the first to lend a hand at church with any event. True, sometimes Beth's giving nature could get on her nerves, but Vonnie was honest enough to realize the differences in their personalities. If she was serious about serving God maybe she should try to be more like Beth.

Quickly regaining her composure, she dropped her hand to her side. "Thank you, Adam. I appreciate your coming. I must admit I was surprised to see your father here."

Adam's eyes followed P.K. as he walked away from the grave site. "I wonder if he didn't care more about Teague than he's willing to admit."

"If he did, then it's too bad he never told him," she said. "For all concerned." Their eyes met briefly before he looked away.

"I'm so sorry about your father," Beth said, slipping her hand into Vonnie's. "If there's anything I can do, you must let me know."

"Thank you, Beth. Tell your mother I appreciate the chicken she sent over."

"I'll come by tomorrow and—well, we'll all have a nice, long visit." She tilted her head, smiling encouragingly. "Would you like that?"

"That's kind of you. Mother is so upset. I'm not sure that she'll be up to visiting. Mrs. Lincoln is going to stay with us a few days to help out, but I'd like your company. The house seems so empty without Daddy—"

She faltered, a lump forming in her throat. The realization that her father would never again come in the back door and call for Cammy hurt. Never again would he hug her and call her "Puddin'." Never again would the aroma of his pipe float through the big house he'd helped build with his own hands.

It seemed so senseless, a man struck down before he could enjoy his declining years. A man who'd worked hard deserved to put his feet up by the fire for a few years at least, didn't he?

As the crowd began to disperse, Beth moved Adam toward the Baylor buggy. Cammy was surrounded by several well-meaning matrons who went on about how sad it was that Cammy was "left alone" in her prime. In clucking, sympathetic voices, they invited her to join their quilting club on Thursday afternoons. It was little more than a gossip group, Vonnie knew, but it would be good for Cammy to be with friends.

Vonnie's gaze moved over the mourners, most of whom were heading back to the house to eat lunch from the food brought in; all except the Baldwins. The five men had ridden away immediately after the ceremony.

It was evening by the time the farm quieted down. The house was so still that Vonnie couldn't stand it. She decided to go check on the ostriches. Suki followed her outside and scampered around her feet, demanding attention, as she walked toward the pens that were built two hundred yards back from the house.

"Settle yourself," Vonnie scolded the dog. "You'll upset the birds acting like that."

The ostriches were accustomed to Suki's interruptions, but they were easily disturbed by anything out of the ordinary.

Ten pens stood in a row, with a pair of adult ostriches in each. The little "waddlebabies" were kept separate, each hatch together in a pen until they were big enough to begin pairing.

The most recent hatch was only a week old, but they were a handsome group. Vonnie liked watching them. They ran back and forth in the pen as if on a very important mission, their brown-gray feathers just covering bodies balanced on legs that looked far too thin to support egg-shaped abdomens and long, thin necks. Large eyes were as bright and curious as buttons; they split their time pecking at various bits on the ground and watching her approach.

"Hello, babies," Vonnie crooned, counting the chicks to make sure they were all accounted for.

Some of the young ones came to the fence and peered up at her, a couple of them pecking at the woven wire fence in curiosity. She slowly walked around each pen, checking that no wires were loose or had slipped and that the edges were all anchored into the ground. The pen material had to be specially made with squares of wire, small enough to keep the adult ostriches from poking their heads through and choking, yet large enough so the little ones could get their heads out if they poked them through.

They weren't the dumbest birds in the world. They just seemed like that sometimes. Curious, they'd try for anything that captured their attention, sometimes getting their heads hung in the fence. More than once, Teague had lost his hat to the lively birds.

If frightened, they'd run pell-mell into the end of the fence, breaking wings, necks or legs in their hasty flight. And they were temperamental. Like humans, some were gentle and some had a temper. Some could be handled and petted; others didn't want to be touched at all.

They could be persuaded to move to another area, not herded there. An adult ostrich could run like the wind, reaching unbelievable speeds. A man on a fast horse would have difficulty catching one, once it got going.

Tears brightened her eyes. But, oh, how her father had loved these funny-looking creatures. Did they miss the sound of his voice, the gentle touch of his hand?

Suddenly Vonnie detected a shadow from the corner of her eye.

"Who's there?"

She peered into the twilight, a frown creasing her forehead. Goose flesh raised on her arms.

"Who's there?"

A figure stepped from behind a tall cactus at the edge of the pens.

"Andrew?" she said, relieved when she recognized him. "You frightened me." A person could get himself shot creeping around the ostrich pens. The hands knew to shoot first and ask questions later.

"Sorry," he said.

Andrew Baldwin was nearly as tall as Adam, with the same wavy brown hair. He was the most serious of the four boys. He'd walked with a limp ever since she could remember, the result of a fall from the loft of the Baldwin barn. He had broken his leg, and the injury had never healed properly. Andrew was rumored to have read all the books in his father's library, a feat P.K. himself had never accomplished.

"Just stopped by to see how you're doing," Andrew said, "and decided to take a look at the birds."

"You gave me a bit of a start," Vonnie admitted. "I'm surprised to see you out this late."

"I wanted to talk to you at the cemetery today. But there were a lot of people around, and you were talking with Adam."

"I'm glad you came."

"Wanted you to know if there's anything I can do to help—"

"Thank you, Andrew. I appreciate that."

Andrew was the odd duck in the Baldwin group. Where Adam was most like his father, Andrew was broody and quiet. No one really knew what was going on in his mind.

The sound of a horse coming at a fast clip drew their attention. Vonnie identified the tall figure astride the big bay immediately.

"Looks like we have company," she murmured, watching Adam dismount.

"Andrew." Adam acknowledged his brother as he approached. "I didn't expect to see you here." His eyes swept Vonnie curiously.

"I wasn't aware I needed your permission to be here," Andrew returned.

Vonnie glanced from one brother to the other. A thread of tension ran between them, and she wondered why.

"Dad's looking for you," Adam said curtly.

"Is he now? He sent you to find me?"

"I don't believe he thinks you're over here." Accusation colored Adam's tone.

The two brothers stared at each other.

"Then I suppose I'll go report in," Andrew stated coldly.

"Thank you for coming by—" Vonnie's words faltered as she watched him limp to where his tethered horse waited.

Swinging into the saddle, he looked back at her, then touched the brim of his hat briefly and a moment later disappeared into the thickening darkness.

Turning around, she gave Adam a perturbed look.

Chapter Six

❧

Removing his hat, Adam ran his fingers through his thick hair. The air hummed with awareness between them. It had been years since they'd been alone.

"What was that all about?"

"Who knows?" he said. "He's hard to figure out."

Vonnie drew a deep breath. Adam still had the power to render her breathless. "What brings you here this time of night?"

"I was checking on a stray. Since I was in the area, I thought I'd stop by, see if you needed anything."

"Need anything?" She wanted to laugh. "Since when have the Baldwins ever been interested in a Taylor's welfare? I thought coming to the funeral would have stretched the 'doing what's right' quotient for the day."

He let her bitterness spill out without interrupting. She

was glad; right now she didn't know what she was capable of saying.

"I guess now that Daddy's gone, P.K. wants to put on a good front for the community, show he's a real human being after all?" She hated the sting in her tone, the harpy inflection. She was more mad at herself than at him. She was the one who hadn't been willing to fight for their marriage.

"I know this has been a rough time for you," he said.

"You're right." She turned away, staring at the birds. "My father dropped dead in the kitchen in front of me, and your father's taking advantage of our misery to show he has no hard feelings for a man who's dead? How magnanimous of him."

"Whatever was between your father and mine is dead and buried. Let it lie."

"I wish I could." Turning away, Vonnie headed back to the house.

His voice stopped her. "I didn't come over to start an argument. Can't we have a conversation without all this animosity?"

Sighing, she lowered her guard. What purpose would it serve to argue? She was being unreasonable and petty at a time she needed his strength more than she needed retribution. She closed her eyes.

"Of course, you're right. I am upset. Thank you for stopping by. Mother and I are coping. We both...appreciate your concern."

When she looked up, she saw compassion reflected in his eyes. A subdued understanding. "I'm sorry about your father, Vonnie. I didn't know him, but I'm sorry for you and your mother's loss."

Pulling her wrap closer against the night air, she studied him. It was the child in her that needed his acceptance, or perhaps it was the woman in her that needed his love.

"I don't know what Momma will do."

"It won't be easy for her."

Maybe if he was less kind it would be easier. Resentment flared anew.

"I think you're here because your father is concerned about propriety, not because you have any real concern for me."

"No," he corrected her. "P.K. doesn't know I'm here, and he doesn't care about propriety."

She bit her lower lip, wanting to believe that he was there for no other reason than he cared for her. Cared deeply.

His voice dropped to a low timbre. "I'm here because I want to be here, and I thought you might need me. That's the only reason."

Her eyes welled with unshed tears when she finally looked up again. "Well, go home. I don't need you, Adam."

Shaking his head slowly, his eyes met hers in the moonlight. For a moment, time faded, and they were young and in love. "I'd hoped you wouldn't make it necessary for me to remind you."

"Of what," she whispered. But she knew. Oh, she knew.

"I wanted to fight for us, Vonnie. You didn't."

Closing her eyes against the truth, she looked away. "I was young, Adam."

"You've had seven years to reconsider." Grasping the reins of his horse, he prepared to mount. "We'd appreciate if you'd let us know when you sell the birds. P.K. knows someone who might be interested in buying a pair."

"Sell the birds? What do you mean, when I sell them?"

He looked down on her from his perch in the saddle. "When you sell out. You can't raise those birds by yourself."

Her chin lifted a notch. "I don't intend to sell my birds. I still have Roel and Genaro and the other hands, in case you haven't noticed."

She saw the muscles tighten in his jaw.

"With Teague gone, I didn't think you'd be keeping the place."

"Mother and I are staying right here. My seamstress work is good. Daddy had some money put away, and with the bridal-gown orders coming in, we'll do fine."

His look was cold and dismissing.

"The birds were Daddy's pride and joy," she added, compelled to defend her decision and stand her ground.

In the past, maybe she hadn't taken a personal interest in them, but now they had taken on new significance. The birds had been special to her father, and he'd seen a future in raising them. She would feel guilty if she sold out after all the hard work he'd put into building the herd. Besides, Adam Baldwin would be the last person on earth she'd let buy the birds.

"I'm keeping the birds."

Stubborn, Adam's expression said. *As stubborn as your father, if not more.*

You are as bullheaded as P.K., hers implied right back.

"Well, the offer holds. When you want to sell out, we'll buy."

"In a pig's eye," she murmured.

Ignoring the less-than-charitable refusal, he wheeled his horse and rode into the darkness.

Vonnie watched him go, listening to the fading hoof-beats. She felt very alone and hated the fact that he could still make her feel that way.

Vonnie rapped lightly on her mother's door before push-ing it partially open.

"Momma, dinner's on the table."

"I'm not hungry, dear. You go ahead and eat. I want to rest a little longer."

"You can't stay up here in this room forever." Vonnie moved to the window to lift the shade.

Two weeks had passed since Teague's death, and Cammy was getting worse every day. She was withdrawing, wrapping herself in a shroud of grief. She rarely left the room she'd shared with her husband. Her face was lined with anguish, and she wept inconsolably at times. The house was like a tomb.

"Vonnie—don't—the light hurts my eyes," Cammy pro-tested, turning her face away from the glare.

"Momma, you have to try."

Mrs. Lincoln came each morning to coax her downstairs, thinking up reasons for them to take a short drive or go into town, but Cammy resisted all her efforts. She spent her days in a chair beside the bed, usually remaining in her dressing gown, sometimes listlessly allowing Vonnie to help her dress.

Each morning Vonnie brushed her mother's hair and wound it atop her head, but Cammy never showed an interest in how she looked these days. Already frail, she had lost more weight. Her clothes hung on her alarmingly sparse frame. She spent her days staring into space as if nothing mattered, and Vonnie knew that to her it didn't.

"I've got a surprise for you today. We're going to visit Audrey." Vonnie hoped a visit with Audrey Schuyler would make Cammy realize how fortunate she was to have her health.

Health was precious, and only when one lost it, or saw it being slowly drained away, did they realize their own good fortune. It had probably been her mother who had told her that.

"What dress would you like to wear?"

"I'm not up to visiting today," Cammy said.

"I think the pink flowered one with the pretty torchon-lace collar," Vonnie ignored her mother's protest. "It'll put the color back in your cheeks."

"No, Vonnie. I don't want to go."

"Franz says Audrey has been feeling better the last couple of days. Here, let's slip off your gown…."

Ignoring her mother's feeble objections, Vonnie maneuvered her arms into the dress sleeves like a rag doll.

"Dear, really, I don't feel up to going anywhere—"

"There, don't you look pretty! Here, let's put your shawl about your shoulders in case it's a bit cooler when we return. I've had Roel hitch the team to the buggy—"

"I don't think so, dear, really—"

Vonnie sighed. She would have liked a good cry herself.

She smoothed the shawl across her mother's shoulders. "Now, we're almost ready to go. It's a lovely day out there— the temperature's nearly perfect. Hard to believe Thanksgiving's just around the corner."

Vonnie bustled around the room, gathering up the things needed for the afternoon outing. Audrey would be the one to set Cammy's priorities in place. Teague was gone. No amount of crying could bring him back. They both missed him unbearably, but somehow she had to make her mother want to live again.

She had to virtually pull Cammy out the door and down the stairway. Oblivious to her mother's weak protestations, Vonnie propelled her outside and into the waiting buggy.

"Thank you, Roel," she said, accepting the reins to the team. "We'll be home before dark."

"*Sí, señorita, hasta luego.*"

Giving the reins a slap against the horses' rumps, Vonnie set the team on its way.

"My, my, my," Franz said, greeting them warmly as they hitched the horses to the railing of the Schuylers' front porch. "What a nice surprise. Audrey will be delighted to see you. Come in. Come in!"

He ushered them into a small but neat living room where Audrey was resting on a sofa, a yellow crocheted throw over her thin legs.

"Oh, how wonderful it is to see you!" Audrey said, holding out both hands to Cammy.

Vonnie relaxed as her mother reached out for Audrey and the two old friends clasped hands. Cammy seemed to momentarily shed the melancholy that had plagued her for weeks. In fact, as she and Audrey talked, Cammy seemed to almost be her old self.

The two women conversed in low tones, and Vonnie settled herself in a chair nearby. Franz escaped to the kitchen, returning shortly with a tray holding a teapot and four china cups.

"Would you pour?" he asked Vonnie.

"Of course."

She performed the small ritual, automatically adding two teaspoons of sugar to her mother's cup.

"Just look at our little Vonnie," Audrey said, accepting Franz's help to sit up straighter so she could sip her tea. He fussed over her, fluffing her pillow, making sure she was comfortable. "Thank you, dear. I remember so well the day they brought you home."

Cammy and Audrey were like sisters. They had spent part of nearly every day together when they were first married.

Though Teague and Franz had served in the war together, it was the women who were close and shared every part of their lives.

"You were the sweetest young'un. A thatch of black hair that never changed. A little button of a nose." Audrey smiled gently. "And a little rosebud of a mouth. And you never cried. Not really. Just a beautiful child in all ways." Her eyes brimmed with emotion for the child that she loved like her own.

Sipping her tea, she then lay back against her pillows closing her eyes.

"Franz and I wanted children. A whole houseful. But, it wasn't to be."

Vonnie made an appropriate remark. It seemed Audrey always talked about her disappointment of not having children. It appeared to weigh on her mind heavily these days.

"Well, I guess one should be careful what they promise." She smiled. "When Franz was off to war, so many months passed without knowing whether he was alive or injured. I got down on my hands and knees and prayed every night that he'd be spared. I promised, 'God, if You'll just bring Franz home safe, then I'll never ask another thing of You.'"

"And you never did," Franz said, his tone tender. "You've never asked for anything."

Vonnie could hear the sadness in his voice and knew that if he could give Audrey anything it would be her health, so they could have many more happy years together.

"But," Franz added, a twinkle returning to his eyes, "you did want your piano back."

"Franz," Audrey scolded. "I did not—it was such a frivolous thing."

Although Vonnie had heard the story numerous times, she played along. "A piano?" she asked.

"A Steinway," Franz said. "Her father bought it for her. Oh, how she loved to play. But we lost everything after the war, and we had to sell the instrument in order to make ends meet." He smiled warmly at his wife, adoration glowing in his eyes. "She did love that piano."

"It was nothing, really. Other people sacrificed more," Audrey insisted. "So many lost families, husbands, sons. What's a piano compared to someone's life? I never missed it. Ever."

"Audrey Schuyler! You're such a fibber!" Franz teased. "I've seen that look in your eye when that piano's mentioned. It meant a great deal to you."

"Go on now," Audrey said, swatting at her husband as he caught her hand and held it. They held hands for a moment like young lovers.

A knot formed in Vonnie's throat. *Oh, to have a love like that.* The kind of love that weathers the hard times and flourishes in the good times. The kind that only grows sweeter as the years pass.

"My wife didn't *just* play the piano," Franz said. "She mastered it. She attended the Sorbonne, you know, and would have played concerts had I not begged her to marry me."

"Begged?" Audrey scoffed. "More like I chased him down shamelessly and pleaded with him to marry me!"

Franz laughed. "When we married, her parents gave her the Steinway as a wedding gift. It was a beautiful instrument, one of a kind. Ivory keys, a fine finish, and a tone that couldn't be matched. When she played, even the birds stopped their singing."

"Why did you sell the piano?" Vonnie asked, though she knew the story well.

"Like many families after the war, land lay without crops, homes were burned, there was no food. When I came home, there was no work." Franz patted his wife's hand lovingly. "So, we had to sell Audrey's beautiful piano."

"Judge Henderson bought it," Audrey said. "Paid a handsome price for it, too. Enough to keep us going until we could get a good garden in and put food aside. It was a few months before Franz could get work, so selling the piano was the only choice."

"Ach," Franz inserted. "The judge bought it for his daughter, but that Carolyn had no touch. She just pounded it—I've heard her!"

Vonnie lifted her cup to mask a smile. Carolyn was quite atrocious at the keys. Tone-deaf, Teague said when he heard her. But Carolyn was possessive about that old piano. She wouldn't hear of it being sold.

"Yes, no one could match my Audrey. When she played, it was like the angels touched the keys. That Miss Henderson, she flitted away from that piano and on to some new fancy, just like she does the boys," Franz said.

Audrey laughed at Franz's irritation, and Vonnie joined her.

"Young people," Audrey said, "are more fickle than when we were girls, aren't they, Cammy?"

Cammy looked up. "Pardon?"

"I said the young aren't like we used to be, are they?"

"No," Cammy murmured. "I suppose not."

The afternoon passed by uneventfully. The talk turned to local gossip. For a while, Vonnie endured the conversation centered on the community's newest engagement, that of Adam and Beth. After a while, she quietly excused herself and disappeared into the kitchen to make more tea.

It was growing late when Vonnie finally stood up. "We should be going, Mother. It will be dark soon."

Nodding quietly, Cammy set aside her teacup.

"So soon?" Audrey protested. "Why it seems you barely got here."

Cammy smiled wanly. "I must confess that I tire easily these days."

"It's been so good to see you," Audrey said, reaching out a hand to her old friend. "Come back soon."

"I will," Cammy said, leaning to kiss a sunken cheek.

Audrey caught her face and held it momentarily. Gazing up at Cammy, she said softly, "I pray for you every night. Teague is in a far better place, you know. It's you who's hurting."

Cammy's newfound resolve momentarily crumpled. "Oh, Audrey…I don't see how I can go on without him," she whispered brokenly.

"Of course you can." Audrey squeezed her hand. "Teague would be ashamed of you if you didn't try."

Audrey's strength was depleted. Vonnie felt guilty for having stayed so long. Franz walked them out to the buggy.

"I hope we didn't tire Audrey too much." Vonnie helped Cammy onto the seat, then arranged a warm blanket around her legs.

"Not at all," he returned. "It's good for her to see old friends. You come back. Soon."

"We will," Vonnie promised. She turned, kissing Franz on the cheek. "The visit has been good for Mother, too."

The sadness in Franz's eyes reminded Vonnie that Audrey's days weren't long, and he too was grieving.

It was late as they turned down the lane to the Flying Feather. Much of the trip had been made in silence, Vonnie and Cammy involved in their own personal thoughts.

"You know, Momma, we're lucky to have each other. We're

not alone. God is watching over us. We need to have faith. I know it's hard, but faith is only a word if we don't practice it."

Cammy studied the horizon, a glint of moisture in her eyes. "I know. But it's easier to speak of faith when all is well."

Gathering twilight bathed the countryside as carriage wheels sang along the road. Vonnie slapped the reins, urging the horses to a faster pace. "It's in times of trouble you utilize that faith."

"I know Audrey's not here for long," Cammy admitted. "It's so sad to think of Franz and what her passing will do to him. He would do anything for her."

"I know, Momma." Vonnie didn't want to think about it, either. Franz and Audrey were so much a part of each other, as Teague and Cammy had been.

"People are kind. They want to say something to help. They say, 'Oh, I know how you feel,' but in fact, they haven't the slightest idea how it feels—the pain—" Her hand came up to touch her heart. "The pain never goes away." Biting her lip, she struggled for composure. "When Audrey's gone, Franz will be alone, but I have you."

She patted Vonnie's knee and then left her hand there, as if to reassure herself that her daughter was indeed beside her.

They were nearly home before she spoke again.

"You know, after your father came home from the war, he never wanted to talk about it. Always said it was too painful."

"I know." That had puzzled Vonnie, since most men

who'd been in the war were prone to talk about their exploits, or at least brag that they were at Bull Run, or had taken part in some other important battle.

"Daddy didn't talk about it at all, even to you?"

"He told enough for me to understand why he hated it so. He wanted to put it out of his mind. I remember Franz mentioned something in passing one day, and Teague was rather curt in telling him never to speak of the war in his presence. I thought he was unnecessarily sharp with Franz, but he said it was a time he wanted to forget."

"What was Daddy like, then?"

A smile curved Cammy's lips. "Oh, he was a rascal when he was young, that father of yours. Wherever there was a party, he got there early and stayed late."

She smiled and paused. Then her face sobered. "But when he came back from the war, he was a different man. The death, the blood, the loss—I've heard others talk about it. It's not something a man wants to recall.

"But when he finally began to come around, he was more like the old Teague. He got those ostriches and seemed to like what they gave him, as if life would get better somehow. He started back to church. His faith just grew stronger day by day. It was amazing to see the miracle of God's love working in that man. Yet so changed. Slower to laugh, never touched a drop of liquor after that. After a while he started working again, and began building the farm." Her eyes grew distant. "Other than the terrible rift between him and P.K.... I always hated that. I believe that deep in his heart, Teague hated it, too. There was a time when he and P.K. were close as brothers." She sighed. "We had a good life together."

Vonnie let Cammy out at the front door of the house, then drove the buggy to the barn, where she handed the team to Roel.

"Be sure and give them some extra oats," she called.

The aging ranch hand tipped the brim of his hat politely. *"Sí. Buenas noches."*

"Good night."

Cammy had already disappeared to her room when Vonnie entered the kitchen. She decided not to push the issue. That her mother had ventured out for an afternoon visit was enough for today.

Climbing the stairs to her attic workroom, Vonnie realized that she was too tired to sew, but the Wilson dress still had a few final touches to be added.

Flipping on the light, she took off her coat and hung it over the hook. Cammy still preferred the use of coal-oil lamps throughout the house, but Vonnie insisted on electrical lighting in her workroom. Teague had contacted the Electrical Light and Ice Plant and paid for the wiring as a surprise for her eighteenth birthday. He had teased her, saying since it looked like he had an old-maid daughter on his hands, he wanted her to bring in some money.

Smoothing her hair, she automatically stepped to the window to look down on the pens. The birds were settled for the night. Moonlight drenched the barn and the outbuildings. All appeared peaceful and serene. Only the emptiness in her heart reminded her of the startling upheaval that had so recently shaken her comfortable existence.

She found her thoughts returning to Franz and Audrey. So much in love, they would be lost without each other.

So much in love.

The way she and Adam had been once. She could close her eyes and see the determined set of his jaw. She knew the way his eyes darkened when he was serious, the joyful lilt of his laugh, knew all his moods. They had walked hand in hand, sharing their dreams.

He had been so intense, so determined they belonged together.

"Promise me," he had urged. "Promise we'll stay together forever."

"I promise...I promise."

Well, forever hadn't lasted long and it had been her fault. She leaned her head against the cool glass of the windowpane. Her inner musings turned to God. "What if I have to make Beth's dress?" The thought made her sick, yet she knew Beth would ask. *"If she asks me, Father, help me to make it as lovely as I can. Take this hurt and anger from me, and fill me with Your grace."*

She stood by the window a while longer, feeling surrounded by God's love. Then a coyote howled in the distance and the moment passed.

Snapping out of her thoughts, she sat down at the sewing machine and attempted to pass the ivory thread through the needle with shaking hands.

Adam, for all purposes, was gone. The marriage was over—never began actually. So why was she pretending she had "rights" to Adam Baldwin—God-given rights.

As surely as Cammy had laid Teague to rest, she must now lay Adam's memory to rest.

Her resolve quickly crumbled and she laid her head on her arm and bit back scalding tears of remorse.

Chapter Seven

❧

Blowing a strand of hair out of her eyes, Vonnie pinned a seam to Jane's slim figure. With a deep, weary breath, she smoothed her hair, tucking the errant strand back into place.

She straightened and circled Jane slowly, examining the wedding dress with a practiced eye. The long train was unadorned. The front of the white satin dress was plain, with three tiny flounces edged with silver at the bottom.

Honiton-point lace was arranged in three flounces, and long trails of orange blossom, with buds and foliage, carried down on either side of the flounced space. Two more trails were brought across the sides at a short distance below the hips, lightly tied together in the center where there was a small droop, and then allowed to fall to the edge of the dress.

The long-pointed bodice was fashioned of white-and-silver brocade, and more Honiton trimmed the top of the bodice to form the upper part of the sleeve. A small wreath of orange blossom was carried all the way around the bust, with a miniature bouquet on each shoulder, and a larger one in the center, mingled with white heather.

The matching Honiton-lace veil would allow Jane's face to be in full view, and would be worn with a small orange-blossom wreath placed on her hair. Tool Bennett had spared no expense on his daughter's wishes.

"Well?" Jane said anxiously.

Vonnie made another slow orbit, while Jane stood on the stool wiggling her fingers.

"Stand still. Don't fidget."

"I'm trying. I'm really trying not to move a muscle. Well?"

Vonnie laughed, unable to stretch out the suspense any longer.

"I think it might be the most lovely dress I've ever made," she finally admitted.

"Oh!" Jane clapped her hands together in delight, then yelped as a pin pricked her. "Can I see it?"

"No. Not until I have the seams stitched in permanently and that last bit of lace tacked to the hem. Then, and only then, will I unveil the mirror. And remember, the day of the wedding I'll replace the artificial blossoms with real ones."

"I can't stand the suspense a moment longer!"

Laughing, Vonnie took another tuck in the waist seam. "It's a rule. Like the one about a groom not seeing the dress or his bride on their wedding day. It's considered bad luck."

"Oh, rules are silly."

"Whatever you say," Vonnie said, her mind already racing ahead to how little time there was before the wedding and how she was going to schedule Jane's last fitting in with the rest of the work she had to finish in the next month.

"Are you all right, Vonnie? Is your mother doing any better?"

"Stand still," Vonnie murmured around a mouthful of pins.

"I can't, I'm too nervous."

Vonnie began marking the seam lines in the dress. "Mother is having a hard time adjusting. It's very difficult for her. She and my father were very close."

Jane sighed. "It's so sad—I hope Edward and I have that kind of marriage."

"What kind of marriage is that?"

"Oh, you know. The kind where Edward can still make me smile when I'm old and wrinkled—a grandmother."

"Lift your arm. Careful," Vonnie said as she methodically adjusted pins. She tried not to think of the dreams she'd once had for marriage and children. She couldn't remember the last time someone had come courting. Was it Peter Kinsley? Surely not. It was nearly a year ago that Peter had escorted her to the Christmas ball. In spite of her best intentions, Adam was always on her mind. *I'm sorry, Lord. My duty is here, taking care of Mother. Adam is betrothed. Why can't I accept that?*

"There, now step out…carefully." Vonnie extended a hand for support. The white silk Honiton flowed over the stool as Jane gingerly stepped out of the gown.

"It feels wonderful to move again," Jane stretched her hands toward the ceiling.

"Will you be wearing the dress afterward? Many wedding dresses are kept and never worn again, but others are being worn on special occasions these days. I've seen brides who plan to wear their wedding dresses to dinner parties after the wedding."

"I plan to put mine away for my daughter."

"Oh, your daughter, huh?"

Jane smiled. "Edward and I want lots of children."

"I'll pray you'll be blessed with a whole houseful."

Taking her day dress down from a hook on the wall, Jane pulled it over her head, settling it around her hips. She had a perfect hourglass figure, one that would enhance the wedding gown's beauty.

"The attendants' dresses are simply exquisite, Vonnie. The new cut on the neckline was exactly what they needed." She smoothed her hair, then began buttoning the front of the bodice. "I don't know how you do it. You've such an eye for design and color. You must have been born with a golden needle in your hand."

Carrying the dress across the room, Vonnie carefully draped the yards of silk and lace over the form that had been adjusted to Jane's measurements. "I've been making dresses since I got my first doll. I fashioned them from bits and pieces of material and lace Mother gave me. It was what I always did," she mused.

While most children played with dolls, Vonnie had idolized Charles Frederick Worth, an English tailor who became the couturier, or designer, for the Empress Eugenie, consort of Napoleon III.

Teague had provided her with any information he could

order about the famous designer, hoping to encourage her gift with needle and thread.

Worth had been the first designer to show dresses made of fabrics of his own choosing. Before, dressmakers had used fabrics provided by their patrons. He was also the first to display his designs on live mannequins, or models.

"I sort of drifted into dressmaking, and then my sewing evolved into designing and sewing bridal gowns. I've been very fortunate that my gowns have been so widely accepted," she admitted. "I've been truly blessed."

"Fortunate to be accepted?" Jane made a face. "Most women would die for a Vonnie Taylor gown!"

Vonnie's gaze skimmed her sewing room as if seeing it for the first time. Long tables she used for cutting materials lined two walls. It was here she drew patterns and measured hems.

Floor-to-ceiling shelves lined the other two walls, framing the one large window that looked out across the Taylor acreage. Teague had accidentally painted the window sill one year, and she'd not been able to open the glass to allow a breeze. Separate shelves held various bolts of silk and lace, and cut dress pieces with patterns still pinned to the material. Her father had made a large Peg-Board to hold spools of thread and to hang her scissors and measuring tapes on.

One long shelf was divided into boxes that contained laces and ribbons and other trims, including ostrich feathers.

Her reputation for creating unique hats was unparalleled. She had been successful dyeing feathers for more flamboyant trims to adorn capes and cloaks.

Drawers beneath the cutting tables were divided, one to hold buttons, another beads and pearls. The work area was efficient, easy to keep neat, and allowed her to accomplish the sometimes tedious work with a minimum of effort.

"Well, I think you deserve every bit of recognition you get. You saw the announcement of Carolyn Graham's wedding in the New York newspaper, didn't you? It made special note that her gown had been 'designed by Vonnie Taylor of Amarillo.' Why, I felt almost a celebrity myself, just knowing you." Grinning, Jane leaned closer. "But, between you and me, I know my dress is going to be much prettier than Carolyn's."

A loud ruckus from the barnyard suddenly interrupted Jane's lively chatter.

"What on earth?" she exclaimed, whirling to look out the window.

"Oh, no!" Vonnie bolted out of the sewing room and down the long stairway, leaving a puzzled Jane calling after her.

"What? What's all that noise? Vonnie, where are you going?"

The birds' distinct squawk combined with Suki's barking, was enough racket to be heard in the next county as Vonnie ran out the back door and toward the ostrich pens.

The big birds were racing frantically back and forth across the pens, throwing themselves against the wire. Dust, mixed with bits of feathers, clogged the air. The sound was deafening.

Glancing around for help, Vonnie realized Roel and Genaro were in town. Who knew when they would return?

At the fence, she paused, unsure of what to do.

The adult birds stood erect at nearly eight to nine feet and weighed close to 350 pounds. When calm, they had a kind of humping walk that reminded one of a camel's gait. But when disturbed, they could move in a ground-covering sprint that left roadrunners in their dust.

"Suki! Suki! Quiet," Vonnie demanded, trying to catch the wildly barking dog to calm her.

Two of the birds had their heads caught in the wire, too frantic to recognize that by turning to one side they'd easily slip free.

"Suki! Sit!" she demanded again, running toward one bird who was in danger of decapitating himself.

"Shh," she soothed, trying to calm the kicking bird. *Lord, help me. I don't know how to calm them!*

Vonnie jumped back at every thrust. This was turning into some kind of strange dance—bird kicking, Vonnie jumping back, then leaping forward to persuade the bird to turn its head and free itself.

"You stupid, stupid—ow!" she screeched as an ostrich, having somehow gotten out of the pen, made an attack from the rear. He pecked first, then kicked, missing Vonnie by inches.

While he missed her, he did manage to kick loose a section of fence. Sensing freedom, birds poured through the break like water over a dam.

Plastered to the fence so tightly, she knew there must be permanent wire imprints on her back, Vonnie watched as her father's "babies" leaped over the barrier and, quickly gaining maximum speed, disappeared over the horizon.

Leaning weakly against the posts, she watched the cloud of disappearing dust, unable to believe what had just happened.

"Vonnie! Are you all right?"

Jane burst out of the house. "What is going on?"

"I—I'm not really sure," Vonnie managed. "Something disturbed the birds…and then…well, everything was happening at once. Oh dear—they're gone!"

"Gone?" Jane lifted her hand to shade her eyes.

"Gone." Vonnie dusted off her gown, coughing as feathers tickled her nose.

"Well, I do declare, I've never seen anything like it! Birds, feathers, all that dust…" Jane suddenly burst out laughing. "I thought you were being trampled to death!"

"And that's funny?"

Shaking her head negatively, Jane held her hand over her mouth to stifle her mirth.

"Well," Vonnie studied the cloud of dust, sighing. "I sure hope they know their way back."

Teague had told her once that the birds were territorial, which meant they would eventually find their way home. She hoped he was right.

Thought she rarely had anything to do with their actual care, their deep-throated roar, much like a lion's mixed with a strange hissing sound, had become familiar to her. They were odd creatures, their size and peculiarities intimidating.

She and Teague had an agreement. "You don't expect me to take care of the birds," she told him, "and I won't expect you to pin lace on wedding gowns."

"Agreed," he had quickly replied with a grin.

She didn't have the patience to baby the birds the way her father did. He would go out to talk to them at least three times a day, and got up in the middle of the night to check eggs when the birds were laying.

He watched to make sure the males were on the nests at night, and that not too many eggs were broken. He attended the birds like an expectant father until they hatched chicks that were hen-size from birth and grew into large birds in six months.

Raising ostriches was tedious work. It required the understanding that there was little one could do to control circumstances, and Vonnie liked to be in control of a situation. But the situation was definitely out of control now.

With a last anxious glance over her shoulder, she followed Jane back into the house.

"Keep that wire tight," Adam called, watching as Joey nudged his horse forward a half step.

The Baldwins were stringing a new strand of wire along the north property line today. Adam kept a close eye on the dark clouds that had hung low in the west all morning, threatening rain.

It was the dry season, but Texas had had more rain in the past thirty days than it'd had all year.

As Joey held a roll across the front of his saddle, making sure the horse kept the wire firm, Adam and Pat stretched and nailed the new strand to posts.

The air was thick with the building storm. Around nine, they'd shed their shirts and bent to the work under the hazy sun.

"Think we can beat the rain?" Pat called.

"It should hold off another couple of hours." Adam stood back, running his forearm across his face to wipe away the sweat.

The men glanced up as the sound of rumbling thunder rolled over the knoll. Adam squinted toward the horizon and tried to make out the cloud of thick dust coming in their direction.

Pat came to stand beside him, his eyes fixed on the bewildering sight. "What do you think it is?"

The three men stared at the strange stampede as it drew closer. Long-necked birds covered the ground at a phenomenal speed, leaving floating bits of feathers and gouged earth in their wake as they headed straight toward the men.

Grazing cattle idly lifted their heads, their eyes widening as they spotted the bizarre entities bearing down on them. Bolting, the herd stampeded, trampling anything in their path to get out of the way.

"Get the horses!" Adam shouted.

Wild-eyed, the horses whinnied, reared, then broke into a gallop and converged on the stampeding cattle.

Joey ran after them, then quickly abandoned the pursuit as the birds approached.

Diving headfirst for cover, the three men crouched low, their eyes focused on the strange scene playing out below them. Awkward birds screeched and bellowed while leaping with their ungainly gait across the ground like crazed ballerinas.

Beef cattle, apparently unnerved by the sight, turned tail

and ran bawling over the horizon, followed in hot pursuit by the birds, who were suddenly outrunning them.

"What was that!" Pat said.

Spitting dirt out of his mouth, Joey sat up. "Did you see that? Are those the Taylors' birds?"

"Whose else could they be?" Adam snapped.

"Well, that beats all I've ever seen." Pat sat up, reaching for his hat.

Rolling to his feet, Adam settled his Stetson low on his forehead. "Come on, we have to get those birds away from the cattle before they run them to death."

"The cattle are in Africa by now," Pat guessed.

"Then we'll have to go to Africa and get them."

Pat and Joey grumbled as they got up, smacking their hats against their thighs to knock a layer of dust off both.

"We're going to have to run down our horses first."

"Great."

"Beats all I've ever seen."

"Why would anyone want to raise those crazy things?"

The three men struck off on foot. It promised to be a long morning.

Hours later, Adam rode into the Taylor farmyard. Swinging out of the saddle, he strode across the front porch and knocked on the solid door. He waited, about to assault the door again when it opened. Jane Bennett stood in the doorway.

"Where's Vonnie?"

"Hello, Adam. What are you doing here?"

Dispensing with pleasantries, he repeated. "Where's Vonnie?"

Jane's amazed gaze shifted from his dirt-streaked face to his dusty clothes. "I—I don't know. She was out at the pens a little while ago. There's been an incident with the birds. I'm staying with Mrs. Taylor. She—she's in her room and—"

Whirling, Adam leaped off the porch and rounded the corner of the house, striding angrily toward the ostrich pens. There was an ominous silence about the place this afternoon.

At the barn, he saw the empty pens, and the gaping hole in the fence.

"Vonnie!" he shouted.

The sound of chickens clucking near the henhouse came to him.

"Vonnie!"

"Stop shouting, please."

Glancing around, he didn't see her anywhere. Then he saw a wriggling form trying to extricate itself from a broken piece of fence on which a dress was firmly snagged.

Anger momentarily drained out of him, then returned. They were her birds. She had insisted on keeping them so she could take care of them.

"Of all the rotten luck!"

Adam's lips curved into an unwilling smile as he heard her muttering.

Tipping his hat back on his forehead, he grinned. "Something wrong?"

"Yes, there is something wrong, and you're going to get an earful if you don't get me out of here!"

"Yeah, looks like you might have a little problem there." He bent to help.

"My back is about to break, Adam! Get me loose!"

"I don't know. Maybe I'll just leave you here to stew."

"Adam!"

Stepping to the fence, he extricated her from the snare. "You wouldn't have been in that fix if you'd used the gate instead of climbing the fence."

"I don't need your advice, thank you."

"I wasn't giving you my advice—I was stating a fact."

She stepped clear, swiping hair out of her eyes. "For your information, I was trying to repair the fence, not climb it."

He glanced toward the barn. "Where are Roel and Genaro?"

"They went into town—I haven't seen them since early this morning."

Straightening, she refused to look at him as she pinned back her falling hair.

Leaning against the fence, his blue eyes skimmed her lightly. "Having a bad day?"

She sighed. "A bad life."

"What happened?"

"I've lost the entire herd of birds."

His anger would have been easier to maintain if she hadn't looked so charming with her hair falling down, a streak of dirt across her sweaty face, her dress soiled and torn from the experience. To this day, she could reduce him to a mooning, callow boy. The sight of her filled him with memories best forgotten.

Crossing his arms, he eyed her sternly. "I found them."

"You know where the birds are?"

"I believe I do."

"Thank you, dear Lord." Relief filled her face. "Where are they?"

"Africa."

"Oh, dear." Her heart sank. She knew they weren't in Africa but they'd probably run twenty miles.

"Yes. Oh, dear."

"I…I don't know what happened. They suddenly started running as if they were scared to death, and before I knew it, they were beating themselves against the fence…. Since I didn't work with them, I…you know, my father—"

His features hardened. "Those birds are a menace. If you can't take care of them, then you'd better get rid of them."

Her hands fisted at her waist, and blood rushed to her cheeks. "Is that why you're here? You came all the way over here just to tell me to get rid of my birds?"

"Your birds stampeded my beef!"

"Oh…really?"

"It took me, Joey and Pat all morning, Vonnie, half a day to round them up!"

"I'm sorry. I have no idea what spooked them."

"Could it be the dog?" he mocked. Suki barked.

"Nonsense! The birds are used to Suki. It wasn't the dog."

He stabbed the air in front of her with his forefinger. "I don't care what spooked them. Don't let it happen again!"

"Well, pardon me!"

"You keep those birds in their pen!"

"You don't tell me what to do, Adam Baldwin!" She kicked dirt on his boots.

Slamming his hat back on his head, he turned and stalked off, rounding the pen in angry strides.

"Come back when you can't stay so long!" she shouted at his fading back.

"Keep those birds in their pens or I'll have ostrich and dumplin's on my dinner table!"

"Ooh!" Kicking a clump of dirt, she stomped back to the house.

Chapter Eight

❦

"Keep those birds together, Joe!"

Adam's brother urged his horse forward as another ostrich decided to take a right turn out of the group.

"There goes another one!" Pat shouted.

Adam kicked his horse and galloped after a bird who had his eye on the far horizon. Galloping ahead of it, he cut it off, turning it back toward the Taylor ranch.

"If we had to herd these pests another mile, she'd get them back in tow sacks," he muttered.

"I don't know why Teague wanted the birds anyway," Pat complained, pulling his mount abreast of Adam's.

"Could be because they made him a lot of money."

"Maybe so, but boy they're big." Pat's eyes traveled the full height of the African male, whose size was stupefying. "I wouldn't cross one."

"I don't know how Vonnie's going to handle them," Adam said.

An ostrich suddenly leaned forward to pluck the hat off Adam's head. For a moment, a game of hat tag ensued among the birds until one fumbled, and the hat hit the dust. Chaos broke out as the three men scrambled to retrieve it.

The hat was flattened. The ostriches fled.

Climbing off his horse, Adam picked up the Stetson and dusted it on his pants leg. Settling it back on his head, his eyes studied the birds, which were, at least momentarily, moving in the right direction.

How did Vonnie think she was going to handle the nuisances with Teague gone?

From what he had heard, she had her hands full with her mother. Alma had mentioned the gossip in town—Cammy Taylor wasn't doing well. She had practically taken to her bed since Teague's death and was hardly responding to anyone.

Vonnie was capable, but with her dressmaking business doing so well, he didn't see how she could oversee the birds, too.

"Joe," he shouted suddenly, "that one's making a break for it!"

Swinging back into the saddle, he spurred his black into a full gallop as a female flapped her short wings and made a dash for freedom.

The sudden ruckus launched the other birds into a faster gait, and their awkward lope began to carry them across the ground at an alarming rate.

It took over thirty minutes to cover the final five hundred yards to the pens.

Leaving Joey and Pat to settle the birds, Adam rode on to the main house.

Swinging down from the saddle, he stepped upon the porch. Pulling off his hat and running his fingers through his damp hair, he rapped on the door, then wiped his sweaty face on his shirtsleeve.

Vonnie opened on the first knock, her wide violet eyes mirroring surprise when she saw him. Her welcome expression cooled immediately. "Yes?"

"Your birds are back."

Her attention slipped to the pens, where Joey and Pat were herding the birds into the runs.

"Well, I haven't gone looking for them because they're territorial, you know." Her nose tilted a notch higher. "I knew they'd come back on their own."

At his dubious look, she added, "And if they didn't, then I was going to send someone to look for them."

She looked tired. It was obvious she'd been sewing. Wisps of hair had strayed from the loose knot at the nape of her neck. Curling strands framed her face. Bits of lace dotted her dress. Deep circles shadowed her eyes. Adam's gut twisted with admiration. Life was difficult for her right now.

"Get someone on that broken fence as soon as possible. Pat and Joey will repair it enough to hold the birds tonight, but it's only a temporary fix."

"I'll have Roel mend the hole immediately."

"They're in the pens," Pat said, riding up to join them. Joey followed close behind. "Don't know if they're in the right ones, but they're all there."

"I'll sort them out," Vonnie smiled. "Thank you for bringing them back."

"Finding them wasn't too hard." Joey laughed, settling his hat more firmly on his head. He immediately sobered.

Suki rounded the corner of the house in a trot and decided to investigate Adam's boot.

Vonnie seemed anxious to get back to her work.

"Well, again, thank you." Glancing at the dog, she frowned. The animal was worrying the hem of Adam's trousers.

"Suki, stop that," she admonished as Adam pushed the dog aside with his boot.

He tried to distract Suki by throwing a stick.

The dog wasn't interested in a stick.

"Could I get you gentlemen some lemonade?" she asked. The group ignored Suki's persistent fascination with Adam's boot.

"Sounds good to me," Pat said, starting to dismount.

"We don't have time." Adam nudged Suki aside for the fourth time and gave the dog a hard look.

Pat climbed back into the saddle.

"Anything else we can do for you, Vonnie?"

"Thank you, Joey. You've all done quite enough already."

"Well, Alma will be waiting supper for us. You coming, Adam?"

"I'll be along in a minute."

Tipping the brims of their hats, the boys reined in their horses and rode off. Suki resumed her busy exploration. The dog still had Adam cornered.

"What is wrong with your dog?" The pet was making a real bid for Adam's attention now, dipping in front of him, then jumping to paw his leg, tail wagging, tongue hanging out.

"She's female." Vonnie grinned, leaning against the door frame. "I'd think you would be used to females trying to get your attention."

Their eyes met and held in silent challenge.

"Suki, stop it!" She opened the door, nudging the dog into the house. "I know you don't want my gratitude, Adam, but you have it. Thank you anyway for bringing the birds home."

"You'd better sell them—"

"No." Years ago the sun rose and set on this man. Now he wanted her birds, not her. Her *birds. Well, thank you, Lord, for making this easier.* The day she sold Adam and Beth the birds would be the day she ate dirt.

When she looked up, she caught him staring at her. "Was there something else?"

"No, that's it."

She swallowed against the dryness in her throat. Wasn't this what she'd wanted? It was over once and for all. No ties, no thoughts of Adam Baldwin. Not ever again.

"Vonnie."

"Yes?"

"I don't know much about birds, but a couple of yours seemed a little droopy. They were acting strange. A few looked sickly."

"I'll have Genaro check them."

Nodding, he put his hat on, then fit it more snugly on his head. "Take care."

"Yes…you too."

"Good night."

She leaned against the door frame, watching him ride away. A sob caught in her throat and she closed her eyes against the aching emptiness inside her.

After a while, she straightened. The ostriches. He said a couple were acting strange.

Exactly what did strange mean? She glanced in the direction he had just ridden.

Strange to him?

Stepping off the porch, she walked to the pens. Dusk had fallen. The ranch hands were settling in for the night. After their daylong adventure, the birds were exhausted. They should be separated, but it was more than she could cope with tonight. Tomorrow she would separate the pairs from the young ones and…

She paused, peering closer through the fence. One or two did look a bit under the weather.

Her heart hammered; she stepped closer to examine a midsize chick standing closest to the fence. The bird stared back at her with large expressive eyes.

Please, she silently prayed, *don't let any of the birds get sick. They're too expensive to lose. Especially now.*

"Vonnie?"

She whirled in response to her mother's voice.

"Yes, Mother?"

"Why are you out there in that heat? And you without a bonnet on your head. Get into the house, child, before you have sunstroke!"

Frowning, Vonnie moved away from the pens. "It's all right, Momma. It's getting dark."

"Dark? Why, child, it's broad daylight! You come on in

now—and tell your daddy I'm waiting supper on him! That man—he doesn't know when to stop. Tell him to come in here and get washed up. Hurry now!"

Vonnie watched as she closed the back door, then through the open window, Vonnie saw her shuffling back through the kitchen.

"Oh, Mother," she murmured. Self-pity overwhelmed her. Her life was falling apart, and she didn't have a shoulder to cry on. If only Cammy was in her right mind. She couldn't tell her about Adam and the marriage, but she could cry on her shoulder. And she could feel safe again.

Safe and loved.

It was starting to feel like a long time since she'd felt either.

Chapter Nine

❦

Late Saturday afternoon, Adam was totaling a column of figures when the library door opened. He glanced up, then, recognizing Andrew's distinctive step as he limped into the room, returned to his work.

"Am I interrupting?"

"No. What's on your mind?"

Penciling in the column total, Adam closed the ledger. It was unusual for Andrew to seek his company. The loner of the four Baldwin boys, more withdrawn and serious about life in general than Pat and Joey, Andrew was the balance weight to the younger boys' impetuousness. As a child he had rarely engaged in boyish pranks, and, as a result, he often drew P.K.'s wrath and seldom his favor. P.K. expected his boys to be boys.

As his sons grew into manhood, it had been hard for

them to live up to P.K.'s expectations. He wanted them to be men. His kind of men. Men's men.

Removing the spectacles he'd worn since childhood, Andrew cleaned the lenses with a handkerchief before settling them back onto his nose. Nearly as tall as Adam, with the same Baldwin leanness, he was a handsome man, save for the fact he rarely smiled.

The chair squeaked as Adam leaned back and stared at him.

"Books closed for the month?"

"Just balanced out. You'll need to look them over, but we seem to be in good shape." For the shape they were in. If the situation didn't improve soon, he'd have to ask Beth to set a wedding date. He didn't take to the idea. Or his deception.

"Has P.K. seen them yet?"

"No," Adam hesitated. "I'm not sure he's that interested in our financial situation."

P.K. still ran the ranch, but the day-to-day matters had been left to Adam.

Andrew's expression sharpened. "It looks as if he's finally about to turn the reins over to you."

"I doubt it."

Adam studied the specially made boot that accommodated his brother's shortened leg. Andrew had never accepted his affliction, nor was he charitable to those who singled him out for pity. He was also the brother who most resented Adam's favor with P.K., and most resented Adam's sense of responsibility toward the younger brothers.

The difference P.K. had made between the two boys was

a sore spot between them since early childhood. P.K. preferred his oldest son and made no bones about it. Adam, his firstborn, was the child who most favored his wife in looks and temperament. When the reins of power were handed down, it was understood that Adam would assume control of Cabeza del Lobo and would be responsible for the ranch.

Adam resented the favoritism as much as his brothers did. He certainly didn't seek it. It created an insurmountable barrier between himself and Andrew, yet he was unable to alter his father's partiality. The younger boys learned to live with it and used it to their advantage, seeking Adam's favor when P.K. vented his fury on them. Andrew had never accepted it.

"Teague Taylor's death appears to have gotten to him." Andrew limped to the sideboard to pour a glass of tea. The boot made a harsh, grating sound against the pine floor. "Maybe the old man's finally realizing that he's not invincible."

"He's not exactly a kid anymore."

Andrew took a bracing sip from the glass, grimacing as the liquid slowly trickled down his throat.

"Think Vonnie will keep the birds?"

"The birds?"

Andrew's lips curled with a mirthless smile. "You've forgotten the ostriches?"

Adam grunted. "Hardly. It took hours to cut them out of the herd and get them back to the Taylor ranch."

"Yes," Andrew mused, staring into his glass. "It seems she has her hands full."

Swinging out of his chair, Adam moved to the file cabinet. "She's a big girl. She can handle it." *And stubborn as a Missouri mule.*

"I'm surprised to hear you say that. I always thought you had a thing for Vonnie Taylor."

Closing the file drawer, Adam sat down again. "Name one boy in Potter County who didn't." One of Andrew's rare smiles slipped through, and Adam caught it.

He grinned. "Didn't you?"

"Yes," Andrew confessed. "I suppose I did."

"Suppose you did?" Adam repeated, pinching his lower lip between thumb and forefinger as he studied his younger brother. "If I remember right, when you were in the eighth grade you cornered her outside school and kissed her."

Andrew took another sip of tea and stepped to the window. "You think she'll keep the birds now that Teague's gone?"

"If she's smart, she won't."

Andrew stared out the window, a pensive look shadowing his features.

"What do you make of her—now that she's grown?"

Adam looked up.

"Who?"

"Vonnie—what do you think of her?"

The question caught Adam off guard. Andrew usually had his own opinions about people and kept them to himself, rarely expressing an interest in what anyone else thought. As far as women were concerned, he'd never been seriously interested in one, at least not that Adam knew about. He'd always thought it was because of the limp and

Andrew's mistaken belief that a woman didn't want to be seen with an "invalid." Adam believed that many a woman would be proud to be on Andrew's arm, but his brother refused to share the belief.

As he grew older, Andrew had ignored the fairer sex, choosing instead to bury himself in his books. Women ceased to be an issue as far as Adam could tell. Vonnie Taylor was the only girl Andrew ever mentioned. Even as a boy, Adam had known his brother had a crush on her.

"I think she's a beautiful woman," Adam said.

Turning away from the window, Andrew smiled. "Pity. She appears to have lost her fascination with you."

Adam ignored the gibe, but the edge in Andrew's voice caught his attention. He knew his brother had resented Vonnie's favoring him. He didn't blame Andrew; he'd have been jealous if he'd thought Vonnie had favored Andrew over him. But that had been a long time ago.

A knock sounded at the library door, diverting his attention. Alma bustled in carrying a tray with two pieces of pecan pie, cups, and a pot of fresh steaming coffee. "Supper's running late, tonight. I've brought something to tide you over."

Adam glanced at the laden tray. "You spoil us, Alma."

Pinching Andrew's cheek as if he was still a youngster, she winked. "*Sí*, but the two of you are worth it."

The housekeeper set the tray onto the desk and added a drop of cream to Andrew's coffee, before bustling out again.

Adam reached for a cup and took a sip of the hot coffee. "Why the sudden fascination with Vonnie?"

Andrew swung to confront him, and Adam recognized the familiar tightness around his mouth.

Meeting his brother's eyes over the rim of the cup, Adam continued. "You just being neighborly, or are you concerned about her?"

Adam cut a bite of pie and savored the rich taste. It struck him as odd that Andrew had been at Vonnie's the night Teague was buried. No more curious than his own unexpected arrival, he supposed, yet it wasn't like Andrew to show such compassion. Not even for Vonnie.

"No particular reason. I'm just curious about what she plans to do now that her father's gone and her mother's no longer responsible. She's a woman alone. Looks like she needs a man to help her. Maybe I should see if I can do anything to ease her load."

Adam's brow lifted. "Who told you Cammy was no longer responsible?"

"I overheard some of the hands talking. Is it true?"

Pensive now, Adam looked away. "I don't know."

"Why not?" The sharp edge was still in Andrew's tone. "You've been over there often enough lately. You should know what's going on."

"Well, Andrew, I don't know what's going on at the Taylors'. It's none of my business."

Staring into his cup, Andrew turned thoughtful.

"What does Beth think about you spending so much time at the Taylor ranch?"

"I wasn't aware I was spending an undue amount of time over there." The conversation was taking a nasty turn. "I took her birds back. You got a problem with that?"

"A problem?" Andrew laughed hollowly. "Is the 'gimp' not allowed to be concerned about a neighbor?"

"Andrew, if you've got something on your mind, spit it out."

"Things never change, do they? Adam's top dog—Andrew's the pitied one."

Shoving his cup aside, Andrew got to his feet and limped from the room.

As the study door closed behind him, Adam realized the rift between Andrew and himself was deepening, and there wasn't a thing he could do about it.

Beth Baylor arrived at Cabeza del Lobo around six.

Alma's eyes crinkled in a friendly grin when she opened the door.

"Oh, how *bonita* you look."

Beth was wearing a dark rose dress with a tight waist, a cascade of lace descending from the top of the neck to the waist. A band of lace decorated the edges of the short, close-fitting jacket, matching that on the hem of the narrow skirt and overskirt. Her blond hair was piled high on her head.

"Adam's in the study with Andrew," Alma said. "I'm sure they won't be long. I am in the kitchen. You can join me there, or perhaps you'd like to sit in the parlor—"

"The parlor, please." Beth peeled off her gloves and handed them, along with her bag, to Alma. "Mmm, something smells wonderful."

"I put a leg of lamb in the oven earlier," the housekeeper told her, leading the way toward the back of the house. "Would you like some tea?"

"I'd love a cup, thank you. It was so dusty on the way here."

As Beth passed the study doors, Andrew burst out, greeting her with little more than a glance.

"Andrew, my goodness, you startled me—"

Her greeting fell on deaf ears as he brushed past her and slowly ascended the stairs to the second floor.

Pushing open the library door, Beth found Adam leaning back in his chair, staring out the window. He turned when she tapped lightly on the door.

"Hello. I know I'm early. Hope you don't mind."

Adam stood up. "Hello, Beth. I didn't hear you come in." Moving around the desk, he lightly brushed her cheek with a cursory greeting.

"It's so nice that we're having lamb for supper."

"Lamb?"

She frowned. "You don't like lamb?"

"It isn't my favorite."

"Oh, dear. You don't like lamb? Does Alma know? No, I'm sure she doesn't or she wouldn't have prepared lamb for supper. Well, not to worry, darling. I'll just go to the kitchen and ask her to prepare something other than lamb for your supper. What would you like? Steak? Chops? Chicken— you like chicken. Broiled, baked, stewed?"

Adam felt his hackles rising. "Don't worry about it. Alma knows I'm not partial to lamb, but the others enjoy it so I can—"

"Eat it, but you're just being nice," she chided. "Really, darling, Alma doesn't mind." Moving closer, she tripped her fingers lightly along the front of his shirt. "After all, it won't be long before I'm responsible for all your meals, and I need to know your likes and dislikes."

"Really, Beth—"

"It's not necessary," she finished for him. "But it is! I

couldn't eat a bite knowing that you weren't enjoying your meal." She bent, giving him a light peck on the mouth. "Relax, darling. I'll go into the kitchen and get the chicken started."

"Beth, I wouldn't do that. Alma doesn't—"

"Like anyone in her kitchen." Beth sighed. "I'm sure once I explain the problem she'll welcome the intrusion. She'll want you to be pleased, won't she? Now, relax and let me do my duty."

Adam released a mental sigh of relief when the door closed behind her.

He wished, just once, she'd let him finish his own sentence.

Beth was back momentarily, and he bit back a grin. She looked like a hen that had just had her tail feathers singed.

"Alma says that you can eat what everybody else is eating, or you can go hungry. 'This is not a cantina.' Those were her exact words. She says she will cook one meal and one meal only. She actually was quite rude," Beth complained. "And I had decided to fix burritos—do you like burritos?"

"I can eat them."

"But do you *like* them, Adam?"

"I don't know, Beth. Do you like them?" He didn't think Spanish cuisine was standard fare at the Baylor table.

Smiling, she said, "I do if you do."

"But do *you* like them, Beth? That's the question."

"No," she said pensively, "I believe the question was, do you like them?"

The standoff was getting on his nerves. "They're all right."

She made a pouty face. "Just 'all right'? It's a woman's place to accommodate her husband, and I desperately need to know your food preferences."

"I don't want to be 'accommodated,' Beth, I just want to know if you like burritos."

The subject was downright infuriating, but for some reason he felt compelled to see it through.

"Dear me, I think we'd better change the subject." Perching herself on the edge of the chair, she wagged her finger playfully at him. "Someone is getting cranky."

Adam drummed a pencil on a chair back, his eyes boring into hers.

"Oh, whatever. Burritos aren't important. There's something far more important we need to discuss."

Adam sat back down at the desk, waiting for the announcement. The bombshell wasn't long in coming.

"I'm going to ask Vonnie to make my wedding dress."

He must have looked blank, because she clapped her hands together gleefully.

"Isn't it wonderful? I know it's extremely extravagant, but Father said I could. Now, the question is—do you want me to arrange for Vonnie to make the shirts for the men, or do you—"

Adam interrupted. "Beth, I don't think that's a good idea."

She paused, blinking. "Why? She makes exquisite bridal gowns."

"I know, but in view of everything that's happened recently, I don't think it's such a good idea. I understand that—"

"Her mother isn't doing well. I know. Cammy isn't

adjusting to Teague's sudden demise, but honestly, darling, I can't imagine anyone but Vonnie making my dress. Why, she's simply the best there is. I wouldn't dream of having anyone else make it. Of course, we'll need to set a date. Early fall or late winter. Maybe spring…spring is nice."

Adam sighed. "I don't think you should expect Vonnie to take on any more than she already has—especially now."

"Darling! I wouldn't 'expect' her to do it, though we've been friends for ages. She'll *insist* on doing it. Don't you see? I want the dress to be absolutely perfect, and Vonnie's the only one I would trust to do it. You'll see, she'll be thrilled I asked her. Why, she'd be crushed if I didn't!"

Adam hardly thought Vonnie would be crushed.

"I'm only thinking of her—"

"Welfare. Of course you are, and that's so thoughtful of you, darling, but really, Vonnie and I will work it out. Now, about the shirts, do you want her to make them?"

He didn't want Vonnie to make the shirts. Or Beth's wedding gown. He attempted to divert Beth again.

"Beth. Vonnie's got her hands full with the ostriches, her mother isn't doing well, and I think—"

"It'll be too much for her? Heavens, no, it won't! She'll welcome the extra money, what with her father gone and all."

Adam shrugged. The woman had her steel-trap mind made up.

She grinned. "You'll see, darling. It will be the most beautiful gown in the world. Do you like pure white silk or off white silk?"

"Either one."

"Or maybe more of a vanilla," she mused. "No. A yummy milk white—cream, maybe, no, magnolia-white—snow-white!

"Yes, snow-white with eggshell lace—no, oyster colored… or perhaps a nice ecru…"

Two birds were dead.

The startling discovery left Vonnie shaken. Genaro and Roel came to the house early with the grim news.

Vonnie hung on the fence, her fingers caught in the wire, watching the ostriches pace the length of the pens. What had caused the birds' deaths? Thankfully, they were not adults, but still it was a costly loss.

The birds strutted around the pen, oblivious to what had happened. Large eyes blinked slowly back at her as they peered over the top of her head. Occasionally they paused to peck at an object on the ground.

It was precisely the pecking that concerned Vonnie.

In spite of her best efforts, the birds had gotten hold of foreign material. Bits of baling wire had been found caught in the deceased birds' throats.

Baling wire!

Teague would roll over in his grave if he knew. Genaro and Roel patrolled the pens every morning and evening to avoid exactly this kind of threat.

The birds were never exposed to rocks or pieces of glass or string that they could pick up and swallow. They could easily choke to death on foreign matter.

Vonnie had even taken to raking the pens herself, picking up any tiny object that might attract the curious creatures. Had they picked up the killing material when they were on the loose?

Teague had lost a few of the birds to illness or bad weather, but never through neglect. She pressed her face against the wire. Her father had been gone less than a month, and already she had managed to lose two of his prized stock.

Drawing a deep breath, she vowed to be more alert. She would talk to Genaro and Roel and they would all redouble their efforts to protect the birds.

"Suki, I'm not very good at this," she confessed to the dog.

Suki yawned widely and sat down on her haunches.

The sound of an approaching horse drew Vonnie away from the fence. Shading her eyes with one hand, she groaned aloud when she recognized the rider, Sheriff Lewis Tanner. Crooked as a dog's hind leg, and the very last person she wanted to see.

Tanner, a stocky man with a dark beard, drew his bay up alongside Vonnie. She fanned dust away from her face, irritated at his thoughtlessness.

"Morning, Miss Taylor. How are you this fine day?"

"What brings you out this way?"

Though Lewis Tanner was a neighbor on the south, owning fifty acres adjoining the Taylor land, there was little neighboring going on between the two families, especially since Teague's death. For years, Lewis had wanted to sell his property but claimed the birds were a hindrance to the sale.

"Got a serious prospect for your land."

"My land isn't for sale."

"Sure it is—little lady like you can't run this ranch."

Suki growled. Saddle leather creaked as the sheriff shifted his massive weight, eyeing the dog warily.

"I repeat. My land isn't for sale."

"Best reconsider. If my prospect saw the birds—" he nodded to the ostriches "—he might not be so eager to buy. As it is, he's offering a handsome price, sight unseen."

"If he'd dislike my birds, then why would he want to buy them?"

He shrugged. "Assets."

She pulled off her bonnet. "They're more than assets to me, Sheriff Tanner. You best move along."

The dog growled, and the horse shied. The sheriff shifted from side to side in the saddle.

"Well now, ma'am, I think I could convince my buyer to keep the birds, if that's your terms. That's something to consider. If you were to sell to anyone else, they might not be so obliging."

Suki growled again and got up to investigate the sheriff's horse.

"Heard they got loose the other day and created quite a ruckus. Heard the Baldwins had to bring them back."

"That was an unusual circumstance, I assure you."

The sheriff's horse shook its head at the dog and sidestepped nervously.

"Suki, get away," Vonnie reprimanded quietly.

"Unusual or not, the fact is they're a nuisance, ma'am. Now, I can sell this property and you can leave the birds here. With your papa gone an' all, you need to be thinking about selling out."

Vonnie's lips firmed.

"Your pa's gone, Miss Taylor, and I hear tell your ma ain't doing so good. Since it don't appear that you can handle those birds, you best get out while the gettin's good." Leaning over, he spit a stream of tobacco on the ground. Wiping his mouth on his shirtsleeve, he smiled. "When you think about it, what choice you got?"

She took offense at his audacity. What made the men in this area so interested in her business, anyway?

"Keep them?" she guessed, realizing too late that the sheriff had no sense of humor.

Lewis Tanner had a reputation for meanness, and he was indiscriminate about whom he vented his temper upon. It was well-known that his friends were men who should be in the sheriff's cells instead of in his parlor drinking moonshine liquor. There were those in the community who wanted Tanner out of office but, fearing swift retribution, no one was willing to challenge his authority.

"Well, little lady." Lewis looked into the distance as if carefully weighing his next words. "If you insist on bein' stubborn about this, I'll have to warn you. Keep your birds where they belong. It'd be a shame if more turned up dead—"

Before he could finish the implied threat, Suki jumped up, barking wildly, leaping at the sheriff's boot and startling the horse.

The ostriches began pacing the pens, flapping their wings nervously.

Glancing at the birds, Vonnie turned back to see the sheriff was trying to bring the big bay under control.

"Down! Down!" she shouted at the leaping dog. "Suki!"

"Remember what I said," Tanner shouted from the back of his plunging horse. With a decided lack of grace, he gave his horse its head and galloped off.

Suki followed after him, barking.

Leaning wearily against the fence, Vonnie closed her eyes, her mind registering his thinly veiled threat. He would do what? Throw foreign objects in their pen?

"What is going on? Was that Lewis Tanner?" Vonnie looked up, surprised to see Franz standing not five feet away, his weathered face lined with concern. She hadn't heard him arrive. She must be unusually tired.

"It was Tanner all right."

Walking toward her, Franz frowned. "What did that snake want?"

"To cause trouble, mostly."

"Anything I can do to help?"

"Not unless you can bring two birds back to life, make Momma come out of her room and stop crying over those old photograph albums, sew a wedding dress…"

"Ah, poor child. Since your father died, everything's fallen on your shoulders. Maybe I can help. The birds? Chores? I would be happy if I could do something for you."

Vonnie straightened, pushing her hair back off her face. "Oh, Franz, you've got your hands full with Audrey and your own chores. I couldn't ask—"

"You didn't ask. I'm volunteering."

Vonnie weighed the merit of his generosity, knowing it

was prompted by their long-standing friendship. She knew he would be hurt if she didn't accept his offer.

"I'd be ever so grateful if you could help me. Since Daddy's gone there are so many things that need to be done, and I simply don't have the time to do them all, and the ranch hands have their hands full."

"Good. Good." He seemed genuinely pleased by her acceptance. "Tell me what I can do first."

Together, they walked toward the house.

"Well, there's a mound of canned fruit that needs to be put on the shelf, water to carry to the birds. They drink a lot when it's this hot."

"I can help Genaro and Roel keep them watered."

"Then there's the step on the back porch. It's about ready to give way. Daddy had planned to fix it the day he died…." Her voice caught.

"I'll get the hammer and nails. Shouldn't take long to fix it."

"There's a loose shutter on the front window, and the wind blew a shingle off the roof last night."

"And then there's the cellar," Franz added. "Teague kept meaning to get to it, but he never did."

"Oh, yes, the cellar. I would appreciate it if you could clean it, so I can get the rest of the vegetables stored."

"Don't worry your pretty head another minute. Franz is here."

She left him at the steps and returned to work. In her sewing room she felt more in control. Familiar things surrounded her—the smell of machine oil, her materials, buttons, threads.

The colorful bolts of cloth soothed her; the sight of lace on satin restored her fortitude. Sewing was something she understood, something she could control. When nothing else made sense, she sought refuge in her work.

But this time it wasn't working.

As she sat down at the treadle sewing machine, her mind was clouded. Would her mother ever get over Teague's death?

It was too soon for the grieving process to be completed, but she was so worried about her. Cammy sat in her room for hours on end, staring out the window. The few times she had ventured downstairs she sat in the parlor, weeping and poring over old photographs of Teague. It was as if half of her, the important half, had been stripped away.

Vonnie sat, sewing forgotten. Didn't she know a little of how her mother felt? Hadn't she mourned Adam? Her loss?

Adam.

Why couldn't she get him out of her mind?

Chapter Ten

✣

The days crept slowly by. Vonnie mailed Emily Wilson's gown to Phoenix and Janie Bennett married Edward Lassitor.

Rising shortly before dawn each day, Vonnie dealt with the housework before fixing Cammy's breakfast, then going to her sewing room. Late fall arrived and with it came new heartaches.

She had established a routine of cleaning one room of the house each day, and today the chore was the kitchen.

Every Monday, she straightened the cabinet and shelves and put things in order the best she could, but the jars of canned vegetables that she and Cammy had put up this summer were always in the way. The shiny jars of tomatoes, corn, green beans and pickles stood row on row, filling the holding room off the kitchen. The rest stood on tables at the back of the kitchen where the canning was done. Franz was busy with other, more immediate tasks, and hadn't finished in the cellar so they could be stored.

Vonnie paused, her hands tightening around a jar of green beans. With Teague gone, the food reserve would last forever.

Perhaps she would give some to Franz. Audrey had been too ill to do any canning this year.

Loading a woven basket with jars of tomatoes, Vonnie elbowed the back door open and made her way to the cellar door and down the steps, where she found Franz diligently at work.

He industriously wielded a broom, clearing the rafters of accumulated cobwebs, brushing stacks of crates and discarded tools.

"Hey! Slow down," she teased. "It doesn't all have to be cleaned today."

Apparently willing to take a breather, Franz propped the broom on the dirt floor and leaned on the handle. Vonnie noticed how twisted and painful his joints looked this morning. Her first impulse was to tell him to let the work go, but then she knew he'd be embarrassed by the gesture. He liked to say he could still outwork any man his junior.

Besides, she needed his help. The cellar was filthy, bug infested. She only came down here when it was absolutely necessary. Both she and Cammy had avoided the dank vault like the plague. If they needed anything, Teague had retrieved the stored goods.

The sound of a carriage pulling into the yard caught her attention.

"More company," she murmured, thinking she didn't need the interruption.

"Leave the basket," Franz said. "I'll put the jars away for you."

The job wouldn't be that strenuous, she decided, so she readily set the basket down. "Thank you, Franz. I don't know what I would do without you."

He nodded and tugged his cap.

Flashing him a smile, Vonnie ran quickly up the stairs. A carriage stood at the railing. Beth Baylor and Hildy Addison were climbing the steps to the front porch.

A flash of resentment went through Vonnie when she saw Beth, but she forcefully pushed it away. Beth didn't know she had once been married to Adam. She had no idea how Vonnie felt, or why.

As usual, Beth looked as pretty as a picture. She wore a vanilla nansook suit trimmed with a deep flounce. The overskirt and waist ran in narrow tucks. Narrow and broad white lace bows of black and white grosgrain ribbon comprised the remainder of the trimming. The perky Italian straw bonnet perched on her head was trimmed with cream-colored serge ribbon and a black ostrich feather.

Beth Baylor was the epitome of fashion, and here was Vonnie, flushed from housework, the odor of the dank cellar clinging to her.

"Hello," Vonnie called out, refusing to give in to her irritation.

"Vonnie!" Hildy turned. "Were you in the cellar?"

"Yes, putting away canned goods. I'm ready for a break. How about some lemonade?"

"Wonderful!" the girls chorused.

Following her into the kitchen, the two women chattered like magpies. Beth and Hildy seated themselves at the large, round oak table while Vonnie fixed the drinks.

"What brings you all the way out here today?" Seating herself opposite them, Vonnie poured lemonade into tall glasses.

"Oh, Vonnie, I am so ecstatic! I can't wait." Beth leaned close. "Father said I could ask you to make my wedding dress!"

Vonnie's heart dropped like a stone. The idea Beth might ask her to make the gown had crossed her mind, but she had hoped against hope that the girl would decide on another seamstress, Eleanor Regan, in nearby Lubbock.

"Isn't it wonderful?" Hildy exclaimed. "I'm so pleased for Beth. I know you'll design something absolutely stunning for her."

Beth doesn't know what she's asking, Vonnie agonized. Make her wedding dress? She'd sooner try eating an ostrich at one sitting.

"How does this sound?" Beth said. "I saw this perfectly marvelous picture in a catalog of a white peau de soie with a full-trained, untrimmed skirt. It had this darling, short, seamless bodice trimmed with lace on the front, set off by a wonderful lace jabot sort of draped diagonally across—sort of like this." She crossed her hands across her trim bustline.

"Oh my," Hildy squealed. "It sounds divine!"

"Simply sumptuous. Then it has this wonderful tulle veil, hemmed at the edge and fastened with orange blossom and a small cluster of the flowers on the sleeves."

"Yes!" Hildy squealed with ecstatic approval.

Vonnie felt her throat close; she reached for her glass. Adam could have spared her this persecution by telling Beth the truth when he asked her to marry him. Beth would understand. Youth sometimes…often made mistakes. Beth wouldn't be particularly fond of others knowing about her fiancé's past folly, but she'd accept the news.

"Well?" Beth asked. "Doesn't it sound thrilling?"

"Thrilling," Vonnie managed. "You've set the date?

"Almost!"

Almost? Vonnie wondered what that meant.

Leaning forward, Beth covered Vonnie's hand with hers, concern flooding her blue eyes. "I know how terribly busy you are right now, but I told Adam I wouldn't dream of letting anyone but you make my gown. Your work is unequaled."

Vonnie bit her lower lip and asked, "Adam knows you want me to make your gown?"

"Yes," Beth said, giving a puzzled look.

"Well, I…don't know, Beth. What with Daddy's death… and the birds…" Vonnie said lamely.

Edging forward in her chair, Beth searched Vonnie's face imploringly. "But you can work it in, can't you? A woman's wedding is the happiest day of her life, and if I weren't wearing one of your gowns, why…why, it just wouldn't be the same. And…the wedding might be as late as next spring. I just can't decide!"

Beth had no idea of the spot she was putting Vonnie in. They had been friends since grammar school. How could she tactfully refuse to make the dress without a more plausible excuse than she was too busy?

"I…it's that there's so much work right now. I've got orders stacked on my cutting table, the birds are taking more time than I imagined, and there's Mother…. I doubt spring will be any slower."

"Oh, yes." Beth patted her hand consolingly. "I understand your mother isn't feeling well."

"Daddy's death has devastated her. She can't seem to get her life back in order."

"Of course," Hildy murmured. She glanced at Beth. "How thoughtless of us to try and put more on you. It's just that we love you and value your work so highly. And spring…well, that's months away!"

"I appreciate that, Hildy, Beth. But I really don't know how I could take on more work right now."

"I understand completely," Beth said. "I'm disappointed, but I understand your dilemma. It's that Adam and I so hoped…"

Avoiding Beth's gaze, Vonnie fidgeted with her glass.

Gathering her purse and gloves, Beth mustered a brave smile. "I'd like to leave the invitation open…at least for a while." She viewed Vonnie hopefully. "Promise you'll at least think about it? It would mean so much to me."

"Beth," Hildy cautioned. "Vonnie shouldn't be pressured right now. If she can't make the gown, she can't."

"Of course. It was inconsiderate of me to press," Beth relented. "Is there anything I can do to help you, Vonnie? I would like very much to make this transition easier for you."

In spite of a multitude of reservations, Vonnie felt herself softening. If she had a Christ-like spirit she would put her pettiness aside and make Beth's special day…special.

"When you set the date, Beth, I'll work with you. It would mean that I have to bring in Nelly Fredicks and Susan Matthews to help. I couldn't possibly finish the dress alone and there will be an additional cost—"

"Oh, the cost isn't important," Beth assured her. "If Nelly and Susan can help, that would be wonderful!"

Right now the nagging feeling of empathy was worse than the thought of making the gown. She felt she would be letting Beth down on the most important day of her life. But it seemed so unfair. How could she make the gown that Beth would wear to marry Adam?

"Well, we must be running along," Beth said. Picking up her bag, she smiled. "I've a thousand things to do before the wedding."

And you have almost seven months to do them.

Where is your graciousness? Vonnie told herself. Your sense of compassion? This isn't Beth's fault. It's Adam's.

Vonnie walked the two young women to the door and watched as they drove off down the lane. Upon parting, Beth and Hildy made vague references to getting together again soon. Soon winter would be here making frequent visits impossible.

Vonnie hoped she hadn't offended Beth. Her request had caught her off guard; she'd handled the situation badly.

Two days later Sheriff Tanner returned.

"Sheriff."

"Miss Taylor," he said, thumbing his hat to the back of his head. "Wondered if you had time to think over our earlier conversation?"

"Regarding the birds?"

"Regarding my buyer. The man has cold cash and he's eager to relieve you of your problems. I hope by now you see the wisdom of selling out."

"I haven't changed my mind," Vonnie said, folding her arms against her body and leaning against the door frame. "I see no reason to sell my land or birds."

"Well, now, that's foolhardy, Miss Taylor." He pointedly studied the outbuildings, pens and surrounding acreage. "Lot of work here for a little gal like you. Genaro and Roel are getting on in years. You think you can keep a place like this going on your own?"

She shrugged. "Men drop by every week looking for work. Young, strong men. Keeping responsible help hasn't been that difficult."

She didn't know why she was against the idea of selling. Plain mulishness because the sheriff was being so pushy, she supposed. At times it would be a relief to be spared so much responsibility. No, it wasn't the request. It was who was doing the asking that got under her skin. Teague had frequently said he had no use for Lewis Tanner; consequently his prejudice had rubbed off on her.

"Heard your ma still ain't doing well. Seems to me selling out would be to your advantage. Heard you got relations in Frisco. Why not sell out, take your ma to California and let her get back on her feet? The change would do her good." He smiled, his beard darker than sin. "If you give it serious thought you'll see I'm right."

Vonnie fought the thread of sudden fear that shot through her. She held his challenging gaze. Why, he was threatening her!

"This is my mother's home. She has no plans to leave. If you want to sell your property you're welcome to do so. I'm not selling mine."

The sheriff's features tightened. "I can't sell my land because of your birds," he growled, pointing a sausage finger at her. "You, little lady, are getting on my nerves!"

Vonnie stood firm. The man was offensive and rude! "I won't be pressured into selling my land, or my birds. Or into moving. Is that clear?"

He took another tack.

"If it's the buyer you're concerned about—" he ran a hammy hand over his cheek "—then I'll buy your property."

She laughed in surprise. "You?"

"Me. I could use the land."

"I don't want to move."

"I'll give you a hundred dollars an acre, plus ten thousand for the house and the birds."

She mentally figured the sum in her head. "That's—why that's—a fortune!" Why, she and Mother could live their life in luxury.

"No."

"No?"

"No. I'm not selling."

"Admit it! With Teague gone, a couple of women can't run this place. It makes no sense."

"This is our home," Vonnie contended.

Tanner's features hardened. "You're being stubborn. You know I'm right. Take the offer."

"I don't think so," she said, wishing he hadn't made the

proposition so tempting. The land and birds weren't that valuable, so why would he offer such an exorbitant amount?

"Take a week," he argued. "Think about it. Talk it over with your mother. You'll see it's a very generous offer."

Yes, it was generous. Too generous. How did a sheriff get that much money?

"You'll not get another one to match it." He fished his meaty hand from his pocket. "I took the liberty of having an agreement drawn up. I'll leave it with you. You sign it, send it to me at the sheriff's office, and I'll have your money within a week."

He extended the paper to her and, after hesitating, she took it. Taking it wasn't the same as agreeing, she told herself.

"Sign it," he urged. "And get on with your life."

"Good day, Sheriff."

After a pointed hesitation, the sheriff turned on his heel and went to his horse. Hauling his bulk astride, he gave her one last glance, then rode away.

Vonnie stepped back and slammed the door, then leaned against it and closed her eyes, fighting the tears that threatened. Furious with herself for letting the sheriff get to her like that, she pounded the door with her fist.

"Adam Baldwin! This is all your fault!"

It was irrational, but somehow it seemed to her, at that moment, that the whole rotten situation was Adam's fault.

"Why didn't you love me enough to fight for me?"

There. She'd said it. To herself, assuredly, but she'd said it. The thing that had been gnawing at her for seven long years. And now that she'd said it to herself, she was going to say it to Adam. He hadn't *loved* her enough to fight for her. Yes, she had insisted on annulling the marriage, but he had agreed. Without a fight.

Her decision made, she grabbed her bonnet and rushed out of the house without thought of consequence.

Quickly saddling her horse, she rode at a fast clip toward the Baldwin ranch with Suki following, tongue lolling out as she loped along behind.

Knowing that Adam would be working outside, Vonnie checked the barn first. She found him there, mucking out stalls.

Dust motes floated in the air. The fragrance of freshly cut hay mixed with that of horse manure and seasoned wood. Her eyes adjusted slowly to the dim barn interior.

She stood in the doorway for a moment, staring at him.

Turning, he caught her staring. "What are you doing here?"

His low voice brought her out of her trance. Lifting her chin, she took a deep breath, then said, "I have something I need to say, Adam."

"Oh?" He leaned on the hay fork. "This should be interesting."

His amusement fed her fury.

"Only the lowest, vilest kind of animal would have his fiancée ask his former wife to make her wedding gown!" Her accusation ricocheted off the barn wood.

He sobered. Straightening, he carefully leaned the pitchfork against the stall. "I didn't want Beth to ask you to make her dress."

"Well, she did."

"And you think I encouraged her to ask you?"

"Why else would she?"

"Well, let's see. Because you're friends? Because you make beautiful dresses? Because you're the best seamstress around? Any of those reasons ring a bell with you?"

She hated it when he was logical.

"Then why didn't you head her off? Why didn't you tell her I was too busy?"

"Because I'm not running your business," he returned. "You tell her you can't do it. Make up a reasonable excuse. You've got too much work as it is."

"You're absolutely right I've got too much work. The birds—"

"Sell the birds."

She gasped "What?"

"Sell the birds!"

"I can't. They're Daddy's—"

"Teague's gone. The birds are yours. You're hanging on to them out of pure orneriness."

Stung and looking for a fight, she planted her hands on her hips. "I'd rather be stubborn than a coward, Adam Baldwin."

"Coward!" he bellowed.

"Only a coward would run whining to the sheriff about my birds."

"Where did you get that cockamamie idea? I don't need Lewis Tanner to take care of my problems. Seems like you need somebody, though, since you can't keep those birds in their pens."

"That wasn't my fault!"

"Then whose fault is it?" He towered over her, his face flushed with heat and anger.

"Yours!" she shouted, suddenly remembering why she'd come here in the first place. "Everything…" Her breath caught. "*Everything's* your fault!"

A puzzled look crossed his face. "My fault? How is your being unable to keep your birds in their pens my fault?"

The words burst into her throat. Before she could stop them, they rolled out unchecked. "Because you wouldn't fight for me. You didn't *love* me enough to fight for me!"

She could have cut her tongue out. How could she have said that? But now that she'd started, she couldn't stop.

He shifted his hand on one hip. "What are you talking about?"

"You didn't love me enough to fight for me." Horrified, she heard her voice break.

He looked as if she'd slapped him.

"Where do you come off accusing me of that? If you re-call, lady, I *wanted* to fight for you. You were the one who said you wanted 'to pretend the marriage never happened.'"

"I was fifteen. You were wiser—you should have known better." To her horror, she was crying.

Anger tightened his features. "I loved you more than my life, Vonnie. It killed me to walk away from you that night. I did it because that's what you wanted."

A sob caught in her throat. "Do you even know the meaning of the word *love?*"

"Oh, no you don't. You're not laying this on me. The pro-blem was you didn't love me."

"I did," she whispered. "I did, Adam." A sob caught in her throat.

Turning away, he clenched his fists and raised his eyes toward the barn loft.

She needed proof that he had cared about her back then, that all these years of mourning him had been justified. "What were we doing the first time we kissed?"

Turning back, he met her eyes. She could never remember him looking so virile, so attractive—so forbidden.

"What were we doing?"

"You don't remember, do you? How can you say you cared when you can't even remember." She remembered every day, every hour, every moment they had spent together.

"We were standing under the juniper near Liken's Pond."

"Where were we when we had our first argument?"

"At the Doughertys' barn dance. You thought I paid too much attention to Lucinda Brown. It was—" he pinned her with a challenging look "—eight-thirty on a Friday night and it was cold out. Unusually cold. I'd just gotten you a cup of cider and you turned on your heel and walked off with your nose in the air."

Her voice dropped to a whisper. "The day I sprained my ankle?"

"You insisted on trying to jump off the haystack, and you landed wrong. You were wearing a blue-sprigged dress with white lace and some other sort of frilly stuff around the collar. And—" he leaned closer "—you were so pretty I wanted to kiss you right then and there.

"I had to take you home on my horse, and if I remember right, I was late getting home. P.K. was angry, but I told him a snake spooked my horse, and it threw me and ran away and I had to walk home. I missed supper that night."

The air in the barn was suddenly deathly still.

"Why didn't you just tell him that we'd gotten married, that I was going to be your wife until the day I died," she whispered. His jaw firmed, and she could see obstinacy flare in his eyes.

"We weren't married at the time."

Furious, Vonnie shoved at his chest, throwing him off balance.

Before she could shove him again, Adam grabbed her arms. "Will you calm down?"

"I am calm."

"You're pitching a temper fit."

They glared at each other for an emotion-charged moment, before he released her. "You're right, we were young, but it's too late to change things now."

Her lips trembled. "Yes, you're engaged to be married."

"You don't have to remind me of that."

Her fingers tingled with the desire to touch him, to brush her fingertips across his face, to explore his rugged features. The realization of what she'd lost was too much to endure.

"I'm sorry I wounded your pride," she said quietly. "I know you'll never forgive me. I never meant to hurt you." Even to her ears her voice sounded small, vulnerable, in the large barn. "I've relived that night a thousand times. If I could change one moment, I would, but I can't."

"That's nice to hear, but it changes nothing."

She closed her eyes, momentarily, before opening them

to look up at him. "I still think you should have ordered Beth not to ask me to make the dress."

She walked out of the barn, head held high, and mounted her horse.

As she rode away, she glanced back to see Adam watching from the barn door. She kneed the mare into a gallop, heading toward the Flying Feather with Suki trotting behind.

Chapter Eleven

Vonnie drove the buckboard into town in late October for supplies. Running the ranch and household was wearing her down. *Lord, what am I going to do if Mama doesn't pull out of her despair? I can't face this alone.*

She tied the team to the hitching rail and turned to see Beth and Hildy Mae bearing down on her.

"How fortunate to bump into you!" Beth exclaimed. "I was going to ride out to the ranch later, but now you've saved me the trouble."

"I have?" What could Beth want now?

"It's about my wedding gown," Beth said. She dropped her voice. "I'm worried sick. You are going to make it, aren't you?"

"Yes, Beth…I told you—"

"Because I wouldn't feel married if you didn't. My goodness, we've been friends forever. Promise me right here and now you'll make that gown."

"I will, Beth. Have…you set the date?"

Beth heaved a sigh. "I think I'm leaning toward a fall ceremony now—definitely fall, if not next winter."

Vonnie smiled, recognizing the sincerity on her friend's lovely face. The uncomfortable situation wasn't Beth's fault. If she had to work day and night, she would make her gown and it would be one of her most lovely works. "Rest assured, Beth. I will make your gown. I thought I had promised you."

"Oh, you did! I just know how much work you have, and I was afraid you might have had second thoughts."

"I've given you my word."

If only the words weren't bitter as gall.

A faint blush of early-winter light filtered through the windowpane. Vonnie rolled to her side struggling to adjust her eyes to the light. The clock chimed six times.

The pane needs cleaning. Maybe she would ask Franz to do it.

No, she couldn't keep imposing on Franz. He had been over every day for the last three months to help. There was a limit to his kindness, and the ladies at church soon wouldn't be able to help with Audrey. Snow would come.

Dressing quickly, she knocked on Cammy's door before going downstairs.

"Momma?"

When there was no answer, she opened the door a crack. Cammy sat in front of the window in her dressing gown, as if she planned to get dressed, like she had every morning for as long as Vonnie could remember. Vonnie knew that was not her intention today. After a while, she would crawl back into bed and sleep the day away.

"Momma, it's a lovely day. Let's bundle up tightly and go for a ride. Maybe go see Audrey."

"No. I'm…not feeling well," Cammy said, passing the tips of her fingers across her forehead in a gesture that was becoming all too familiar.

Vonnie suppressed a sigh. "At least get dressed. I'm making pancakes for breakfast. You love pancakes."

"I'm not hungry—"

"Mother, if you don't come downstairs," Vonnie threatened, "I'm going to dress you like a rag doll and personally carry you down!" It must be a hint of Teague's temper surfacing that made her impatient with her mother today. But, Vonnie reminded herself, Teague had never lost patience with Cammy.

The older woman's lower lip trembled. Opening her mouth, she quickly closed it again. Her mouth curled down at the corners; tears welled in her eyes. "I'm a burden on you."

"Momma," Vonnie said, knelt beside Cammy's chair and took the thin, cool hands in her own. "You're not a burden to anyone. I worry about you. It's not like you to sit up here and do nothing. Daddy would be heartbroken to see you like this. He liked you doing things, knitting, cooking. You know it's true."

Cammy focused on her daughter's face. "You're right," she said. "You're right. Teague would be disappointed with me, wouldn't he?"

"Yes, Mother, he would."

Cammy's fingertips briefly touched Vonnie's cheek. "I'm sorry, darling child. I have been a burden. I miss your father so. He's been gone so long."

"It's all right to miss him, Momma. I do, too." Every day was a trial without Teague's revitalizing authority. No thunderous sound of his laughter, no voice calling out unexpectedly, "Puddin', get out here! There's something I want you to see!"

"He was such a fine man," Cammy whispered. "So good. I don't know what's wrong with me lately. It seems I can't...think clearly."

"I know and it's understandable, but you've got to try. Begin by getting yourself dressed and coming downstairs to breakfast. I'm making the best blueberry pancakes you've ever tasted!"

"You do that," Cammy said, her eyes brightening, "and I'll eat a whole stack of them."

Hugging her tightly, Vonnie felt tears stinging her eyes. Today was going to be a turning point. Soon life would be normal again.

"Ten minutes, Momma."

Tripping downstairs, she hummed a tune. Maybe she *was* beginning to pull out of her grief. Oh, the sorrow hadn't lessened. She knew that. But maybe Momma wouldn't drown in it.

She got out the fixings for pancakes, pausing to stare past the blue-and-white checked curtains to the ostrich pens. What if Mama never got any better? What would they do? She set the big blue mixing bowl in the center of the table and dropped into a chair, hands gripped tightly together. *"Lord, be with her. I can take care of her physically, but I can't clear her mind or give her a reason to go on living. If it be Your will, give Momma back to me. Please."*

Ten minutes later, Vonnie had the big iron skillet hot and the pancake batter mixed.

"Where are those hotcakes?" Cammy asked, stepping into the kitchen. She was dressed in a dark blue wool dress that had been one of Teague's favorites. Vonnie felt so relieved laughter bubbled up inside her.

"Sit yourself down at the table," she said, pouring a cup of coffee. "And get your mouth set for a feast."

Fifteen minutes later, their plates nearly licked clean, mother and daughter lingered over cups of coffee. For the first time in months, the atmosphere in the kitchen felt normal. Comfortable, effortless, relaxed.

"This is good," Cammy said. "I didn't know how much I'd missed sitting at this table with you."

"I've missed you, too, Momma."

"I haven't been myself lately, have I?"

Vonnie smiled. Cammy had always possessed an inner strength that many admired, and it wasn't likely to change, but during the months since Teague's shockingly sudden death, she had wavered—understandable for a woman who had lost a vital part of herself. Hopefully, they were putting that behind them now. Together, they would go on without Teague, remembering the joy he had brought into their lives. Now if she could put Adam in the same box, tie it neatly and resume her life, too… Cammy had an abiding faith in God that would see her through awful tragedy. Did she have that same deep faith? Sometimes she feared she didn't…not like Momma.

Sighing, Cammy studied her hands. "It's been so…difficult. Your father and I have been together so long—"

Vonnie squeezed her hand, then jumped when someone pounded on the back door.

Startled, Cammy sat up straighter. "Who would come visiting so early in the morning?"

"I don't know," Vonnie hurried to answer the impatient summons. Opening the door, she saw the hired hand, his face a mask of concern.

"Roel? What's wrong?"

"*Buenos dias*, Señorita Taylor. Two of the birds, they are very sickly this morning. Someone's been in the pen…you should come quickly."

"Two more?" Vonnie breathed. "Momma, I've got to check the birds."

"Go ahead," Cammy waved Vonnie out the door. "I'll take care of the dishes."

"Thanks, Momma."

Vonnie followed Roel out to the pens, and she immediately saw that he was right. Two of the ostriches were "drooping" again. Standing alone in separate corners of the pen, they looked dull and listless.

Entering the holding crib, Vonnie approached the rooster closest her. The adult male was smaller than the hen, with prettier feathers. His bright red legs meant he was breeding now.

"Quiet," she crooned, not sure she knew what she was doing. "I want to look at you a bit."

Slowly edging closer, she held out her hand until she reached the bird. Cautiously, she circled him, keeping an eye on him but out of reach of his feet in case he decided to kick. This morning he was too ill to be combative.

Smoothing feathers that suddenly seemed dusty and ugly, Vonnie examined the bird. Just the day before, the animal had seemed perfectly healthy.

"Roel, did anything disturb the birds last night?"

"No, *señorita*. I'd have heard them."

Roel was right. Someone had been in the pens. "This bird has several cuts, bad ones, on this side of his neck. Get me the salve from the shed, will you?"

"*Sí*, immediately."

Roel returned with the jar of salve, and Vonnie applied it to the fresh cuts. Moving to the other bird, she examined it and found the same cuts and abrasions. She treated the bird accordingly.

When she was finished, she handed the salve back to Roel and then walked the full length of the pen, running her bare hand along the wire.

"Ouch!" she cried softly. She shook her hand, flinging drops of blood across her skirt. Investigating the injury, she found a fresh cut across her index finger. Wrapping a handkerchief around her finger, she bent to examine the fence.

"How can this be?" she exclaimed softly.

A short piece of wire was wrapped around the fence where two pieces came together to form a square. Enough of the ends had been left sticking out to catch and slice, but not enough to be readily seen. It would take someone running their hand over the wire to find it.

"Or the birds rubbing along the fence," she muttered. "Roel, come here."

"*Sí?*"

"See this?"

Bending closer, Roel focused on the jagged end of wire. "*Sí*, but I do not understand. I checked this section of fence early this morning."

"We'll walk every foot of wire, running our hands along every inch. Wear gloves—you'll cut yourself. Locate every bit of ragged ends, and remove it immediately. This wire was intentionally rigged to injure the birds."

"*Sí*…but who could have done such a thing?"

"That's a good question," she mused. "A very good question."

Vonnie thought about the answer while they both walked the fence. Who would want to hurt the ostriches? Sheriff Tanner came to mind. He wanted her to sell the birds. Failing that, he wanted her to sell him her land. Either way, the birds would be gone, and that was all he wanted.

But would he go this far?

Yes, she decided. Lewis Tanner would go as far as he needed to achieve an end.

The question was, what was she going to do about it?

After that, Vonnie went to the pens first thing each morning, running her hands along the wire to make sure there were no barbed spurs to harm the birds. Either Roel or Genaro performed the same ritual at dark, as well as listening for any disturbance during the night.

Cammy was less inclined to seclude herself in her room lately, but her apathy had returned. Again she retreated into her own world.

For once, Vonnie was too distracted to worry about her. Between watching the birds and trying to keep up with her sewing, there was scarcely a free moment.

One Sunday morning, Vonnie convinced Cammy to dress and attend church with her. Out of habit, they sat in the same pew they'd occupied since Vonnie was born.

Automatically holding the songbook for Cammy, Vonnie kept her eyes away from the Baldwin pew, but she knew what she would find. Beth smiling up at Adam, looking for the world like an angel as her lilting soprano blended harmoniously with his baritone in a spirited rendition of "Blessed Assurance."

Someone seriously needed to bless her assurance.

The times she'd sat in this same pew and watched Adam and Andrew make faces at her…

More than once, P.K. had thumped his sons on the head with his knuckles to settle them down.

Her mind snapped back to the service as the pastor stood and opened his Bible.

After the sermon, folks greeted friends and neighbors. It was a social hour, the hour of brotherly friendship.

Vonnie and Cammy made their way outside and ran into Judge Henderson, his wife, Maddy, and daughter, Carolyn.

"Camilla, it's so good to see you out and about again," Maddy exclaimed, "and Vonnie, you look lovely. One of your designs?"

"Yes, it is." Vonnie's hand self-consciously smoothed the

skirt of her dress. The striped, changeable rose silk trimmed with black velvet bands and Vandykes of white Irish guipure lace was striking. The buffalo felt hat trimmed with black velvet and black ostrich feather gave the ensemble a French look she had copied from a catalog.

"It's been so long since we've seen you," Maddy chided. "You must come for tea this afternoon. We'll have a long visit and catch up on things. We'd so love to have you."

"Why, that would be lovely," Vonnie said. "Wouldn't it, Mother?"

"I don't know, Maddy." Cammy sounded vague. "Maybe not this time."

Maddy wasn't going to take no for an answer. "Nonsense. Shall we say four o'clock?"

Cammy glanced imploringly at Vonnie.

"That's very kind of you, Maddy. Of course, we'll come." Vonnie said. "We'll see you at four?"

"At four. We'll be looking forward to it!"

Grasping Vonnie's hand, Carolyn grinned. "I have so much to tell you." Bending closer, she whispered. "Have you heard that Priscilla Nelson is seeing Lem Turner?"

"No!" Vonnie gasped. "Since when?"

"Since last week."

"I thought Lem was seeing Nola Richards."

"So did I, but apparently he isn't any longer. I'll tell you everything at tea this afternoon."

"I'll be there," Vonnie promised.

Back home, they ate a quiet dinner of roast chicken with mashed potatoes and green beans. Afterward, Cammy wandered into the parlor while Vonnie washed the dishes. She found her mother looking through the picture album, and crying.

"Oh, come see, Vonnie. Look here."

"Momma," Vonnie chided. "Why don't we put the album away? You should rest before we go to the Hendersons'."

"In a while," she promised. "Come, sit with me. There's something I want you to see."

"I've seen the pictures a hundred times, Momma."

"Please." Cammy patted the seat beside her. "Share a moment with me."

Sighing, Vonnie sat down beside her mother and glanced at the photo she indicated. It was of Teague, dressed in a Confederate uniform. Her father looked so young. He had been quite dashing—quite attractive until the day he'd died. How she missed his calm, insightful presence.

"Doesn't your father look handsome in his uniform? See how wonderful he looks? Why, he's barely aged at all, don't you agree? I must remember to tell him so—though it will surely embarrass him."

Vonnie's heart fell. In spite of all her recent expectations, her mother was living more and more in the past. She had begun to talk as if Teague were away on a trip and would walk through the door at any moment.

"Why, I told your father the other day that when I look at him in his uniform, I fall in love with him all over again."

"You mean you talk to Daddy...in spirit, don't you, Momma?"

"Yes dear...in spirit," Cammy answered vaguely.

Turning the page, her fingers caressed the worn photographs taken when she and Teague were first married.

"He knows that after I met him I never looked at another boy. He used to laugh at me, but it's true! I fell in love with him at first sight. I was fourteen…. I'd never met a boy who could make my heart pound with giddiness the way Teague did."

Tears glistened in her eyes. Her fingers touched the brown-tinted photo. "When will he be home, Vonnie? He's been gone such a long time. Nearly as long as when he put on this uniform and marched away."

"Momma—" Vonnie started, and then stopped.

She could tell Cammy a hundred times that Teague was never coming back, but her mind could not comprehend that the heartbeat of her life was gone, never to return. Sometimes she envied her mother's fantasy. At least the strength of her hope sustained her.

"Momma, you must rest before we visit the Hendersons."

Cammy looked up, anxious. "Oh, my. Leave again? What if Teague comes while we're gone?"

"He won't," Vonnie assured her.

"You'll leave a note for him, won't you? In case he should? I wouldn't want him to come home and not know where we are. He worries about us, you know. Why, when you were a baby he'd wake up nights stewing about you, wondering if you'd marry properly, if the man would treat you good."

Vonnie patted her mother's hand. "Why don't you go up and change back into your new dress with the white lace collar. You look so pretty in blue."

"Yes, I will. Thank you."

After Cammy went upstairs, Vonnie remained on the settee, holding the photo album.

Oh, Daddy, what am I going to do? Momma's so bad, and I don't know what's happening to the birds.

Teague's image stared up at her, cold, unseeing.

By three, Vonnie and Cammy were in the buggy on their way to tea. A sharp wind rocked the carriage as it sped along.

Judge Henderson's three-story house sat at the end of a street shaded by beautiful, old oaks in the summer. The wide porches wrapped around three sides, and during the warm months one could sit there in the cool of the evening, smell the flowering shrubs and watch the sun paint the town muted shades of yellow and purple.

Within the large rooms, the snowy white walls were a perfect backdrop for the dark, handmade furniture. The hardwood floors gleamed with polished care.

Carolyn's room took the whole front of the second floor. The lush living quarters had been the envy of her friends when, as girls, they'd lain awake in the big four-poster bed and giggled over what boys they were interested in, and who'd been kissed first.

"Here we are," Vonnie said, drawing the buggy up in front of the house. Judge Henderson sat on the porch, napping in a large, white wicker rocking chair, oblivious to the wind. The arriving buggy woke him.

"Afternoon, ladies," he boomed, getting to his feet to greet them.

"Afternoon, Judge," Vonnie called. "Lovely day, isn't it?"

"That it is," he agreed, ushering them into the house.

"There you are!" Maddy exclaimed from the stairway

when they entered the house. Latching onto Cammy's arm, Maddy squeezed it affectionately. "I'm so glad you've come. Come into the parlor where we can be comfortable. Tea will be served later."

The judge ushered Vonnie into the parlor where a fire burned brightly in the fireplace. Cammy hadn't said a single word on the trip over, and now she was looking around as if she didn't recognize where they were, although they had been the Hendersons' guests a hundred times.

"Can you believe Thanksgiving will be upon us next week?"

"It is hard to comprehend." The first Thanksgiving without Daddy.

"Vonnie, your dress is exquisite!" Carolyn cried upon entering the room.

It got to be a tiny bit embarrassing that each time Carolyn saw Vonnie in a new dress she marveled aloud at her friend's sewing ability, but Vonnie appreciated the praise. She sorely needed a lift to her spirits.

Carolyn kissed her. "Honestly, Vonnie, you amaze me. I can hardly believe that the shy young girl I shared a primer with is now so incredibly talented and dreams up marvelous designs for dresses straight out of her head."

Vonnie smiled her appreciation for the compliment and sat next to Cammy by the fire.

The group made small talk for a few minutes, about the weather, a new mercantile being established in town and how it might affect Garrett Beasley's business. Cammy said little, looking occasionally to Vonnie for assurance. It hurt to see her mother so vulnerable, so uncertain.

Vonnie found herself avoiding the judge's eyes all afternoon. His knowledge of her earlier marriage made her uneasy, although he had closely guarded her secret for years. He spoke fondly about the upcoming holiday festivities, and how much he looked forward to the season.

Carolyn chatted incessantly about upcoming parties and Christmas soirees.

The conversation touched briefly on the recent trouble with the ostriches. It was commonly agreed that the wire incidents were unfortunate, a nuisance that must be avoided. The injured birds were healing properly.

The chime on the front door interrupted the conversation.

"That must be Franz and Audrey," Maddy announced. "I asked them to join us."

The Hendersons and the Schuylers had been friends nearly as long as the Hendersons and Taylors. The men had fought on the same side during the war. It had been the judge who suggested the lamplighter job to Franz.

The four of them, and Cammy and Teague, had spent many an evening together, listening to Audrey play the piano.

Over the years, the three families shared the good and the bad, as old friends tend to do.

Vonnie heard the judge's hearty laugh from the foyer, then Franz entered with Audrey holding tightly to his arm. It was obvious her health was failing, but her smile was as bright as ever when she saw Cammy and Vonnie.

"Momma, Audrey's here." Vonnie's eyes plaintively urged her mother to respond.

"Why, Cammy, don't you look lovely," Audrey said, coming over to place a kiss on Cammy's cheek.

Vonnie glanced at Audrey apologetically when Cammy didn't respond, but Audrey's look clearly said she understood.

Maddy brought tea and served while Audrey and Franz caught up on the recent happenings in the community.

"And Cammy, how are you this lovely day? How nice you look in blue." Audrey tried to draw her into the conversation.

Cammy ignored the question, sipping her tea indifferently. She turned to her daughter and said, "You know, Vonnie, dear, you should see those nice Baldwin boys more often—Adam and Andrew? They're such fine boys—handsome young men. Eligible, too…"

"Mother," Vonnie admonished, feeling color flood her cheeks. "Adam is engaged to Beth. Have you forgotten?" she gently chided.

"Forgotten? No," Cammy mused. "Well, yes, perhaps I knew that." She looked up again. "Have you considered them proper suitors?"

"Adam and Andrew?" Vonnie couldn't believe this turn of her mother's conversation—didn't want to believe it.

Not here, in front of the Hendersons and Schuylers!

"They're good men…your father doesn't care for them, but he's hardened—always has been…. If you like them, you tell them they can come courting. You leave your father to me." A smile softened her lips. "I know how to handle Teague Taylor…always have, always will…"

Vonnie apologized, the full impact of her mother's condition striking her. It was frightening. "I'm sorry… Mother is a little distracted today—overtired—"

"It's all right—" Audrey began.

"The cellar is evil."

Vonnie's cup rattled on her saucer. This behavior had gone beyond grief.

"Mother—"

"It's evil. Bad. Bad!" Springing to her feet, Cammy screamed. "I won't go down there. Not ever—you shouldn't make me…"

Maddy squirmed uncomfortably. Vonnie could see her distress; the outburst was so out of character for Cammy.

Reaching for the teapot, the judge's wife smiled at her husband. "More tea, dear?"

Clearing his throat, he held out his cup. "Just a tad more, Mother."

Vonnie quietly laid her hand on Cammy's hand. "There's nothing wrong with the cellar, Momma," she soothed. "Don't you remember? Franz cleaned it for us recently."

Her mother's fear of the cellar was legendary. Cammy had always had an abnormal fear of the tight, small place.

"I won't go down there," Cammy repeated, her voice strained and tense.

"The cellar is as neat as our parlor—"

"It certainly is," Franz declared. "I spent the good part of a week going over every inch—"

"No!" Cammy sat up straighter. The expression on her face startled Vonnie. She wore a mixture of fear and loathing. "No! I'll never go down there. Never!"

Chapter Twelve

✤

"Cammy isn't herself today," Franz excused, offering a reassuring smile. "If it makes her feel any better, I'll clean the cellar as many times as it takes to set her mind at ease. Don't worry your pretty head about it."

"Have you heard that Beth has chosen rose for the bridesmaids' dresses?" Carolyn asked.

"No, I hadn't heard that." Vonnie wished the floor would open up and swallow her…and her mother.

"I thought surely she'd insist you make her dress," Carolyn blurted, then looked as if she wished she'd bitten her tongue. "I mean—"

"She did." A knot formed in Vonnie's throat. "When she and Adam set a date we'll talk further."

"Oh, of course." Carolyn nodded. "Of course no one knows what the date will be."

"Oh, my," Audrey crooned, eyeing the piano. "My lovely old piano—"

Audrey got up to run her hands over the fine wood lovingly, her eyes filled with sweet memories. "I never tire of seeing it."

"It is a beauty," the judge agreed. "And I must confess, it's done nothing but gather dust these past few years. That girl of mine played it long enough to learn a song or two, and then got bored with the whole idea."

Vonnie recalled Carolyn's musical talent: heartbreaking!

"Daddy, you have to admit your nerves have calmed down once I stopped playing." Carolyn laughed. Turning to Cammy, she giggled. "He said that piano practice was far too kind a word for what I was doing. He said it was more like premeditated slaughter of fine music when I sat down to play."

Audrey laughed with the others at Carolyn's self-deprecation, though they all knew it was true. The girl had absolutely no sense of rhythm. Her piano teacher, Vonnie remembered, had given up out of sheer frustration.

"I'd like to buy the piano back," Franz offered quietly.

"I fear," Clive said gently, "that the piano has become a part of us. I'm hoping our grandchildren will be more musically inclined, but Audrey is always welcome to play as often as she wants. We so enjoy her fine talent."

Carolyn smiled. "I am perfectly dreadful at the keys."

"Oh," Audrey sighed. "We could never afford to buy it back anyway."

"But you'll play for us, won't you?" the judge encouraged.

Audrey sat on the bench and lovingly opened the lid to expose the keys. Her fingers lightly touched the ivories, up and down, up and down. Glancing around, she smiled. "What would you like to hear?"

Carolyn turned to her father. "What was the song you always wanted me to play, but I absolutely could not do it? Instead, I'd have the teacher play it for me and you listened with such enjoyment. Oh, what was it?" Her brow furrowed. "It was one by Johann Strauss, right?"

With a smile, Audrey nodded, then her fingers flowed up and down the keys, and a hauntingly sweet melody filled the room and captured her audience with its irresistible beauty. The room's occupants sat spellbound, breathless, as she bent over the keys, her frail body moving with the music's emotion.

Vonnie glanced at Franz and smiled when she saw the clear pride in his face as Audrey played on. They listened, recognizing Audrey's love for the music and the blend of artist and instrument. From one piece to another, until, exhausted, Audrey straightened from the keyboard and the last notes faded into the late afternoon.

"My, oh, my," Maddy said. "You are gifted, Audrey. Thank you again for sharing your talent with us."

"Thank you for loaning me the use of your piano," Audrey returned.

"Well, I'll make fresh tea," Maddy said, gathering their cups.

Vonnie took the opportunity to wander out onto the side porch for a breath of fresh air. Judge Henderson followed. The fragrance of wood smoke curling from the chimney scented the late afternoon air.

"You're still grieving over Adam, aren't you?"

The judge lit a cigar. His words caught Vonnie by surprise. Emotion welled to the back of her throat. Was she so transparent?

"No one will ever know your secret," he calmly stated. "I must admit, I can't ever recall another circumstance like this one." He winked at her playfully. "When you put your foot in it, little lady, you really put your foot in it. P.K. and Teague would have had a royal fit had they known what you and Adam did." He chuckled. "It would have been worth a king's ransom to see it."

"I fail to see the humor," Vonnie said drily.

He could be trusted to share her secret, and she so desperately needed to talk to someone who understood.

"Forgive me," he said. "I realize the situation is anything but humorous to you. I know you hurt deeply over Beth and Adam's pending marriage."

Vonnie hugged her waist, fighting back tears.

"I do have one question."

Vonnie could guess what it was. "Whatever possessed us to do such a thing?"

"No, if my memory serves me, I know what prompted you to do it. My question is, why haven't you or Adam told Beth?" His expression softened. "She needs to know."

Vonnie studied the quiet street, the houses lined along it. Sounds drifted to her—a dog barking in the distance, the breeze rustling the juniper tree in the side yard. She tried to think of a reasonable explanation to a question she had been asking herself.

"Adam feels the information would only hurt her. It was one afternoon…and the marriage never began."

"No…I suppose not," the judge agreed. "Still—"

"Still."

Vonnie knew Beth should be told. It would only be fair.

"It's my fault, you know. Adam wanted to tell our parents that day, but I wouldn't allow it. Being in our parents' favor meant so much to me. Too much. I know that now." She touched a handkerchief to the corner of her eyes. "Adam's feelings should have come first."

Had she taken her own advice, today she would be his wife and Beth wouldn't be planning his wedding.

The judge drew on his pipe thoughtfully. "I suppose one might argue why Adam didn't take the matter into his own hands?"

"Adam loved me enough to do as I asked. I asked him to have the marriage annulled. In doing so, I wounded his self-esteem."

Promise me you'll stay with me forever, Vonnie.

I will, Adam. I promise. Forever.

She sighed. "I was so foolish. I'm older and wiser now. A woman can't hurt a man's pride the way I did Adam's and not expect to suffer the consequences."

"Oh, my child," the judge said, resting his hand on her shoulder. "Wisdom is never easy in matters of the heart."

"I'm such a fool." She bit her lower lip, hard, hoping to stop threatening tears from spilling over.

"You're still in love with him. After all these years."

Her lower lip trembled.

With a sigh, he pulled her to him, his hand gently patting her back. "Oh, how tangled our lives can become. Does he know?"

"No!" She pulled away. "He can never know. Please, Judge Henderson, you must promise me!"

"I won't breathe a word of it," he vowed. "But the question remains, what are we going to do about this?"

"There's nothing I can do. Adam is marrying Beth." She turned, her back firming with resolve. Bitterness choked her. She had no one to blame but herself.

"Dear me," the judge said. "You're willing to let the man you love marry another woman? Just like that?"

"Adam doesn't share my sentiments."

"You're sure of this?"

"Reasonably certain."

If he shared her love he wouldn't be marrying another woman, regardless. Regardless of P.K.'s thirst for more. She changed the subject.

"Sheriff Tanner has made me a generous offer on the land and birds."

"Do you want to sell?"

"No. At least I don't think I do." She paused. "To be perfectly honest, I don't know what I think or want."

She stared out across the lawn, wishing she could turn back the clock and make her troubles go away.

"What would you do, Judge?"

"Sell out."

She turned. "Sell out?"

"God may be opening a new door for you and your mother. You feel Adam is lost to you. A woman can't run a ranch and take care of those birds. Spend some quiet time with God. Open your heart to His leading. He'll show us what to do if we take the time to listen. If what you say is true, that you don't intend to interfere in Adam's future, then it would behoove all concerned if you were to take Cammy back to San Francisco so that she can be near her family. Perhaps there, she will adjust to her loss. The birds must be a great deal of trouble. Why not start a new life in California? With your talent, you needn't worry a day about finances."

Vonnie paced a step or two away, trying to distance herself from the truth.

"I don't know —maybe that would be best."

"You and your mother would be sorely missed, but I'm confident it's the best all-around solution."

"I keep hoping Mother will get better. She still thinks Daddy's going to come home at any minute. If I take her away before she's accepted that he's gone, I don't know how it will affect her."

"The decision is most difficult, but you must consider what's best for the both of you. How will seeing Adam and Beth together affect you? Will you be able to set aside your love and not be resentful when their children come along—"

"Judge…Vonnie…are you going to stay out there all afternoon?" Maddy called.

Taking a deep breath, Vonnie turned to go inside.

"Promise me you'll think about what we've discussed," the judge urged. "I know you've been singled out to have wisdom far beyond your years, but it's all really quite simple. Trust God, Vonnie. He loves you and He wants the best for you. Let Him guide you in the path you should take.

"And, either you love Adam and are willing to fight for

him, or you move to California and make a new life for yourself…without him."

How she wished it were so simple. Yet she knew he spoke the truth. If she stayed here, not a day would go by that she wouldn't think of Adam and see Beth at his side. How could she do that?

"I'll give it serious thought," she promised.

Leave Amarillo and Adam. Forever? Could she do it?

"I'm sure you'll make the right choice." Extending his arm, he gave her a paternal smile. "Shall we go have that tea?"

Pulling the handkerchief over the lower half of his face, Adam spurred his horse into a gallop. He was riding drag this morning while his brothers bunched the herd closer. Moving cattle to higher pasture was a tedious, dusty job, considering the animals had been left to range free all fall. Winter was close; the animals would need feed soon.

He'd looked forward to the ride. It gave him time to think. But he detested it for the same reason. Beth was talking fall wedding, eleven months away. He had to agree or think of a reason he couldn't marry her.

He gave a sharp whistle and cut a stray back into the herd.

Vonnie. He'd avoided the inevitable as long as he could. The way she'd looked this past Sunday, sitting in the Taylor pew with her mother. Beautiful, self-assured, confident.

There was a rumor floating around that Lewis Tanner had made her a handsome offer for her land. Tanner had been heard boasting around town that he had an eager buyer for the Taylor ranch and they wanted the birds, too. He must not have been around the birds.

Adam knew the ostriches were worrisome. They'd done a fair job of spooking his herd a third time. Baldwin beef had been scattered over nearly a hundred acres. It took two days to round them up and cut the birds out of the herd.

When he took the birds back to Vonnie, she seemed almost unconcerned. Told him he should get calmer cattle.

Their conversation had ended in an argument, nothing out of the ordinary these days.

Beth had mentioned the trouble Vonnie was having with the ostriches. Jagged fences, strange disturbances, the birds getting out periodically. That had never happened under Teague's watch.

Were the troubling incidents due to lack of experience or calculated interference?

Lewis Tanner wanted Vonnie's land. Why? Did he want it badly enough to sabotage the birds? If he had a buyer as eager as he claimed, how much were they willing to pay? Enough for Tanner to try to force Vonnie to sell? Enough to buy her out for a healthy price and pocket a hefty profit?

But Lewis wouldn't be able to sell his land as long as Vonnie owned the ostriches.

Hold up, Baldwin. She isn't your concern, he reminded himself. It was something he had to remind himself far too often lately.

Whistling, he turned two more strays back into the herd.

How far would Tanner go? As far as he needed. Adam knew that with certainty. The man would do anything for a buck.

He used his power to punish and for his own benefit. And, at the moment, it looked like Vonnie was his next target.

If she got one of her stubborn streaks and refused to cooperate—as he suspected she would—how far was Tanner willing to go to make her sell? Enough to hurt the birds? Enough to hurt her?

He bristled at the thought. If Tanner thought he'd get away with hurting Vonnie, he was sadly mistaken. Adam would personally see to that.

Back off, Baldwin. It isn't any of your business.

Giving another sharp whistle, he rode into the herd, determined to get his ex-wife off his mind.

On Tuesday there was a knock at the door just as Vonnie finished cleaning up their lunch dishes. Glancing in the parlor as she passed, she frowned when she saw Cammy with the photograph album cradled in her lap.

"Mother, close the book. Please."

When she opened the front door, she saw the sheriff. Tipping his hat, Lewis didn't bother with formalities. Vonnie assumed this wasn't a social call.

"Shouldn't be surprised to see me. Told you I'd be back," he said curtly.

"Told you not to bother."

Tanner quickly came to the point. "Have you reconsidered my offer?"

"I have, and the answer is no. I'm not going to sell the land. To you or anyone else."

Actually she hadn't decided one way or the other until the moment she opened the door and saw him standing there. Other than P.K. Baldwin, Lewis Tanner was the last man on earth Teague would want her to sell to.

Tanner's eyes narrowed. "I gave you a better offer than you'll get from anybody else. More than the land is worth."

"I realize that. And I also have to wonder why."

"Because you've got me over a barrel!"

She doubted that. Lewis Tanner never let anyone best him. There had to be another, more self-serving, reason.

"The answer is no. I don't want to sell."

Tanner's face flushed red-hot. "You'll be sorry. Real sorry."

Lifting her chin a notch, she confronted him icily. "Are you threatening me?"

Spinning on his heel, Tanner stomped off the porch, mounted and rode off, leaving Vonnie with a knot in her stomach as large as a fist and an even bigger sense of impending doom.

Slamming the door shut, she sagged weakly against it.

He is *threatening me.*

Chapter Thirteen

❦

Eyeing the long plank tables laid on wooden sawhorses in the churchyard for the all-day meeting, Vonnie sighed. Dinner on the grounds was part of the church's holiday events. Thanksgiving was coming up, and every woman in the community had outdone herself hoping her culinary contributions would outshine her neighbor's. The weather held; today November sunshine filled the courtyard.

The tables groaned under a baked turkey, sweet potatoes, cornbread dressing, vegetables and desserts. Amanda Fischer's Mile-High Buttermilk Coconut Cake with lemon filling occupied the place of honor. No one could outshine Amanda when it came to cakes.

"Oh, Vonnie." Beth rushed up, dragging an obviously reluctant Adam behind her. Vonnie averted her gaze, trying not to make eye contact. She sneaked a look only to find Adam staring determinedly at the ground.

"We still can't agree on a wedding date," Beth said. "What do you think? Fall or winter? I'd thought for certain fall, but I've changed my mind again. I'm such a picky Annie, I declare."

"Whatever season you prefer," Vonnie said. "That's a decision you and Adam must make." She couldn't listen to this. Her pride hurt too much to set the date for the Baldwin/Baylor wedding. Surely the Lord wouldn't think less of her if she failed to comply; surely, He understood her reluctance.

"Winter." Beth lifted a hand to her forehead. "Winter— yes. A lovely winter wedding. Winters can be dreadful around here. What if there were a snowstorm and no one could come. Or ice? No, winter isn't good."

Or maybe never. Vonnie caught her hateful thoughts. Oh, how she wished she could be more charitable about this— genuinely happy for Adam and Beth. Beth didn't deserve her envy or her lack of enthusiasm.

Beth tilted her head to one side. "How *do* you feel about late fall? That would give you oodles of time to make the dress."

"Yes."

Beth frowned. "Yes what?"

"What you said. Late fall." Anytime, just get this over with.

"Late fall, a day like today. Hmm. November would be lovely."

Vonnie noticed that Adam pretended unusual interest in

a neighbor's rig. She wondered if he was even listening to the conversation.

"Of course, holidays *and* a wedding…" Vonnie almost choked on the words.

"Oh. Yes, the holidays." Beth pursed her lips. "I'm leaning toward springtime."

"That too," Vonnie said, desperate to escape. She had to get away from Beth before she disgraced herself by bursting into tears. "I'm sorry, but I need to check on Momma."

Her eyes met Adam's for one brief instant before she walked away. She sensed his gaze following her across the churchyard.

Spring. Summer. Winter. Fall. What did it matter? The event couldn't be far enough away to suit Vonnie.

The holidays passed in a blur. Thanksgiving. Then Christmas…a sad day in the Taylor household. No lit candles, no turkey. Vonnie read the Christmas story from Luke, but she didn't think Cammy heard her.

They went to bed early. She could hear her mother crying long into the night.

Straightening his string tie, Adam shrugged into his dress jacket. Dinner with Beth. He stared at his reflection in the mirror. How much longer could he perpetuate this farce? He didn't love Beth. He'd never loved her.

"Having supper at the Baylors'?"

Adam paused at the library door. P.K. was sprawled in front of the wide window that allowed the room a scenic view of snow-covered fields. It was the elder Baldwin's favorite room.

"I'm on my way to Beth's now. Alma taking care of you?"

"She always has. I'm sure she has some kind of gastric torture planned for my supper. Your brothers are off tonight, too."

"Oh? Andrew?"

"Yes…strange thing. He must have found an interest in town. He's gone enough, lately."

It was unusual for Andrew to be away from the house in January. The weather was too bad. He was more inclined to stay home and bury himself in a selection from his latest book order from back East.

"Andrew and a woman? She must be amazing to get his attention."

"Uh-huh. Say hello to Leighton and Gillian for me," P.K. said.

Darkness had fallen when he looped his horse's reins over the hitching rail in front of the Baylor house. A stiff breeze blew from the north, suggesting snow any minute.

Leighton Baylor had carved a niche for himself and his family in the community. The shrewd businessman owned the local sawmill. As sole proprietor, he made a healthy profit for himself.

"Mama was about to give up on you," Beth scolded when she opened the door.

"Sorry, as I was leaving, I stopped to talk—"

"To P.K.?"

Adam nodded.

"Adam," Gillian trilled as she came to the door, wiping her hands on a cloth. "What a delightful pleasure. Let me take your hat."

Adam removed his hat and handed it to her. "Good evening, Mrs. Baylor."

"For goodness' sakes, when are you going to call me Gillian. We're about to be family, dear."

"Gillian," Adam corrected.

"Make yourself at home. Beth, take Adam—"

"Into the parlor. I am, Mama." Looping her arm through his, Beth smiled up at him and escorted him through the doorway. "Daddy, Adam's here."

"I can see that," Leighton said, getting up to meet them. He winked. "You look like you could use something to warm you. Temperature's dropping."

Adam took the cup of hot coffee and silently saluted Leighton, a man who wore his success with comfortable ease.

"P.K. sends his best."

"How is the ol' coot?" Leighton chuckled, settling himself in an overstuffed chair and motioning Adam to a matching one.

"Well. Thank you."

"Still favoring that leg of his?"

"It bothers him from time to time, but he manages."

"Stubborn as a donkey. Always was. Wouldn't admit he isn't as young as he used to be, even if that leg gave out on him completely."

"Dinner is on the table," Gillian announced from the doorway.

"Roast beef," Leighton murmured. "Act like you like it."

The dining room, now devoid of Christmas finery, was square, with a rectangular table set with Gillian's best. Eggshell china with a rim of gold and cups so thin that one could almost see through them. Knives and forks matched with gold plates that gleamed brightly beneath a crystal chandelier that must have cost as much as half the houses in Potter County.

The table setting did justice to the silk wallpaper that Gillian had ordered from Boston in the spring. Beth made a point of telling Adam that her mother had taken great pleasure in finding a tablecloth and napkins to match the flower pattern, so he was to be sure to comment on the striking design.

Should he get it over with and comment now, or wait?

Gillian spared him from the decision. "Leighton, your usual place. Adam, at the other end." She gestured one way, then another with her hand.

Beth sat on Adam's left; Gillian sat to his right. Leighton said a perfunctory grace. Adam could see he was uncomfortable with saying prayers aloud, but bent to Gillian's wish for a dinner blessing.

After the amen, the women started dishes of roast beef, boiled potatoes, carrots, squash, string beans and cabbage around the table.

"Has Beth told you she's chosen rose for her attendants' dresses?" Gillian asked Adam.

"Yes, I believe she mentioned it."

Gillian slanted him a sly look. "Your favorite color. You mentioned once that your mother was partial to it."

He looked up. "I did?"

"Yes. Do have more carrots, Adam. I made them with that brown-sugar glaze you favor so much," Gillian urged.

"Thank you." Adam spooned more carrots onto his plate.

"Beth made the rolls. You must have more than one."

"Thank you."

"I thought about white flowers. With some greenery," Beth said.

Adam glanced up. "White flowers?"

"For the wedding."

"Oh."

"Butter for your potatoes? Though I'm not sure that's the best choice." Adam knew Gillian was Beth's stepmother but they acted alike and talked incessantly. How did Leighton stand this constant chatter?

"No, butter's fine," Adam said.

"No, I'm talking about the flowers."

"More roast?" Gillian asked, extending the plate toward him.

Adam's head started to throb. He couldn't keep up with the changing topics.

Vonnie. How restful she could be when she wasn't angry at him.

His attention moved to Beth then Gillian. Could he face a life with these two chattering magpies?

Beth buttered a roll for him. "What day was it that we drove out to Paul Sandler's place to look at that team you were thinking about buying?"

"I don't know…Thursday, maybe."

"No, it couldn't have been Thursday. That's when I went to see Carolyn. Tuesday. It was definitely Tuesday. Anyway, did you notice the house? It was so homey, so impressive. Could we think about building one like it?"

"I suppose we can think about anything we want."

"No, silly, I'm serious. Didn't you just love the Sandlers' house?"

* * *

Later, Beth sat by Adam and poured coffee while her mother settled herself opposite them, armed with a barrage of dinnerware catalogs.

"I thought this one was quite nice." Gillian spread a gazette on the footrest. "And this one, though I like the first just a little better, don't you?"

"Oh, I don't know…it's nice, but…oh, what do you think, Adam?"

"I don't—"

"Care for it, either," Beth inserted. "He doesn't like it, Mother. How about this one?"

Adam conscientiously studied the choices. Flowers and leaves, flowers alone, flowers on top of flowers, flowers mingled with flowers, or a small clump of flowers on a plain white plate?

"Or this one. I rather prefer it, don't you?"

He studied the picture. "Grapes and leaves?"

"It's different. It would surely set a fine table. What do you think, Mother?"

"I rather like it," Gillian observed. "And this silver pattern would go quite well with it."

Hours passed. "Rose or pink?"

"What's the difference?"

"Well, rose is soft and pink's a little harsher, but if you like rose, then rose it will be. Don't you agree, Mother. Pink is a little harsh."

"What does Adam think?"

Setting his glass aside, Adam smiled wanly at his bride-to-be. "I'm sorry, Beth, Leighton, Gillian, but I have to be going. There're a couple of strays that need my attention.

When the door closed behind him he shut his eyes, thanking God for the relief. And silence. Blessed silence.

The cold night bit through his heavy coat. He headed for the ranch in an easy lope, enjoying the falling snow. He hadn't gotten a moment alone with Beth…a moment to tell her, to ask her forgiveness. He should have never conceded to P.K.'s wishes. The day was coming when he had to break off the engagement. Couldn't Beth sense his feelings? How was he going to do it without hurting her deeply and causing her shame? He didn't know.

He'd ridden for several minutes when the sound of an approaching conveyance caught his attention. Drawing his horse to a walk, he turned to look over his shoulder to see who might be out for an evening ride. He frowned when he recognized the horse.

The sled whizzed around him and he got only a brief look at Andrew, finger to his hat in mock salute as he passed with Vonnie at his side.

Adam stared after the couple. *Where* had they been? And what was Andrew doing with Vonnie at this time of night?

Had she waved at him as the sled bowled on down the road?

Turning off the main road, he kicked the horse into a gallop, taking a shortcut to the ranch. He was in a rare foul mood by the time he reached Cabeza del Lobo.

Leaving the saddle before the horse came to a complete halt, he strode toward the house and immediately went to the library. Several cups of coffee later, he sat down at the desk and waited for Andrew's return.

Two hours passed before he heard his brother's uneven gait crossing the porch. The clock in the hall struck eleven.

Andrew paused, crossing the foyer, casually assessing Adam. "Where's Father?"

Adam ignored the question. "What were you doing with Vonnie Taylor tonight?"

Andrew's brow lifted curiously. "Doing with her? Enjoying an evening ride. Why?"

"Leave Vonnie alone."

"Since when do I need your permission to court a woman?"

Adam curbed his anger and poured himself another cup of coffee. "Just leave her alone."

Andrew's laugh was short. "My dear brother, must I remind you that you're engaged to Beth? What I choose to do with Vonnie, or she with me, is our choice and frankly none of your business."

Adam hated to admit it, but his brother was right. He had absolutely no right to tell Andrew who to see. But Vonnie? He couldn't take that.

Beth should be his first concern, but he couldn't stop thinking about Vonnie. God forgive him, he couldn't stand seeing Andrew with her.

"You know how P.K. feels about the Taylors."

"Yes. It didn't make sense when we were children and it doesn't make sense now. Whatever was between Teague and P.K. is six feet under now."

"Just stay away from her, Andrew. She's off-limits. There's no use upsetting P.K."

"Adam? Andrew?" P.K. descended the stairs, his hair standing on end as if he had been roused from a sound sleep. "What are you two doing up so late?"

Adam sat at the desk again. "Sorry we woke you, Dad."

"Do my ears serve me right? Are you two arguing over the Taylor girl?" He stood in the library door.

Neither Adam nor Andrew answered.

"Of all the women in the county, you've picked a fight over Vonnie Taylor? Can't you boys control yourselves? Like the serpent in the garden, one little gal you can't have, and I'll be a fool if that's not the one you want!"

"Dad—" Adam began.

"Do you think I'm blind? Do you? Don't you think I saw you making eyes at her all those years, mooning around like a lovesick calf?" P.K. fixed Andrew with a tyrannical look that allowed no discussion. "I warned you then, and I'm warning you now, leave Vonnie Taylor alone!" His voice shattered the quiet night.

He pointed at Adam with the cane he seldom surrendered to using.

"You've got Beth Baylor halfway down the aisle. Get that Taylor woman out of your head! You, Andrew, don't let me catch you with her again. Don't even look in her direction. I won't have it. You hear me? I won't have it! Now, both of you, get to bed!"

Andrew turned, shuffling into the hallway.

"Get to bed!" P.K. ordered Adam, before turning and following Andrew up the stairway.

Adam remained seated, resentment burning like a live coal in his stomach.

He was a grown man. A man with the responsibility of a ranch of more than 73,000 acres, controlling more than a million acres surrounding Amarillo and keeping three brothers in line; still his father persisted in running his life. When was it going to end?

This marriage to Beth hadn't been his idea. P.K. had even chosen his wife. The coal in his stomach burned hotter. Being the firstborn son of P.K. Baldwin carried great responsibility. He had a duty to perform: marry Beth and make the best of it. But could he do it? Could he sacrifice a woman he loved for duty? God would not shine on the marriage, Adam knew it.

"Son?"

Adam looked up to see P.K. framed in the doorway. He suddenly looked old. Old, disappointed and beaten.

"Yes, Dad?"

P.K. turned repentant, almost childishly so. "I'm sorry I have to come down so rough on you. You'll understand when you have sons of your own."

Even P.K.'s voice sounded tired, defeated, sad.

"I only want what's best for my boys. Ceilia said I was too hard on my boys. Maybe I am, but I love you, son. I love all my boys. It may not seem that way to you, but I do."

The show of affection was uncharacteristic for P.K. and, Adam knew, difficult.

Silence prevailed, then Adam said, "What really happened to make you hate Teague Taylor so vehemently?"

For a long moment it appeared P.K. was going to ignore the question. Walking back into the room, he moved to the window, looking out over the falling snow.

He began slowly. "It was a long time ago. During the war, Teague and I served together, warmed at the same fire, ate from the same plate, rubbed each other's feet to keep them from freezing. Closer than brothers, we were."

Adam waited, tense with anticipation, aware the mystery was about to unfold.

"We were on our way home—worn out, sick at heart. Our uniforms, such as they were, were in rags. We'd gone twenty-four hours without sleep and a decent meal, and that had been only what we could scavenge from a few farmhouses.

"Late in the day, we came upon a family. Dear Lord, it was hot. So hot you could fry an egg on a rock.

"The family was Irish, a man, his wife, two sons and a small daughter." His tone was lifeless now. "I don't know how it happened—none of us knew how it happened. One minute we were all looking at each other, then El Johnson pulled his pistol and then the farmer pulled a gun and fired."

P.K.'s eyes glistened with unshed tears as he recalled the awful moment. "We could smell their sweat, their blood, death…."

Adam held back immediate questions that sprang to his mind for fear of breaking his father's concentration on the long-past events that had haunted him and driven an irreversible wedge between Teague Taylor and P.K. Baldwin.

"We got shovels and buried them. The sight of that little girl—" P.K. turned away, pain searing his features.

Drawing a deep breath, he whispered, "Johnson and Teague scavenged the wagon and found a black velvet pouch containing jewels."

The silence stretched. Finally, Adam prompted him again. "Jewels?"

"Jewelry. Heirlooms…things the family wanted to protect from both the North and South. Apparently they'd hoped to keep the cache safe until the war was over. Of course, they didn't count on running into us." He drew another deep breath, bitterness seeping through his voice. "Johnson pitched the bag to Teague."

"Teague took the jewelry?"

"Oh, he argued, but he rode off with the pouch! Later he tried to tell me he threw the jewels away, all of them. Claimed any profit we got from them would have been blood money, which might be right, but that family was dead. There wasn't anything we could do to change what happened. Any one of us could have put the money to good use."

"Teague threw the jewels away?" Adam repeated, trying to make sense of P.K.'s accusations. "You know this for certain?"

"Said he did," P.K. snapped. "Never saw him do it, never believed he did."

"If he didn't want the money, why would he lie to you and say that he had thrown them away?"

P.K. shook his head. "Why did Teague do anything? He sure fooled me. I thought he was a godly man."

"I believe that he was."

"A godly man wouldn't do what he did."

"Dispose of jewels that were ill-gotten?"

"Take the jewels in the first place."

"Maybe he didn't have a choice."

"Every man has a choice. I saw that pouch in Teague's hand when we rode off."

"And thirty-three years passed and you, who claim to be a pious man, didn't go to Teague, a fellow brother and godly man, and ask him why he took the jewels. You just let the hate fester and grow into a wound that never healed."

"The ride between his farm and mine is the same distance."

"Maybe he didn't feel he had anything to explain. Maybe he resented the fact that a friend would think that he did."

P.K. grunted. "You might as well know I did go once, shortly after the incident, accused him of keeping the jewels for himself. He denied it. Got so mad he threatened to shoot me. Ordered me off his property and told me never to set foot on his land again and I didn't.

"Folks have believed all along he got those birds honest. Never believed that cock-and-bull story about 'someone in a traveling show paying off a bad debt.' I think he took those jewels, sold them and bought those birds to fatten his pockets. That's what I think.

"Doesn't matter now," P.K. said impatiently. "Vonnie's Teague's daughter through and through. By the way, another one of those birds got loose this afternoon, chased a steer halfway to town."

Adam shook his head.

"Bull's fine. The bird lost most of its feathers, though." P.K. chortled. "Had the boys lock him up in the barn. You take him back tomorrow and tell that Taylor woman she's got to sell those birds before I shoot every last one of them. You hear?"

"You wouldn't shoot those birds and you know it." P.K.

might bluster, but he was a good man. "Besides, you just told me to stay away from her."

"This is a business. Do as I say."

When P.K. left the room, Adam sank back into the chair. Something didn't ring true with P.K.'s story, but he couldn't put his finger on what it was. He could ask Vonnie, but he'd swear she knew nothing about what had happened between the two once-best friends. If she'd known, she'd have told him the reason behind the bitter feud.

He stared out the window, rubbing his temple. No, something was wrong with the story. Even if his father's version was right, he could see P.K. was wrong. Teague was an honorable man. Always had been. He was right about the jewels being blood money. None of the men involved in the tragedy could claim the bounty. Nevertheless, the money would have most likely warded off the financial crunch P.K. was now facing. That "blood money" could have helped save Cabeza del Lobo.

He leaned back in his chair and ran a hand over his chin. Teague had had the reputation in the community of being an honest man in his dealings. Granted, in view of his strong personality he had been either well liked or despised. There was no middle of the road when it came to Teague Taylor. But to Adam's knowledge, no one had ever accused him of being dishonest, except his once-best friend.

Swiveling around in the chair, he stood abruptly and left the library.

Chapter Fourteen

❧

Sliding the barn door open, Adam faced the ostrich. It was late, but by gum, he was taking the bird back to Vonnie tonight. No six-foot pile of feathers on stilts was going to take up barn space at Cabeza del Lobo.

Why not admit it's her you want to see, Baldwin? You don't care about the ostrich.

I'm returning the ostrich. Nothing more. Taking it back, dumping it in a pen and getting out of there. You want to ask her advice about Beth. Face it.

How did he break the engagement in a compassionate way? Vonnie would know.

The bird ceased its anxious pacing. Turning, he blinked down at Adam with wise eyes.

After rejecting several options, Adam decided to try looping a rope around the bird's neck to control him. He hoped this one was more cooperative than the others they had returned a few days earlier. Without Pat and Joey to help, he knew it wasn't going to be easy to get the bird back to the Taylor ranch alone, and Andrew was in no mood to help. The snow wasn't going to help any.

"All right, boy, you and I are going for a little walk. You don't give me any trouble, and I won't give you any."

Looping a lariat, he began swinging it loosely above his head. He had the bird's attention.

The ostrich was curious enough about the rope that he held his head fully erect.

With a leisurely swing, the loop fell easily over the head and settled at the shoulders.

Taking a half hitch around a post, Adam tethered the bird. Saddling his horse, he began the five-mile journey to the Flying Feather.

It was much later when Adam got there. Adam thought that if he owned the bird it would have been dead on arrival.

As he corralled the ostrich into the courtyard, he caught a shadow from the corner of his eye. He was certain a form darted out of the cellar and disappeared around the corner of the house.

Sitting up straight in the saddle, he squinted, trying to locate the hazy figure. The moon slid behind a cloud, obscuring his vision. By now there was nothing to see.

Frowning, he glanced toward the house, where a light burned in Vonnie's attic workroom. If she was awake and working, he might as well tell her that the bird was back.

Nudging the ostrich to the hitching post, he secured it there, alongside his horse.

He moved beneath the window, and picked up a handful of pebbles and tossed them at the glass. A moment later, Vonnie looked out.

He motioned for her to open up.

She shook her head and painted at the sill. Stuck. He remembered Teague painting it shut. She appeared at the back door a moment later "Adam, do you have any idea what time it is?"

Removing his pocket watch, he held the dial up to the lighted snowscape. "Twelve forty-one."

"What are you doing here?"

"Looking for you."

"Great day in the morning. Why are you creeping around at this time of night?"

"I brought your bird home."

He was suddenly as nervous as a schoolboy. He remembered everything about her: her smell, her smile. Her. That was the problem. He remembered *her* and not Beth.

Her brows lifted. "You have one of my birds?"

Turning, he motioned to the ostrich tied to the hitching post.

"Elmer?" She wilted with relief. "Thank goodness. We looked everywhere for him."

"Really?" His eyes locked with hers. "I suppose that was what you and Andrew were doing? Looking for Elmer?"

The brows came up again. "Excuse me?"

"You and Andrew. Earlier this evening, when you passed me on the road. Didn't look like you were searching for any bird."

"Are you referring to the incident earlier this evening

when Andrew, who is no more than a casual friend, and I passed you on your way back from seeing Beth?"

"I'm engaged to Beth," he said, as if that marked the difference.

"Andrew is a grown man. When are you going to stop protecting him?"

He ignored her question. "Andrew doesn't have any business taking you for a buggy ride."

She leaned against the door frame, looking up at him. "A Taylor isn't good enough for him, either?"

"Now, don't go twisting my words. That's not what I meant and you know it." He stared at her, frustrated. "Where do you want me to put the bird?"

"I'll take him. I was coming out to ride Elsie anyway."

He had already turned to walk away when her remark registered. Turning back, he looked at her, then at the bird.

"You're going to do what?"

"I'm going to ride Elsie. Daddy rode her all the time. It's great fun."

He turned to look at the bird then glanced up at the falling snow. Then back to her.

"Ride one of those things? You're out of your mind."

Her chin lifted a notch. "They're faster than horses, you know."

They were faster than bullets, from what he'd seen. And about as safe.

Pulling on a worn coat and pair of gloves, she pushed the screen open. Stepping down off the porch, she clucked to Elmer, who was tied to the hitching post.

"You've been naughty, Elmer. Genaro's going to fix that

latch in the morning. It's obviously too easy for you to get open. Bad bird."

She led Elmer to his pen as Adam curiously followed behind.

"In you go," she said, opening the gate.

Elmer went in without an argument.

"How do you do that?" The bird had gone out of its way to aggravate him.

"Some are very docile," she said. "Daddy worked with them a lot. Elmer and Elsie are a pair that he's had for quite some time. Carrie and Carl are another. He began riding those four a while ago."

She stepped inside the pen and shut the gate behind her, but didn't slip the latch.

Adam watched with half curiosity, half concern for her safety, while she walked among the birds, talking to this one, patting that one. Lanterns strategically hung from poles, illuminating the pens and blowing snow. He could distinguish the males by their black markings; the hens had silver-and-brown feathers.

"Down, Elsie." One of the females dropped to the ground, and before he could stop her, Vonnie mounted the bird.

Struggling back to its feet, the bird and rider loomed high above him. Sitting far up on the back, clasping underneath the wings, Vonnie laughed, riding easily as the bird strutted around the pen.

"Some men have been known to use the ostrich as a saddle horse," she proclaimed.

"Some men are nuts, too."

"Coward."

"I'm the only sane one here," he muttered.

"Want to try it?"

"No, I don't want to try it."

"Scared?"

"Smart."

"I dare you to try it."

"No thanks."

"Double dare you. Triple dare you! Double, triple, quadruple dare you!"

It was a familiar dare with them, beginning when they were in the third grade. Anything he did, she tried.

And anything she did, he had to prove he could do better.

"Come on, scaredy-cat. I've seen you ride broncs and bulls."

"You be careful."

"Elmer knows you now. Try it. He'll get down for you. Mount him as you would a horse," she said.

"A horse, huh?" He studied the nine-foot, gangly creature. "Funny-looking horse," he muttered.

He hesitated, then his curiosity got the better of him. Sliding inside the gate, he made his way toward Elmer, who was standing near the bird Vonnie was riding.

His eyes slid warily over the creature. "You riding that one?"

"Uh-huh. Elsie's my favorite. Down, Elmer," she ordered, and the bird obliged by squatting.

Adam awkwardly mounted, clutching Elmer's neck when the bird lurched awkwardly to his feet.

"Oh, boy."

Laughing, Vonnie led the way out of the pen. "Come on, chicken!"

Adam held on, wondering if he had lost his mind. Riding one of the stupid things! He hoped his brothers never got wind of this! "Slow down, will you!"

"Burk-burrrrk, burk-burrrrk, burk," Vonnie clucked.

"Funny, Vonnie, funny. Where are you taking me?"

"Outside the pens."

"Forget that," he said.

"You'll be fine. I'll control Elsie and Elmer will follow his lady."

Vonnie let the gate latch behind them, then led the way across the barnyard. They made a strange sight, riding ostriches across the snowy hills. Soon they were loping toward an open field where she'd ridden before.

"Take it easy," Adam warned. The sheer height of the bird alone made a formidable perch.

"Okay." Grinning, she flanked the bird and set off. Elmer followed. In a few minutes the birds were running freely.

"Slow down!" Adam shouted, his words lost in the wind. Once he got the feel of the bird, he relaxed and began to enjoy the experience.

The birds flew over the ground, with both riders holding tightly beneath their wings. The wind rushed by, raising Adam's spirits. Snow stung his eyes and nose.

Elsie loped along at a jarring gait, passing Elmer, Elmer passing her, her passing him.

Breaking into a head-on dash, the two birds raced across the open range at remarkable speeds.

Vonnie's laughter came to him as she looked over. His masterful ease in the saddle had resurfaced.

Grinning at each other, they rode for over an hour, racing side by side over the open range.

After they finally brought the birds back into the pen, Vonnie ordered them to squat. As they dismounted, she gave each an affectionate pat, then closed and carefully latched the gate.

Adam leaned on the fence, watching her.

"Well, what do you think about my birds now?"

"I have to admit, they're not what I expected."

Her wind-kissed features sobered. "They're not what I expected, either. Daddy always took care of them. Momma and I had little personal contact with them, but now, I realize, like people, they each have their own strengths and weaknesses."

Smiling, she gazed up at him. He had never seen her looking prettier. The cold wind had blushed her cheeks a rosy red, and her hair had come loose, falling over her shoulders in wild disarray. He wanted to kiss her—kiss her and never stop. *Forgive me, Lord. Forgive my desire.*

"I'm actually beginning to enjoy them, and I've become quite attached to some of them. I guess that's part of the reason I refuse to sell to Sheriff Tanner. That, and he's such a worm. I'm not ready to let the birds go. Maybe I never will be."

They walked back to the house. Snow had accumulated in the farmyard, and a relaxing calm had settled over the ranch. The wind and the sound of two sets of footsteps moving in perfect rhythm.

"It's your decision," Adam said. "I can't say I'm overly fond of the birds. P.K. would like to see them go."

"He's upset about them getting out, isn't he?"

"He doesn't want the cattle spooked. You can see his objection. We have to protect the stock."

Sighing, Vonnie turned to face him. Snowflakes lay on her shoulders. "Adam, I am sorry about the inconvenience they've caused. I don't know how they keep getting out. A lot of strange things have been happening lately."

"Do I have to tell you to be careful?" Should he tell her about what he thought he saw when he first rode up tonight? If he was mistaken, she would worry unnecessarily. "I mean it, Vonnie. Lock your doors and be alert."

"Don't worry, I'm careful. Genaro's on night watch. Roel takes day watch. And Franz is here during the day. Except for Elmer getting out this afternoon, nothing has happened for a few days. Maybe it's all been a series of coincidences."

She was silhouetted against the house. He couldn't see her face clearly, but it didn't matter. He knew her face as well as his own.

"And maybe not. Maybe someone is trying to force you out."

"I thought of that," she admitted. "And the wire incident almost convinced me of it—yet, I can't be sure."

"What happened with the wire?"

"Someone has been cutting the fence, leaving sharpened ends sticking out, enough for the birds to cut themselves. They get hurt, they get infected and sick. We've been checking the fences morning and night, but the incidents continue. Someone knows our schedule—they know how to avoid us."

"You think someone is purposely sabotaging you?"

"Has to be. It couldn't happen by itself. I think it might be Lewis Tanner, but again I'm only speculating. No one has seen anything suspicious going on, nothing that can be traced to Tanner."

Adam wished now he had pursued the shadow that moved from the cellar. It could have been Genaro, but the ranch hand was tall and this figure was short. They'd reached Adam's horse and he stopped, turning her to face him. They gazed at each other.

"Maybe this is all too much for you to handle."

She grinned. "You've been after me to get rid of the birds. Maybe you're the one causing all the trouble."

He slowly returned the grin. "Have I ever given you any trouble?"

"You've been known to," she confided, her voice barely a whisper now. She impulsively hugged him. "I'm sorry, of course you haven't. I don't know what I would have done without your 'roundup' services lately."

The hug caught him by surprise. After the briefest moment, his arms closed around her, and they held each other.

Vonnie pulled away and stepped back, apologizing. "I'm sorry. I don't know what I was thinking. I only wanted to thank you…on Elmer's behalf."

Her attempt to lighten the moment was obviously contrived, but Adam graciously accepted the effort.

"First hug I've had from a bird. Wasn't bad." he said, putting his foot in the stirrup. He hesitated. Stepping down, he took off his hat. Worrying it in his hand, he said softly, "I want you to know, Beth is serious. I'm going to have to set a date."

He watched her face change. The glow left her eyes.

"I know." She swallowed. Adam watched her fight to remain detached.

"I agreed she could set the day." His voice sounded flat. She gave him a wan smile.

"A bride's privilege."

"It has been in the past."

"Vonnie…" He paused. "I don't know if I can marry her."

"How can you not?"

He nodded, his earlier convictions faltering.

"Well, best wishes. Or is it congratulations one gives the groom? I can never remember."

"Me either." Neither fit the occasion.

Placing his foot back in the stirrup, he mounted. When he looked down at her, his insides tightened. "Why don't you just say it?"

She bit her lip. *Please, he prayed, don't let her cry.*

"Say what?"

"That I'm a despicable man for springing Beth on you the way I did. I had my reason, but I guess it doesn't make me look any better. Family is a good thing, but sometimes it can be a burden."

The words hung between them like a heavy rope.

Summoning a smile, she whispered, "Yes, family responsibilities come first. Beth will make you happy. I want nothing but happiness for you."

Pain touched his heart briefly.

"Adam."

"Yes."

"I did love you."

Their eyes met in the moonlight. "I loved you, too, Vonnie."

"Have a happy life," she whispered.

Nodding, he reined the horse and rode off.

Vonnie was up early the next morning. Beth's dress, or rather the thought of Beth's dress, had kept her awake all night. Did Adam have serious doubts? About the wedding? Was it possible he had discovered that he was an honest man who couldn't live a lie?

She was supposed to be a Christian. Love your neighbor as yourself. God couldn't be pleased with the way she coveted another woman's man. She sighed. She knew all the right words, could make the proper arguments, but living by the Word was a lot harder than talking about them. She remembered her savior's prayer in the garden. *"Nevertheless not my will, but thine be done." God's will be done in this matter.*

Dressing quickly, she twisted her hair into a knot at the base of her neck and went to check on the birds before fixing breakfast. Franz was already at work, rewiring the fence along the back side of the pens to make sure the adult male birds couldn't push free again.

"Good morning," she called.

Franz slowly straightened, and once again she wondered if he wasn't taking on too much work. Still, she knew the small salary she'd convinced him to accept was a help to him and Audrey.

"I have a fresh cherry pie. Audrey sent it especially for you."

"Audrey makes the best cherry pie in the county," Vonnie said, accepting the tin that Franz had wrapped in a dish towel and kept beneath the seat of his buggy. "We'll have a piece with our lunch. Audrey's having a better week?"

"No, she just needs to keep busy. Enjoy," he said. "Now, I must finish the fence."

Carrying the pie into the kitchen, she stored it in the pie safe, then filled the coffeepot with water and set it on the stove. After stoking up the fire, she turned to the cabinet to get the container of coffee.

"Mother," she called. "Are you coming down this morning?"

Silence reigned upstairs. Cammy had not been down once this week. She had taken all her meals in her room, eating and drinking sparingly.

Jerking open the cabinet door, a scream tore its way from Vonnie's throat as the freshly severed head of an ostrich fell out, striking her in the chest.

Stumbling backward, she gasped, her screams filling the kitchen as the head bounced across the floor.

The back door flew open, and Franz ran in, his face a mask of bewilderment. "Vonnie?"

"Oh! Oh! Oh!" She stood frozen, staring at the bright splash of blood on the front of her dress.

He eased her out of the room, consoling her. "Stay here, little one."

She collapsed against the wall in the hallway, eyes closed, her hands lying palm up in her lap. She suddenly felt faint and sick to her stomach. *Dear Lord, who was doing this to her?*

"Vonnie? What is it? Are you hurt?" Cammy called from the top of the stairs.

Realizing she couldn't let Cammy see the ostrich head, or even know about the accidents that had been happening lately, Vonnie dropped the front of her apron so her mother wouldn't see the blood.

"A snake," Vonnie called. "In the wood box. It startled me. Franz is taking care of it."

"Oh, my," Cammy murmured. "Your father will have to be more careful when he brings in wood. Teague? Did you hear that? There was a snake in the wood box. It scared Vonnie out of a year's growth."

"Everything is all right now," Franz said, carrying a towel with the severed head wrapped in it. "I'll dispose of it and notify Tanner."

"Th-thank you," Vonnie managed. Her heart was beating so fast she could hardly catch her breath.

Frowning, Franz paused in the doorway. "Will you be all right?"

She wanted to cry. She wanted to scream in rage and in fear, but she wasn't capable of either at the moment.

"I don't know, Franz. I—I never expected it to go this far."

"Who could be doing this to you?"

"I don't know. Maybe Sheriff Tanner. He wants me to get rid of the birds. He's offered to buy me out—for a hefty sum. But I don't want to leave, and there's Momma. This is her home, and I'm not sure I could get her to leave. I don't know what I'm going to do."

It was getting to be too much. The accidents, the work, the constant pressure.

"I don't know, maybe I should sell out, before it gets worse."

"You can't let Lewis Tanner scare you off your own land! It might not be Tanner at all. It could be anyone. Teague had his enemies, you know." Franz frowned. "And P.K. Baldwin was his biggest."

"I know, but it isn't just the birds, Franz. It's everything combined. If someone wants the birds gone so badly they would resort to this—" her gaze focused on the front of her blood-splattered dress "—what would they be willing to do next?"

"It's no secret that some people don't want the birds here," Franz agreed. "They don't understand their nature, and anything diffcrent is something to be feared."

"You're right. I can't let whoever it is drive me off my land. And once they get that through their heads, hopefully, the sabotage will stop."

"That's my girl." Squeezing her shoulder supportively, he smiled. "You be strong, *liebchen*. Soon things will be better. This has been a troubling time for you."

With a lighter spirit, Vonnie straightened. She had to put the incident behind her. "Thank you, Franz. I don't know what I'd do without you."

"It is my pleasure to be of service," he said, with a courtly bow. "Now, I return to my work."

Her appetite gone, Vonnie fixed a light breakfast for Cammy, then set off to Beth's house. By the time she arrived at the Baylors', she was thinking more clearly.

"It is so good to see you," Gillian enthused, leading her toward the parlor. "Hildy and Carolyn are having tea. Won't you join them?"

"Yes, thank you."

Beth looked up when the two women entered the room. "Oh… Vonnie, I wasn't expecting you."

It wasn't the most enthusiastic greeting she'd ever received, but Beth was already awash with wedding jitters. "I thought if you had a few moments we might go over a few details. I'd like to sketch your gown on paper before I start."

"Oh, this is truly wonderful," Carolyn exclaimed. "I can't wait to see what you have in mind!"

Vonnie glanced at Beth, expecting some sparkling expression of delight. Instead, her friend seemed a little too quiet, her usual exuberant expression subdued.

"If you still want me to make it."

Beth smiled. "Of course I want you to make my dress. It wouldn't be right if you didn't. We've been friends for so long."

Gillian disappeared, returning with a second steaming pot of tea and fresh cinnamon buns.

"Did you hear, Momma?" Beth asked. "Vonnie wants to discuss my gown."

"Oh, thrill!" Gillian set the tray on a side table then clapped her hands. "Oh my. I've looked forward to this day since you were a child!"

"Yes, I know, Momma," Beth mused. She glanced at Gillian. "You don't think I'm marrying too young?"

"I was your age when I married your father."

Beth nodded, sighing wistfully. "I grew up so quickly."

Was it her imagination or was Gillian more excited about the wedding than the bride? Vonnie took a sip of tea and watched Beth halfheartedly nibble on a warm cinnamon bun.

"How is Camilla?" Gillian asked, refreshing Carolyn's tea. "I do hope she's feeling better."

"She is still in mourning," Vonnie said. "It's been difficult, keeping things from her…." Vonnie paused, realizing her slip of tongue.

"Things? What things?" Hildy asked.

"A few odd things have been happening lately. Someone tempered with the fence and the ostriches got loose. Then it seems someone has been putting things in the pens for the birds to pick up. They choke easily, you know. And there are the bits of wire that have been cut in the fence so the birds can hurt themselves. But the worst—" she shuddered "—took place this morning. Someone…put a severed ostrich head in my cabinet."

"Oh, my," Gillian whispered, grasping the teapot handle.

Carolyn gasped. "How awful!"

"Franz was there, and he disposed of it. Otherwise, I don't know what I would have done. The most frightening thing is, how did someone get the head inside my house without me hearing him?"

"I'll bet it's that horrible Lewis Tanner," Hildy said. "He wants you off that land. He's telling everyone who'll listen he'll get you to sell out. He'll offer whatever it takes."

"Do you think even he would do such a horrible thing?" Beth asked.

"Beth, we're talking about Lewis Tanner," Carolyn reminded. "He'd do anything to get his way. You know that!"

"Hmm." Beth drifted off absently.

"Or P.K." Vonnie voiced her suspicion before she thought.

A pall fell across the small parlor.

"Adam's father?" Beth asked.

"Vonnie," Carolyn said, hushed. "Surely you don't think P.K. is doing this to you?"

Vonnie realized she'd spoken out of place.

"Not really. I suppose at this point everyone is a suspect in my mind."

Although the awkward moment passed, the allegation had put a strain on the visit.

Vonnie left shortly after, promising to keep in touch. Plans for Beth's gown would get underway soon.

Chapter Fifteen

❧

"Beth, slow down. What are you saying?"

Adam stopped dead in his tracks and stared at Beth, who was babbling. He had been stacking hay in the barn when he recognized the sound of his fiancée's carriage whipping down the road. He'd waited for her, then listened in mounting fury as she told him about Vonnie's experience with the ostrich's severed head that morning.

"Adam! Vonnie found a—"

"I know what you said."

"Then why did you ask—"

"How did someone get into the Taylor house to plant the head in the cabinet?"

"Vonnie hasn't a clue, the poor dear. She said she locked up the night before, as usual. My goodness, I don't know what I would have done," she said, adjusting a windblown lock of hair. "I mean, to have a…a head fall out of the cabinet and hit you and get its blood all over you…and on the floor! It…it must have been perfectly awful." She shivered.

"Was it an adult bird?"

"She didn't say. Oh, Adam." She grimaced. "How perfectly dreadful, to have one of your…pets…die like that. Who could do such a horrible thing?"

"The birds aren't pets, Beth. They're stock—like cattle—Vonnie's livelihood."

"Adam, she's a seamstress, not a cattleman. Honestly, the way you jump to her defense you'd think you had some sort of personal interest in her personal welfare. The birds are a nuisance, and she should get rid of them before something perfectly wretched occurs. And, by the way, she thinks your father might have something to do with all the trouble she's been having lately. He wouldn't do something that awful, would he?"

Reaching for his saddle, he threw it across his horse, his features tight as he cinched the belt. "Excuse me, Beth, I was on my way into town."

Beth blinked. "But, Adam, I just got here."

"I'm sorry, but I have—"

"Business, I know." She paused. "Vonnie's agreed to make my gown."

Adam let the remark pass.

"Sometimes…" She stopped.

"Sometimes what?"

"Oh, I don't know. Marriage is so final."

He nodded. "Final as a broken mirror."

* * *

Adam rode into town before noon. The dusty street was nearly empty. Tossing the reins over the hitching rail, he glanced through the open door of the sheriff's office.

"Tanner."

The sheriff shifted his bulk in the wooden chair behind the desk and looked up as Adam walked in.

"You want something, Baldwin?"

Resting both palms on the desk, Adam angled toward the sheriff.

"Get off the Taylor girl's back."

"You her keeper now?" Tanner leaned backward, resting beefy hands across his belly. "Thought you were hitchin' up with the Baylor girl."

"What do you know about what's going on at the Taylor ranch?"

The sheriff got up to stoke the potbellied stove.

"Someone put an ostrich head in her kitchen cabinet. Nasty…real nasty." He chuckled.

"Stay away from the Flying Feather. Far away." Adam's tone left no doubt of his intent if the sheriff didn't back off.

Tanner shrugged. "Don't know what you're talkin' about."

"I think you do."

The sheriff perched on the edge of the desk and hooked his thumbs into his belt.

"You don't run this town, Baldwin."

Adam straightened, meeting the sheriff's hostile stare.

"When you start picking on women, killing their stock and leaving severed heads in cabinets, you're stepping over the line."

A muscle jumped in the sheriff's jaw, and his hand shifted to the gun on his hip.

"Get out of here, Baldwin, before I throw you out."

Stepping closer, Adam planted his forefinger in the center of Tanner's chest.

"If I ever prove that you've had anything to do with what's been going on, you'll answer to me, personally."

Tanner managed a derisive snort that wasn't entirely convincing.

"If one more bird is found dead out there, I'm coming after you. Comprende?"

"Get out of here, Baldwin."

"Mark my words, Lewis."

Tanner's voice turned belligerent. "I've got nothing to do with what's going on at the Taylors'. All I've done is offer to buy her out."

"Remember what I said."

Adam turned and walked out.

The sun sank behind the large juniper in the backyard. The Flying Feather was settling down for the evening. It was that special time of night that Vonnie most favored. The day was finished, work done, the animals fed and quiet. Even the ostriches were settled early.

Stepping off the porch, she wandered toward the pens, wrapping her shawl tighter. What was she going to do with the birds? Sell, like the sheriff wanted? Or stand up to him and try to raise and control them herself?

Linking her fingers in the fence, she pressed her face against the wire and studied the birds.

What would Teague have done? That wasn't a fair question. Teague always stood up for what he believed, even if it meant a fight.

But what did she believe was right? Staying on the ranch? Was that the right thing to do? Was it the right thing for her mother?

Cammy wasn't improving. That was clear. A letter from her aunt in San Francisco arrived today, but even when she read it to Cammy, it was as if her mother didn't recognize who had written it.

Both of Cammy's older sisters lived in San Francisco, in a house that she'd once described as "princely." Teague himself had admitted that the family had money and hadn't been happy when Cammy married him. Not long after the wedding, the two sisters moved to San Francisco, expressing the hope that Cammy would soon grow weary of the "quaint" life and join them. But she never did. She loved Teague too much. Of course, all that changed when Teague won the birds. Cammy had as many assets as her sisters.

But Teague was gone. If Vonnie sold the ostriches and the ranch, there'd be nothing to keep them here. And it was certain that she didn't want to stay in town once Adam and Beth were married.

She continued to hang on to the fence, staring at the birds without really seeing them.

Suddenly she had the feeling she was no longer alone. A finger of fear trickled up her spine as she searched the lengthening shadows.

When Andrew stepped out of the darkness, both relief and a touch of anger washed over her.

"Andrew? Is that you?"

He stepped nearer, the rough ground exaggerating his limp.

"Sorry. I heard what happened this morning." His breath formed a heavy vapor. "You shouldn't leave your cellar door open."

"Oh?" She glanced over her shoulder. "I didn't realize it was open."

Strange. She clearly remembered closing it that morning after Franz had finished storing the last of the canned goods.

"Keep it closed. Anything can wander in there."

"Thank you, I'll remember," she said, turning back to the house. "I was about to take a walk," she invited. "Join me?"

It was a lovely night. The air smelled crisp and clean. Patches of snow lay about. They walked for a while, talking. At times it almost seemed that Adam was walking beside her and yet, Andrew wasn't Adam, no matter how comfortable she felt with him.

"Tell me about the trouble this morning," Andrew said.

She told him about the severed head and its frightening implications.

"Was the rest of the animal's body found?"

"No, we could find nothing."

"Do you suspect someone here at the Flying Feather is responsible?"

"I thought of that." The hired hands? Mother? She laughed at the thought. Mother loved those birds and would have no reason to harm them. But…she wasn't thinking clearly these days. Then there was always Tanner. He didn't seem the least concerned about her incident.

"How did the culprit get into the house?"

"I don't know, Andrew. The doors are locked at night."

"No one heard anything strange this morning? The animal's scream?"

"Nothing," Vonnie conceded.

"Did Tanner ask about any of this?"

"No, and I found that strange. He didn't seem concerned about details."

The hour grew late when they walked back to the house. Andrew offered a few suggestions, but no answers.

Blue eyes, so much like Adam's, assessed her with brotherly affection. "Be careful, Vonnie. I'd hate to think of anything happening to you."

"Thank you, Andrew. I will."

Bending, he brushed her cheek with a kiss. "If you feel you can leave Cammy for a while, we'll take a sleigh ride Saturday night. More snow is likely to fall."

"I'd like that."

A few minutes later she heard the sound of hoofbeats fading.

At times like this, it was impossible for her to believe that any Baldwin could mean her harm.

Even P.K.

Chapter Sixteen

❧

"Momma, I'm going for a ride. Eugenia's here with you."

Vonnie knew that it mattered little to Cammy whether anyone was there or not, but she didn't want her mother to come downstairs, find Vonnie gone and not know where she was.

"You take as long as you need," Eugenia told her. "Just as long as I'm home by dinnertime. My cat gets fussy if his meals aren't on time."

"Thank you. I won't be long."

Saddling her mare, Vonnie rode slowly until the house faded from sight. If only she could leave her problems behind as easily.

Kicking the mare into a gallop, she let the wind whip freely through her hair. It was early, but a heavy frost glistened on the ground.

She rode toward the canyon, thinking she might find peace. How long had it been since she'd felt carefree? Many months, but it seemed like years. Since her father died? Or before? Since she and Adam had married?

Suddenly the ring of hammer against wood penetrated her consciousness. Her focus followed the sound, and she saw Adam's big bay in the distance, a rope wrapped around the saddle horn with the other end attached to wire, stretching it taut so Adam could nail it to a post.

Had she ridden this direction without realizing it, looking for him?

Adam straightened, hooked the hammer in his back pocket, and signaled his horse to keep stretching the wire as he moved to the next post. The sharp wind had stung his features bright red.

She'd thought he was handsome when he was seventeen, but the years had added character to his face and substance to his body. Muscles that had been lean were now heavier and mature. Where he'd once been a charming boy, now he was a striking man.

How could she consider staying in town once he and Beth were married? It would be impossible. Moving to San Francisco with her mother now seemed the only answer. Her seamstress business was growing; she was known back East. With a little word-of-mouth advertising and lots of hard work, she could build an even larger clientele in California. Beth's dress—or the beginning—was on her cutting table. Should Adam's bride's dress be her last here in the county?

Adam glanced up and spotted her. Straightening, he

removed his gloves. Planting his hands on his hips, he studied her as she rode toward him.

Her mouth was suddenly as dry as winter clay. Not even a wind disturbed the thread of tension between them.

She wished he would say something. Anything, except stare at her. She would say something, but she couldn't think of anything. His face was shadowed by the brim of his hat; she would have liked to see his eyes. His expression.

"I…was riding."

"Yeah," he said, pushing his hat to the back of his head. "Little cold for riding, isn't it?"

She glanced around. "Where's Pat and Joey?"

"I was riding fence alone and found a section down. Decided to put it back myself. What are you doing out here? Lose more birds?"

"No."

She started to dismount, and he stepped closer to give her a hand. Her knees suddenly felt like applesauce, and she blamed the condition on lack of exercise for several days. It was a lame excuse, she knew. Lack of exercise didn't cause the problem; it was Adam affecting her this way.

"Just riding?" he asked.

"Yes, I needed some time alone."

"Your mother okay?"

"The same."

They paused beside the fence posts.

"Any new *accidents*?"

"No. Andrew stops by to check. He'll let you know if there's any more trouble."

His expression was taut and derisive. "Andrew is very obliging lately."

"I appreciate his help."

"You're flirting with trouble."

Her eyebrows lifted. "Flirting?" She was offended by the implications. "I've never flirted with Andrew!"

"Looks like it to me."

"I have not!" Then the thought struck her. "Why, you're jealous!"

"Ha!" He laughed hollowly. "Jealous of you and Andrew?"

"You have no reason to be."

His gaze raked her boldly. "You visited with him the other night, didn't you?"

"Yes. Not that it's any business of yours."

When a silence descended, she felt compelled to change subjects. "What should I do about Tanner?"

He picked up the canteen and took a long drink. After wiping off the rim, he extended it to her. "What do you mean, what should you do about him?"

"Should I sell out to him? Or should I stay?" She took a drink from the canteen.

He drank from the canteen again, then ran the back of his hand across his mouth. "What do you want to do?"

"I don't know. Tanner might not be behind the trouble, but he hates the ostriches. If he wants to buy my land, he's going about it the wrong way. Then again, who knows? Maybe I'm on the wrong trail. Tanner may not be causing the trouble. Why not Roel or Genaro, or even Franz, for that matter?"

"Or P.K.?"

Glancing away, she realized the town had been gossiping again. "I shouldn't have said that."

"You shouldn't have thought it."

"Do you know for certain your father isn't doing this?"

"Now you are talking crazy."

Nearby, a small stream gurgled. Melting snows lapped the banks.

"Don't worry about Tanner."

She glanced up. "Why not?"

"We talked, and I don't think he'll be bothering you again." He pulled his gloves on.

"You talked to him?"

"He claims he isn't the one causing the trouble."

"Do you believe him?"

"No, but then there's not much I believe unless I see it for myself."

When had he become so cynical? she wondered.

"Then you do think he would have killed the bird to scare me?"

"He's capable of it." He turned to her, his face serious now. "You be careful, Vonnie. I—" He stopped; she knew that whatever he'd planned to say was about them and he would never complete the thought—not openly.

"Just be careful," he finished, his eyes lightly skimming her.

Warmth flooded her, followed by the usual wave of sadness that accompanied thoughts of him. They would have had children by now...one, two. She shook the thought aside. He had been hers once, if only for a brief time. But that time had been enough to alter her life forever. She would never look at a man in the same way as she did him; no man would ever touch her heart in the same way, or as deeply.

Chapter Seventeen

❧

Vonnie rode into the barn lot of the Flying Feather, wishing she'd not wandered so close to Cabeza del Lobo.

She was still in love with Adam Baldwin as surely as the sun came up each morning. Loved him more than the day they'd run off to get married. She'd tried to deny it, told herself Adam wasn't worth the grief he caused, but the love did not diminish, it only grew.

She tried to believe he was a part of her past. A pleasant memory. For years she'd buried her feelings. What had brought those feelings back so strongly now? The fact that he was going to marry another woman. He was going on with his life. And she should move on with her own.

After unsaddling her mare at the barn, she went to the house.

"Oh, there you are," Eugenia said, laying her crocheting

aside. The house smelled of fresh-baked apple pie. For a moment Vonnie was overcome by a feeling of déjà vu. The house seemed almost normal.

"Hildy, Mora, Beth and Carolyn stopped by. I told them I didn't know when you'd be back."

"Sorry I missed them," Vonnie murmured. Leaning over, she patted Suki. "I guess Beth was checking on her dress?"

Eugenia sighed. "For a bride-to-be, Beth doesn't seem real enthusiastic. Is she feeling poorly?"

"Not that I'm aware."

"I put a pie in the oven. Thought Cammy might enjoy a piece later."

"Smells wonderful. Did Mother come down?"

"No." Eugenia glanced at the empty stairway. "I'm afraid not."

"I've heard her moving around."

Gathering her materials, Eugenia eased into her slippers. "I'll take the pie out as I leave."

When the door closed, Vonnie climbed the stairs, peeked in on Cammy, then retreated to her sewing room and closed the door. Being back in her room was comforting, but it didn't take away the weight of the day.

She was thankful she'd missed the girls' visit. She wasn't up to socializing this afternoon.

Picking up the dress she was hemming, she tried to concentrate. After a few minutes of ripping out more than she saved, material lay pooled in her lap, the needle exactly where she'd abandoned it.

She wasn't sure how long she had sat there before she

heard a wagon roll into the yard. When she went to the window to investigate, she saw that it was Franz.

He laboriously climbed down from the seat, then disappeared into the barn. She supposed he was planning to finish sorting out a harness that hadn't been touched in years. He'd told her he could repair and oil it, and then she could sell it, get it out of the way and into the hands of someone who could use it. Besides, it would give her a few extra dollars, he'd said.

She was far from destitute, but it never hurt to be cautious.

She wanted to pay Franz more for all he was doing for her. She planned for the proceeds from the harness to go to him. It was the least she could do, in view of all he'd done to help, and the money would be welcome for Audrey's medical expenses.

Restless, she tossed the dress aside and ventured downstairs. As she entered the barn, she heard Franz softly whistling a German Christmas carol.

Letting her eyes adjust to the dim light, she saw he was polishing a harness. He had it stretched over the side of a stall, whistling as he worked.

"Hello, Franz. Cold today, isn't it?"

"Ah, Vonnie," he said, looking over his shoulder. "It is a fine day, indeed."

She wasn't sure why she'd come to the barn. Just needed someone to talk to, she supposed, and Franz was like a second father. If anyone understood love, he did.

"Audrey feeling stronger today?"

His hand momentarily rested on the harness. "My Audrey is very tired."

Sinking onto a bale of straw, Vonnie sat quietly for a moment, watching him work.

Glancing up, Franz frowned. "Something bothering you, little one?"

"I'm sorry. Your problems make mine small in comparison."

"You have problems? A pretty little thing like you? You should be married, you know. With a house full of children."

Studying her hands, she said softly, "That's the problem, Franz. I love someone I can't have."

Franz rubbed the harness to a dull shine with an oily rag. "This is a sad thing, to love someone who already has a wife—"

"Oh, he's not married," she corrected, "Yet."

He looked up. "Ah, then it is Adam. Yes?"

"He's not married, but he is engaged," she confessed, which admittedly was nearly as bad as being married. She wondered if she was that transparent, or if he was unusually perceptive. "Yes, Adam. I've loved him forever." Leaning back, she stared at the rafters piled high with hay. "Once I thought he loved me, but he doesn't anymore." Sighing, she stuck a piece of straw into her mouth.

"I was so naive. I thought we'd love each other forever, that P.K. and my father would solve their differences, whatever they were. P.K. would accept the fact that Adam and I were in love, and Daddy would give us his blessing. But now Daddy's gone, and Adam is going to marry Beth Baylor." She drew a deep breath, blinking against hot tears suddenly burning her eyes.

"Love is a complicated state," Franz consoled.

She shrugged. "I can sell the ostriches, and my immediate problems will be over. Mother's sisters want her to come to San Francisco to live with them, and maybe that's what she should do. I don't know."

"Making a decision too quickly can be a bad thing," Franz cautioned. "Too many times we live to regret it."

She loved Franz's quiet way, his precise way of speaking with the heavy German accent that had not softened over the years.

"What would you do, Franz?"

His voice gentled. "Ah, *liebchen,* I cannot tell you what to do. I, too, have a great many worries."

"I know. Audrey's illness has been terribly hard on you." She felt small for bending his ear on her trivial problems.

"Sadly, there is nothing we can do for Audrey. You have been good friends to her." He let the harness hang while he added more oil to the cloth. "But perhaps there is something I can do for you. Advice, for whatever it is worth."

"I always value your advice. What would you do?"

"They are only my thoughts—"

"Please, Franz."

"Your father worked hard to build this ranch. I would not sell it. And I would not sell the birds. That, too, was your father's dream. He was a good man."

"Yes, he was," she said.

"But perhaps a change would be good for your mother. This is a place that…has many memories for her. Perhaps too many memories."

"Yes, maybe I am being selfish. Judge Henderson thinks

the move might be good for her. I only thought staying here would be more comfortable for her."

"For some it would be this way, but for Cammy, perhaps a new place, without the memories, would be better for her. For a time."

"Then you think I should accept Aunt Josie's invitation to live with them in San Francisco?"

"At least go for a very long visit," he said. "Cammy would be near to those who love her. I know my Audrey would like that, if she had family left. Perhaps the wound could then begin to heal."

"Yes. Heal. What a wonderful word," Vonnie murmured. "But there's the ranch to see about, and Momma can't make the trip by herself."

"I will stay here at the ranch, see that the ostriches are cared for until she is settled."

"I could be gone for some time," she said.

"I will bring Audrey with me, if that is all right with you. The change might do her good, like your mother."

"That's a lot of work for you, Franz. I couldn't expect—"

"I am an old man, but not helpless," he gently reminded her. "Besides, Roel and Genaro are here to help, and the other ranch hands."

Vonnie's face turned sober. "I know. I didn't want to impose on your goodness, Franz. You've done so much for me already."

"Then you will allow me to help you?"

"I…let me think about it, Franz. I'll talk to Mother and see how she feels about visiting Aunt Josie and Aunt Judith."

"And if she will go?"

"Then, I'll take her there permanently."

Franz returned to cleaning the harness, and Vonnie stared out at the ostrich pens, her mind no more settled than before. What Franz said made sense. If she stayed, more than likely there was nothing but heartache ahead.

The birds strutted around the pens, occasionally pecking at the ground. They would be drumming soon, males and females trying to attract one another in preparation for egg-laying season. Her father had enjoyed the process of choosing the best birds, pairing them, planning for the laying, and then the hatch.

They'd been through numerous hatchings and care of the new babies, and while it had been a tedious process—making sure newborn legs didn't bow, carefully measuring their feed—her father had reveled in it. She smiled, remembering his joy at having fifty percent of the little hatchlings survive. A very good percentage, he'd boasted.

"My father loved this ranch," she said, more to herself. "I feel I'd betray him by selling."

"You will decide what is best."

"My father was a fighter, wasn't he?"

"That he was," Franz agreed.

"He would stay and fight."

Franz cleaned the harness, softly humming as he worked the oil into the dry leather.

"But if I lost Momma, too…"

Suddenly the answer was clear to her. If the move would restore her mother to her former self, that would be Teague's wish.

"Thank you, Franz."

"You have decided what you will do?"

"Not entirely. But with Daddy gone, Momma not herself, Adam getting married, what is here for me?"

"Then you will sell?"

"I think it's my only choice." She patted the old man's arm. "Thank you, again. Give Audrey my love, and tell her I'm praying for her."

Judge Henderson settled more deeply into his favorite chair and sipped his coffee, watching Adam stare out the window at the deepening twilight.

"What did you find out?"

The judge studied the bottom of his glass. "Tanner has a serious buyer. Spoke to him about it this morning. He had a question on the title, so it was easy to find out who the prospective buyer is. A speculator from back East. Money. Plans to move out here as soon as the deal is closed."

"So, Tanner was telling the truth."

"It seems he told the truth about wanting Vonnie's ranch, too. His buyer is willing to pay her whatever it takes to get the land."

"But it wouldn't be beyond Lewis to threaten her, to frighten her into selling out to him?"

"Ordinarily, I'd say no, but in this instance, I can't be sure. From what Tanner tells me, he won't be making a penny on Vonnie's land. Purely a bonus for his buyer. His land is sold, providing the buyer comes to terms with the ostriches being there.

"Something is always going wrong over there. Frankly, I'm puzzled by what's happening." Adam stepped away from the window.

"A severed head falling out of the cabinet. What a cruel, hateful thing for someone to do."

"I can't imagine how it was accomplished. Killing the bird without creating a disturbance, then getting into the house. Who, other than Tanner, wants to see Vonnie gone? And why? If Tanner has a buyer for his land then he has no motive."

"Teague had no enemies?"

"I'm sure he did—doesn't every man?"

"He and your father didn't get along," the judge suggested.

"P.K.'s a thorny old goat, but he wouldn't sink this low, even if he had a motive, which he doesn't."

His father had hated Teague enough to strike out, but he would never seek bitterness and revenge on Teague's daughter. Sure the family needed money, but Baldwins wouldn't stoop so low as to harass a woman.

"P.K. and Teague didn't care for each other and that's the bottom line. P.K. wouldn't go out of his way to create trouble for Teague, and he wouldn't go to any effort to help him out. Teague's gone. Past forgotten."

"You don't have to remind me what P.K.'s like," the judge grunted. "Don't know how you've put up with him all these years."

"I know him better than anyone," Adam said. "Hard, unyielding, unforgiving, but evenhanded and fair. He's never dealt under the table, you know that."

Even if he lost the ranch, P.K. would do what he felt was right. Adam remembered his father talking about the jewels. He'd have taken those all right, but that was different. Wasn't it?

"Then who is doing this to Vonnie?"

"I don't know," Adam said, going back to stand at the window. The thought was keeping him up nights. "I don't know."

Chapter Eighteen

❧

Vonnie snipped a thread and pushed the needle into a pincushion before shaking out the dress she'd finished hemming.

"One more completed," she said aloud, her elation only slightly diminished by the knowledge she had one more to go.

A knock at the front door sent her attention to the clock on the wall.

"Three o'clock already?" she murmured.

Time had gotten away from her again. Quickly hanging up the finished gown, she ran downstairs to answer the door.

"Beth." Vonnie smiled. "I'm sorry, I lost all track of time."

"That's all right," Beth said, stepping inside. "I'm a little early, by at least two minutes, and besides, I know you've got loads of work and I so appreciate your making time to fuss with me."

"I have the basic dress basted together." Vonnie led Beth upstairs to the sewing room. "Think you'll see that the gown is coming along nicely." A cold March wind rattled the shingles.

"Of course, at this stage, Nell, Susan and I can make any changes you'd like—"

"I'm sure it will be lovely," Beth said absently. She stepped to the dress Vonnie was working on. "This is nice."

"Thank you. When your gown…"

Beth seemed more interested in the second dress.

Vonnie spread three versions of the same design across her drawing table.

"You see how this neckline goes here? I've seen you wear it before and it's very attractive. Of course, the lace creates a lovely line, softer, feminine. And, with that, I thought of the sleeve with a point over the wrist, with the lace trim peeking over the edge. Lace will cover the front of the skirt and—"

"It's fine. Really."

Vonnie laid the design aside, her eyes avoiding the small diamond on the third finger of Beth's left hand, Adam's token symbol of a contract undertaken for life. But Beth didn't seem her usual bubbly self today. She hadn't for weeks now. Was she ill?

Beth glanced up. "Did I tell you the date? October first."

Vonnie smiled. "Lovely time of year."

"Yes. October first." She stepped to the sewing table,

perusing the sewing items. "Mother and I decided the men's suits would be dark rose, with white shirts."

"Rose?"

"Adam hates the color."

Somehow that didn't surprise Vonnie. Rose.

"Carolyn is hostessing a tea for me, girls only, of course, a week from Saturday. You'll be there?"

Vonnie put the sketches away in a drawer. "Of course. May I help?"

"No. Carolyn's doing it all."

Silence.

"I haven't mentioned it," Vonnie said, "but I may be selling the ranch and moving Mother to San Francisco. Her sisters live there and would like to have her come be with them. I think the change will do her good."

"Moving." Beth turned to look at her. "When?"

"I don't know. Soon, I think."

Was it her imagination or was Beth behaving even more strangely today? Her exuberance was missing. Her zest. Beth couldn't know about her relationship with Adam.

"Sheriff Tanner has a buyer for the ranch. I suppose it will depend on how soon they want possession."

Beth's eyes clouded. "I'm so sorry. I'll miss you."

She laid a hand on Vonnie's arm, giving her a comforting squeeze. Vonnie caught a hint of uncertainty in Beth's eyes, as if she needed reassurance. About what? The marriage?

"I'll miss you, too," Vonnie said, and sincerely meant it. Beth, Hildy, Mora and Carolyn had been her friends as long as she could remember.

She'd miss everything here. Friends, the town, her comfortable life. Starting a new life and a new business wouldn't be easy, but it would be easier than staying here and watching Beth and Adam together. Watching them move into a home, start a family. Her heart ached for the dreams that would never come true now.

Beth's expression sobered. "Oh, Vonnie, life is changing for all of us. Sometimes I wish…"

"You wish what, Beth?" she asked gently.

"I wish we could have stayed younger longer, having fun, no responsibilities, and no worries."

"What are you worried about, dear?" Vonnie realized that, in spite of everything, she loved this childhood friend. "Surely you're not having doubts about marrying Adam."

"Certainly not. Adam is such a dear man…devoted friend. I am so very lucky to be marrying him, aren't I? It's…oh, I don't know. Pre-bridal jitters months early, I guess." Beth changed the subject. "Did I tell you Daddy bought an automobile?"

"Really?" Vonnie asked.

"I took Adam for a ride the other night. I think we'll probably be buying an automobile when we're married."

"That's nice."

Vonnie had never seen an automobile, but she had seen a picture of one in a magazine once. She didn't think she'd like one.

Beth left after a while. Vonnie stood at the window and watched the buggy rattle out of the yard before she went to the kitchen to have a cup of tea, hoping it would help relieve the headache that had started at the nape of her neck and seemed to be getting more intense by the moment.

She took a steaming cup to Cammy, tried to persuade

her mother to come downstairs for a spell, then gave up. Cammy was content to stay in her room with the photograph album, believing that Teague would be coming home any moment now.

Sometimes it seemed Cammy thought Teague was still at war. Other times she seemed to know that the war was over and Teague had survived, but believed that he was in town, or on an errand, and would be home shortly. Sitting down at the kitchen table, Vonnie kneaded her temples. Shoving her half-empty teacup aside, she got up.

Thinking fresh air would help her headache, she decided to take the carriage into town. She asked Roel to keep an ear out for Cammy since he was replacing a board on the front porch.

"I'm sure she will sleep all afternoon, but if she should call for me, please look in on her."

"*Sí, señorita.* Do not worry. I'll be right here until it's too dark to work."

Vonnie planned to look at new threads and buttons, anything to take her mind off Adam and Beth.

The town bustled today. Seeing people going about their everyday lives made her feel better.

Guiding the horses to the hitching rail in front of the mercantile, Vonnie climbed down and wrapped the holding rein around the post.

Shaking the wrinkles out of her skirt, she stepped onto the sidewalk, only to come hard up against someone.

"Oh, sorry," she said automatically. Her head lifted when a pair of strong hands steadied her.

"Where's the fire?"

"Buttons," she stammered. "Ran out an hour ago."

"Had to come into town for feed," Adam said at the same time. He was still holding her arms; her hand still rested on his chest. She noticed there was a button missing on his coat and almost mentioned it, stopping herself in time. Beth would be sewing his buttons, not her.

"I have to go," she managed.

"Yes…good to see you."

His hands left her arms, and she suddenly felt a shiver move over her, a cold breeze on her skin.

Tipping his hat, he said quietly, "Don't dawdle long. Ladies shouldn't be out after dark."

She made herself turn away and go inside the mercantile.

"Hello there, Miss Vonnie. Haven't seen you in several days," Mr. Beasley called out from the rear of the store. "Something you need?"

"I want to look around a bit," she said, longing to lose herself in the bolts of cloth and ribbons.

"Take your time. I'll finish filling Adam's order. If you need anything, sing out."

"Thank you." *Adam's order.* Was she hexed?

She walked along the ready-made dresses, forcing interest in material and design, knowing those in the catalogs she got from back East were much more recent than Mr. Beasley's.

"Garrett?"

Adam's voice coming from the front door caught her by surprise.

"Yes?"

She peered around the tables stacked with bolts of calico and cottons.

"The wheel on Vonnie's buggy is loose. You got a bolt about four inches long?"

"I may have," the storekeeper said. "Let me see what's back here."

"Oh, dear," she murmured, realizing that it was too late for the livery to repair the wheel.

"Can you fix it?" Vonnie called, keeping a safe distance.

"Enough for you to get home. Then Genaro or Roel will have to take it off and fix it right. The axle may need to be replaced."

"Here," Mr. Beasley called out. "Will this work?"

Adam examined the bolt the storekeeper handed him.

"That should do it. Do you have a piece of heavy wire? About two feet long?"

"I have that."

"Vonnie, it'll take about fifteen minutes," Adam called.

"Can I help?"

"No," he said, closing the door.

She browsed a few moments longer before wandering outside. Adam had shed his heavy coat, laying it over the hitching rail. As he bent to look closely at the tilting wheel, she picked up the coat and automatically examined it. Two buttons were missing.

"Will this do?"

Mr. Beasley came out of the store and handed Adam a length of heavy wire.

"That will work," he said, and thanked him.

The storekeeper turned to Vonnie. "Did you find anything you wanted?"

"Yes, I did," she said, taking Adam's coat inside the store with her.

Ten minutes later she'd purchased and sewn two buttons on the garment and tightened the others. When she went outside, Adam had finished resetting the wheel, sliding in the temporary bolt and wiring it into place.

"That should do it," he told her. He stood back to survey the wheel. "It will hold until you get home, if you don't drive like a crazy woman."

"When have I ever driven like a crazy woman?" she asked.

He grinned.

"I hear you've taken a ride in Leighton's new automobile?"

He looked up, and she quickly looked the other way. The blue of his eyes always caught her by surprise.

"You talk to Beth?"

"She stopped by this morning. We had a nice visit."

She resisted the urge to ask if Adam had noticed Beth's recent preoccupation. It was really nothing they needed to discuss.

He leaned on the hitching post, smiling.

"Well." She realized she was taking up too much of his time. "Thank you for repairing the wheel."

"Have Roel check all of them."

"I will, I will."

She felt his hand on her waist as he helped her aboard.

"By the way, I sewed two buttons on your coat and tightened the others. Beth would thank me." She returned his smile. "She would want you looking your best."

"Alma's tried to get the coat away from me for days. She thanks you."

She reached for the reins. "Maybe Alma could use some help." Keeping up with three men took time and effort.

"You know P.K. wouldn't have anyone new in the house."

She wanted to ask—oh, she wanted to ask, but she had no right. After all, it wasn't any of her business. Still…

"How does he feel about Beth?"

Adam picked up his coat and slipped it on. He buttoned it slowly, taking his time before answering.

"He likes her."

"Beth is a special girl," Vonnie admitted.

"Yes, she is," he said, his eyes never leaving hers.

"Well, I'd better be on my way. Ladies shouldn't be out after dark."

"Evening, Miss Vonnie, Adam."

Vonnie looked up to see Franz setting his stool beneath one of the lampposts. Without her realizing it, evening had approached and Franz had begun his rounds.

"I didn't realize it was so late," Vonnie said.

"I started my rounds early," Franz said, picking up his stool again. "Audrey is worse today, and I wanted to be home with her this evening."

"I'm so sorry. Can we help in some way?" Vonnie asked.

"No. I wish you could," he said, sadness in his voice.

Moving on to the next lamp, Franz slowly worked his way down the street in the twilight.

"I must be on my way," she said.

"See you Sunday."

"Yes, see you at services." But not for long; she and Mother would be leaving for San Francisco soon. Then there would be no more chance meetings, no more Adam.

Vonnie slapped the reins against the horses, and the buggy rolled off.

Chapter Nineteen

Adam sat in front of the fireplace, lost in thought. Beth was a kind and lovely woman, if a bit naive. Only one hitch. He didn't love her. He'd tried to tell himself that what he was doing was all right as long as no one got hurt. But Beth would be harmed if he married her. She would be denied love, the kind of lasting love a man or woman needed. The kind he had for Vonnie. With all the problems, he loved her more now than he had seven years ago.

Beth fussed over him like a mother hen.

Vonnie made him feel like a man. He'd never catch her without an opinion on china or lace, and she wasn't afraid to voice it. Being with her was like drinking from a cold well on a hot day. She might be bullheaded, but so was he. He had a hunch God had made that mulish woman for him and he'd been too full of pride to accept the blessing.

Was it too late—even now—to correct the mistake? He didn't want to disappoint P.K., but he'd disappoint him even more by marrying Beth.

He knew what had caused his foul mood. A man had to do the right thing. He couldn't marry Beth, not even to save Cabeza del Lobo. He'd known that for weeks, but every time he'd been around her he couldn't find the words to break off the engagement, say the words that would hurt this decent, fine young woman. She deserved a husband who loved her, not a marriage of convenience based on what she could contribute in a monetary way. P.K. would throw a fit seeing all his fine plans fall apart, but in the end he'd see the wisdom of Adam's act.

The whole scheme had been wrong from the start and he'd been a fool to go along with it. Now he had to tell Beth, then his father. He'd rather try to lasso a tornado than face either one of them. He'd take the Reverend with him to soften the blow. Tomorrow, he promised himself.

Tomorrow he was going to do what he should have done months ago.

He was in the barn shoeing a horse when Andrew found him. He had to admit, he was in a rare temper. He glanced at his brother.

"I noticed your black was favoring his left front foot yesterday. Have you checked the shoe lately?" Adam pumped the bellows, holding the iron shoe he was shaping in the coals.

"No," Andrew said. "But I will, if you're in the mood to replace it."

"Bring him over and we'll see if that's what he needs. Could be he has a stone bruise."

"Could be a bruise," Andrew said. "I was out in the north section the other morning, by the stream that cuts through the west corner."

Adam stilled, his expression turning serious as the mention of the location brought his encounter with Vonnie to mind. "Were you, now?"

"Saw you and Vonnie there."

Straightening, Adam let the tongs hang loosely in his hand as he waited for Andrew to go on.

"Thought you were engaged to Beth."

"I am."

Adam hated saying it, wished that it wasn't so. Andrew took a step toward him, his hands balled in fists at his side. "Back off, Andrew—"

Before he could finish, Andrew threw himself at Adam's middle. The breath exploded from him, and he staggered back against the side of the barn, cracking his head.

Reflex brought both arms up to break Andrew's hold on him. Andrew fell back, caught himself on a post in the middle of the blacksmith shed, and came up swinging, catching Adam squarely on the cheekbone.

Lunging, Andrew swung, but Adam dodged the blow. When Andrew swung again, Adam gave up trying to avoid a fight and countered with a hard right, connecting solidly with Andrew's jaw.

In the next instant, they were both rolling around on the

floor, straw flying in all directions, some blows connecting, others meeting only air. When they both came to their senses, they each had bloodied noses and Andrew's shirt was half torn off.

They stood, breathing hard, glaring at each other, knowing the physical blows were finished but still raging inside.

"What's the matter with you?" Adam demanded.

"You have no right to be with Vonnie when you're engaged to Beth!" Andrew shouted.

"I'm not with Vonnie!"

"You don't care about her. You're just going to hurt her."

"There's nothing between me and Vonnie. She was riding that day and happened on me fixing the fence." Adam repeated.

"Beth deserves to know what kind of man you are."

Adam studied his brother, filled with angry humiliation. "You thinking of telling her?"

"I might."

The last thing Adam needed was for his brother to tell Beth that he'd been with Vonnie. She'd be hurt and feel betrayed by both a friend and her fiancé. He didn't want that. He might not love Beth, but he'd never hurt her.

He picked up his jacket and headed for the house, work forgotten. Washing off at the pump, he dried with his shirt before going into the house. Later, he examined his face in the mirror over the washstand. There was a deep cut on his cheek, a lump on the point of his chin, and by morning he'd have a glorious shiner.

"Women," he muttered.

"Boys, dinner is ready," Alma called up the stairs.

Finishing his wash, Adam changed into clean trousers and shirt, then went down to face P.K.

Andrew looked even worse than he did, Adam decided. His bottom lip was split, his cheek bruised, and his eye was beginning to turn purple.

P.K. shook out his napkin as Alma bustled around setting dishes on the table.

"What did you boys do today?" she asked.

"Looks like they met up with a wildcat," Pat said.

"Yeah," Joey echoed. "Must have been a big one. Cat step on your toe?"

"Pass the tortillas," Adam ordered.

"Well, what was it about?" Pat pressed.

"Looks to me like someone I know forgot they were grown men," Alma sniffed.

"I stepped on a rake," Andrew murmured.

"And you?" She nudged Adam.

"Broke through a rotten board in the hayloft."

"Uh-huh," Alma said. "Fell through on your face? I was not born yesterday, Adam Baldwin. Your mother would be ashamed, the way you fib. It is no matter if you two want to act like fools. Some people have better sense. Vonnie Taylor for one."

"Vonnie Taylor?" Pat asked, reaching for another tortilla to scoop up his refried beans. "What's she got to do with Adam and Andrew fighting?"

"I hear she is selling the ranch and moving to San Francisco. Her mother has sisters there, you know."

"She's selling the Flying Feather?" Joey asked.

"*Sí,* to Sheriff Tanner. He has an offer for his ranch, I am told, the new buyer will buy Vonnie's place also. It is the talk of the town."

Adam noticed that P.K. was ignoring the conversation, concentrating on his plate.

Alma poured fresh coffee. "If you want to know what I think—"

"That's enough," P.K. said quietly.

Alma sniffed and waddled back into the kitchen.

Chapter Twenty

❧

Adam was in a bad mood by the time he reached Beth's that night. To top everything else off, his eye throbbed like a boil.

The Reverend sent a worried look. "Are you certain about this?"

"Yes sir. I'm certain."

The older man straightened his tie. "Then let's get it over with."

"Oh, dear me!" Beth exclaimed when she opened the door and saw Adam and the Reverend. "What happened to you?"

"A little accident."

"A little accident! Sake's alive! Your eye looks dreadful. Mother, come see what's happened to Adam!"

"It's nothing," he said.

"Adam!" Gillian exclaimed. "You poor thing! Come sit down, and I'll get a piece of steak to put on it. Cordy Lou, bring a piece of meat for Adam's eye. And Reverend. How good to see you!"

"It's nothing," Adam repeated. "You don't need to fuss."

Beth led the two guests to the study. "You poor dear, would you like something to drink? Of course you would. Cordy Lou, bring Adam and the Reverend something warm to drink when you bring the beef!"

Adam said, "No, I just—"

"Want me to stop fussing over you. But your poor eye— and Cordy Lou always has a pot of coffee on the stove."

"Fine." Adam said. "Bring the coffee." He sat down.

Gillian left the study, closing the door behind her.

Beth tried to examine his eye. "Really, Adam, what happened? It looks as though you've been in a common brawl."

"He fell through a loose board in the loft," the Reverend supplied.

"Fell!" Her hands flew up to cover her mouth.

"I wasn't hurt." Fighting with Andrew, behaving like Cain and Abel over a woman. He could be hardheaded and even blind at times, but God had a way of backing him into a corner when he was out of line. And marrying Beth was out of line. Out of line in the eyes of the Lord, out of line to Beth. She was a good woman who deserved a man who would love and care for her until death. He wasn't that man. Much as he respected and honored his father, he couldn't marry a woman he didn't love. Why had he ever thought that he could?

He had to break off the marriage. The insanity had gone

on for too long. He wasn't man enough to question the families' dispute many years ago, but he was now. He was going to unearth the real source of the Baldwin/Taylor feud, a grudge that had shattered more than one life. One Teague Taylor had taken to his grave.

Vonnie might not have the same wild love she'd had for him years ago. They were both older and wiser, but he had to know her feelings and he couldn't until he set Beth free.

Beth sighed. "Let's take a walk. The Reverend can visit with mother and father—"

"Not tonight, Beth."

"Oh, let's do! It isn't so very cold, and you look like you're a bit out of sorts."

"Beth." Adam focused on her. "Can we have a moment in private?"

She glanced from the Reverend to him. "Is something wrong. Something's wrong isn't it? You arrive unexpectedly, sporting a black-and-blue eye, with the Reverend, and refuse to say what's happened. Someone died, didn't they? Who? Someone close…?"

"Beth." He took a deep breath. "There is something wrong, and there has been for months. I'm here to set it right."

The Reverend urged softly. "Please, Beth. Sit down."

"Momma, breakfast is ready! It's another fine day outside."

"I think I'll rest a while longer."

Lifting the shade, Vonnie let light into the bedroom. "Nelly and Susan will be here soon. We should have Beth's dress finished by early next week."

"That's nice, dear."

"You have another letter from Josie and Judith. Shall I read it to you?"

"From Josie and Judith?" Cammy raised, looking confused. "Yes, please."

Vonnie read the chatty letter aloud, all about the sights of San Francisco, the lovely bay, the tea they'd hostessed earlier in the month.

"'We do so hope you are considering our invitation to stay with us,'" Vonnie read. "'It has been so long since we've been together, and our eagerness to see you grows. We look daily for your letter of acknowledgment. Your loving sisters, Josie and Judith.'"

"Wasn't that nice?" Vonnie said, refolding the pale pink sheets of stationery that held Josie's spidery script.

"Yes, it was," Cammy agreed, her hand caressing the photo album that had become her constant companion.

"We'd need to leave soon, you know. While there's a break in the weather."

"I don't know."

"Wouldn't it be nice to see your sisters again?"

"Teague is so busy."

"Think about it, will you, Momma?"

"I'll think about it," Cammy said vaguely, her attention already wandering to the photo album in her lap.

"I'll bring your tea."

Returning to the kitchen, she prepared blackberry tea and set it on a tray to carry upstairs. As she passed from the kitchen to the stairs, she noticed that the back door was ajar. Frowning, she thought back, certain she'd closed it the night before, as she always did.

Her heart pounded when she remembered the severed head incident. Setting the tray aside, she cringed as she heard Cammy's fragile cup strike the floor and shatter.

Racing up the stairs, she slowly pushed the door to her sewing room open.

"No!" she cried. "No!"

She couldn't believe her eyes.

Beth's wedding gown, which had been so near completion, now hung in ragged ribbons on the dress form. Someone had slashed the fine silk from waist to hem. The delicate peau de soie lace was shredded. Tiny, exquisite seed pearls lay scattered across the floor.

Stunned, Vonnie slowly backed from the room.

"Vonnie?"

Spinning around, her heart in her throat, Vonnie nearly fainted in relief when she saw Eugenia standing in the open doorway.

"Child! You're white as a sheet. What's wrong?"

"S-someone—" Vonnie pointed to the destruction.

"Oh, sakes alive," Eugenia whispered, her eyes wide with fright. "Who on *earth* could have done such a wicked thing?"

"I d-don't know. The dress was perfect when I left it last night. I—I just don't—"

"We've got to get the sheriff, now!"

"Yes," Vonnie said. "I'll send Genaro. He was at the barn when I came in."

Her knees suddenly too weak to hold her, Vonnie sank into a chair while Eugenia sent Genaro for Sheriff Tanner. Suki seemed to understand that something bad had happened, jumping into Vonnie's lap to lick her face. Who could have done such an awful thing? And how could they have gotten inside to do the damage?

The idea that someone had come into the house during the night, while they were sleeping, was as frightening as the incident with the ostrich's head.

She had no idea how long she sat there before Eugenia interrupted her thoughts.

"Vonnie? Sheriff Tanner's here. I'll be with your mother if you need me."

Suki sprang off her lap, barking at the sheriff as he approached.

Vonnie looked up. "Sheriff?"

Lewis Tanner loomed over her. "Hear there's been another incident."

"In there," she said. "Someone's destroyed…Beth Baylor's wedding dress, sometime during the night."

"Someone got in during the night?" Tanner stepped to the door of the sewing room and took in the devastation. "What was your mutt doing, sleeping? Did you leave a door open?"

"No. I thought I didn't. I always make sure all the doors are locked before retiring, but the back door was ajar earlier. Eugenia, did you come in through the back door?"

"Yes, but you were upstairs." She excused herself and went upstairs.

The sheriff strode into the sewing room and looked around.

"Nothing here. The window's locked."

"Stuck," Vonnie corrected. "I can't open it."

Bending down, he picked up a pair of Vonnie's sewing shears from the floor and held them for a moment before laying them on her cutting table.

"I'll look around outside, see if any of the hands heard or saw anything, but if it's like the last time, nobody will have heard anything."

He started toward the door, then paused.

"It's none of my business, but this is a sure sign someone is out to get you. You were smart to take my offer. You best leave before someone gets hurt."

Vonnie met his dark gaze. "You have the ranch now. Why won't you leave me alone?"

Tanner frowned. "You sayin' you think I did this?"

"Did you?"

His face flushed a deep crimson. "I have a legitimate buyer, made you a good offer and you've accepted. I don't need to play games to get what I want."

Laying her head in her hands, she whispered, "Why would anyone want to do this to me...to Beth."

"Have you told anyone that you're sold out?"

"No...not yet." It was all still unreal to her. Mother. Daddy gone. Everything gone.

Tanner broke into her thoughts. "I'll go talk to your men now."

Unable to deal with the devastated workroom, Vonnie went to see if the commotion had disturbed Cammy.

"Momma?"

Cammy stood in the middle of her bedroom, holding her dress as if she'd forgotten what she was about to do. Eugenia sat on the couch.

"What was that noise earlier? Did you drop a plate?"

"Yes, a teacup. Sit down, Momma. We need to talk."

"Oh, you broke a piece of the good china, didn't you? Naughty girl."

Vonnie could have cried. Mother had regressed to when Vonnie was a child, and a sense of hopelessness washed over her.

"It wasn't the good china. Remember when we talked about going to see your sisters?"

"Josie and Judith? They were always such bossy things."

"You remember them, Cammy." Eugenia tried to help.

"It's been a long time since you've seen family. It's time we took that trip to California." Vonnie couldn't tell her that she had sold the birds and the ranch. She wouldn't understand. Vonnie couldn't fathom how their lives had changed so swiftly.

"I don't know." Cammy twisted the dress in her hands.

"We need a change of scenery. You start thinking about what dresses you'd like to take, and I'll arrange our transportation. Eugenia is here. She'll be happy to help you pack."

"Josie and Judith." Cammy nodded vaguely, as if she were only now realizing who the two were. "It might be nice."

"I've forgotten your tea," Vonnie said. "Eugenia, would you mind to bring Momma's tea."

"Not at all. I can spend the day if you need me."

They went downstairs where Eugenia began sweeping up the shattered china.

"I thought I'd clear this away."

"Thank you. I'll make a hot pot for Momma." Vonnie hesitated. "I've sold the ranch and birds to Sheriff Tanner."

Eugenia turned. "Oh, my dear."

"Momma's sisters have been wanting her to come stay with them since Daddy died. I thought a visit might be good, and if everything goes well, we'll stay."

"Oh, child," the older woman said, reaching out to her. "I do hate to see you leave here. We've been neighbors nigh on to thirty years. But it might be a good thing for Cammy. A new place, being with family again."

"Thank you. We'll miss you dearly."

"And I'll miss you, but you do what you must do."

"Yes…well, I'll fix that tea. Maybe you can help Momma sort through her dresses? She doesn't know about the sale. Please don't say anything. She wouldn't understand. I would like to leave by the end of the week."

"I'll help with the packing," Eugenia said, patting Vonnie's arm. "I know how difficult this must be for you. You go fix that tea and I'll see to your mother."

The Baylor household was quiet when Vonnie rode her horse into the yard. She shook her head, thinking of the devastating news she would bring, the upheaval in Beth's life. She knew about upheaval. She'd had more than her share recently. Dismounting, she tied the reins to the porch and mounted the steps. Gillian answered the summons almost immediately.

"Good morning, Mrs. Baylor. Is Beth in?"

Shaking her head, Gillian whispered, "She's in the parlor. I haven't been able to get her to eat a bite."

Vonnie wondered at Gillian's hushed tone. Beth couldn't know about the dress. Was she ill today?

"Come in, come in." Gillian shooed her into the foyer. "I'll make a pot of tea. Maybe you can get her to drink something." The older woman wandered off, talking to herself under her breath. Vonnie glanced at the closed parlor doors. Removing her gloves, she stepped to the doorway and carefully slid open the double doors. Beth sat in front of the fire, staring at the flames. "Beth?"

The bride-to-be glanced up at the sound of her name. "Yes? Vonnie?"

"Hi." Vonnie stepped inside the room, pulling the doors closed behind her. "I'm glad I found you home this morning."

"Oh." Beth offered a whimsical smile. "I had planned to spend the day with Hildy, but come in. Warm yourself by the fire."

She strode to the fireplace, grateful for the invitation. March cold winds blew. Taking a moment to gather her thoughts, she unbuttoned her heavy fleece coat. "Beth, there's been an accident."

"Oh?" Beth looked up. "Someone I know?"

"Not someone, but something." She sat down on the stool, grasping her friend's hands tightly. "I'm so sorry. Someone entered my sewing room last night and destroyed your gown."

For a moment the only sound in the room was a log popping and the ashes showering to the grate. "I know this is dreadful news, but we have time to order a new dress. The wedding is months away—"

Beth held up a hand. "Stop! There isn't going to be a wedding."

Vonnie paused to catch her breath. "Now, Beth, a bought gown won't be so bad. I'll have time to make alterations, add whatever trim you want."

Beth met her concerned gaze. "There isn't going to be a wedding. Period."

Vonnie couldn't find her voice. At first elation filled her. Adam wasn't marrying Beth! Then compassion. Adam had broken Beth's heart. How could he?

Or had she broken his?

"Tell me what happened?"

"Adam stopped by last night." Beth's eyes teared up. "He had the biggest shiner you ever saw, but he wouldn't say how he got it—other than some babble about 'falling through a loose board.' But it was more, much more. Eventually the reason for his visit came out. He broke off the engagement."

"Oh, Beth, I'm so sorry."

Vonnie's head reeled. Adam had broken the engagement. Adam?

"No." Beth dabbed at the corners of her eyes. "He was right. We both knew that what we had together wasn't right. Not in the way of 'lasting' right. I loved Adam. I believe in his way he feels deep affection for me, but deep affection isn't enough to last 'till death do us part.' He was wise enough to recognize that and spare us both considerable grief."

"You're all right with this?"

She turned, her nose bright red from crying; she wasn't completely all right. What bride-to-be who now wasn't ever cherished the thought of this hour. But Vonnie knew that Beth was strong, and Adam, for whatever his reason, was right. In her heart she knew that Adam would never love a woman the way he had loved her, but she wasn't sure that was why he'd broken the engagement. Adam had changed, matured. Maybe he had simply decided he would not do his father's bidding.

Taking her friend into her arms, Vonnie held Beth tightly as the young woman sobbed.

She blinked back tears, realizing what she'd done. She'd sold the ranch to Tanner and she and Cammy would be leaving for San Francisco imminently.

Timing never seemed to be her and Adam's strong point.

Late that afternoon, Vonnie glanced at the trunk that Eugenia had dragged in from the spare room and had begun to fill with Cammy's dresses. The neighbor had spared no time in packing.

"I think she should take the green dress, don't you? It would be perfect for afternoon tea," she said, carefully folding the pale green batiste. "I'll have to get some extra hat boxes—"

"Vonnie, come look at this picture."

"Momma, no. Put the album away."

"No, come see this. See how handsome your father is."

"Momma—"

The day had already been hectic. First Beth's dress, then news of Adam and Beth's broken engagement. She couldn't face much more, and yet she fought to keep from going to Adam to ask why. Why now?

"Please dear. It will only take a moment."

Vonnie surrendered, going to kneel beside Cammy to look at the pictures that fascinated Cammy and seemed to give her some sense of comfort.

She pointed to a photo that showed five men standing together, each in uniform with their rifles beside them. "See how handsome he is in his uniform? How young they look. That's Daddy, and P.K."

Vonnie glanced at the picture, recognizing the men though they were young. "That's Franz standing beside Daddy, isn't it?"

Cammy suddenly clutched the photo album to her chest. Vonnie frowned. "What's wrong?"

The woman's eyes widened in fear and her lips trembled.

"I don't want to go to the cellar! Don't make me go to the cellar! Teague said I never had to go there. Not ever!"

"It's all right, Momma." Vonnie soothed, alarmed at her mother's reaction.

"I hate it down there," Cammy snapped.

"You don't ever have to go down there."

"I don't want to go…I don't want to go…"

It took some time to calm her mother, but Vonnie was finally able to pry the photo album from her mother's hands and persuade her to lie down.

Eugenia remained with Cammy most of the day, sorting through her wardrobe, while Vonnie packed her sewing materials.

That evening, exhausted after the stressful day, she moved through the house turning out the lamps.

As the wick died away, the front parlor window shattered, spraying glass across the rug.

Smothering a frightened scream, Vonnie watched, horrified, as a rock bounced across the room and came to rest at her feet.

Heart pounding, she ran to the window to look out.

A shadow with a distinctive limp separated itself from the woodshed and made its way quickly back across the open space to the barn.

Andrew?

Letting the drape fall back into place, she picked up the rock and unwound the piece of paper wrapped around it.

Holding the paper in trembling fingers, she read the cryptic message.

"Sell out while you can," it warned.

"Andrew," she whispered. "Have you been doing this to me?"

Chapter Twenty-One

❧

Staring at the thirty-three-year-old newspaper, Adam studied the article and the accompanying picture.

"Find what you're looking for?"

"I think so," he said, closing the huge drawers that contained the dusty back issues in the back room of *The Weekly Amarillo News*. "Thanks."

"Anytime," the editor said, closing the door and locking it.

Coming out of the newspaper office, Adam paused on the sidewalk. He finally had the answer to one question. Now on to the other.

Later that morning he knocked on Franz Schuyler's door. Dr. McDonald answered his knock.

"Sorry to disturb you, Doctor. I need to speak to Franz."

"Audrey's very ill this morning, Adam. Perhaps another time?"

"Sorry, I'll come back later. Is there anything I can do?"

"I wish there were, But no, there's nothing."

Adam turned and spotted Sheriff Tanner walking toward him. Usually content to let the sheriff past, Adam stopped him.

"Tanner."

"Baldwin." The sheriff tipped his hat.

"You remember El Johnson, the guy who rode with my father, Teague Taylor and Franz during the war?"

"Yeah, I remember him."

"Where is he now?"

"Now?" Tanner lifted his hat and ran a hand through his graying hair. "Last I heard he'd moved from Austin to twenty or so miles from here. Why?"

"Did you ever know the real reason behind Teague and P.K.'s hatred?"

Surprise crossed the sheriff's face. "Don't reckon I do, not for certain. You've lived with the feud all your life. Don't you know?"

"Bits and pieces, things P.K.'s chosen to tell me. I have a feeling the trouble runs deeper than a squabble over jewels." He had a hunch the feud had festered until no one knew for certain what it was about.

"Don't know what I could tell you about Johnson other than I heard he's a hermit—don't let many folks come around."

Adam nodded. It figured.

"Heard the wedding's been called off."

News travels fast. "It has."

"Suppose you've heard about the trouble out at the Taylor place—Beth's bridal gown?"

A muscle in Adam's jaw firmed. "What trouble?"

"Good grief, man. Are you living in a cave? It's all over town. Someone broke into Vonnie's workroom sometime during the night and slashed the Baylor girl's gown to ribbons."

Beth's gown. Guilt flooded Adam. He'd broken her heart, shamed her and now someone had destroyed her gown. He had started to leave when Tanner began to walk on. Then the sheriff stopped and turned back to face Adam. "You do know the Taylor girl has sold out. Lock, stock and barrel."

Adam's mind went blank then numb. Recovering, he shook his head, trying to clear his head. "Vonnie wouldn't sell."

"Better check your facts. She did sell. To me. Brought her a fair price and she took it. Her and her mother is leaving for San Francisco before the end of the week."

What started as a bad twenty-four hours had bloomed into a nightmare. Vonnie had sold the Flying Feather? To Tanner? Had she lost her mind?

"I don't believe you."

Tanner shrugged. "I won't lose any sleep over it. I'm telling the truth."

"Why would she sell to you?"

"Well now, maybe that's a question you ought to ask your pa." Tipping his hat, the sheriff moved on. The whole conversation didn't make sense. P.K. wouldn't know why Vonnie would sell her land and birds to Sheriff Tanner. The thought that his father cared anything about a Taylor was laughable. He turned on his heel and stepped off the porch, anger warring with temperance. If Vonnie was here right now he'd wring her pretty neck! It had taken him years, but now he knew. He wasn't mad at her for wanting the marriage annulled. He was mad at himself for letting her talk him out of it. All these years he'd felt less a man. He'd taken vows before God and he—not only Vonnie—had failed to honor them. Pride had let him walk away without thinking about the ramifications. Sure, they were young and crazy, but neither had been a babe regarding God's commandments. They *both* knew better.

It took a day and a half to track El Johnson down. He found him, a hermit, living not twenty miles from Amarillo. Adam surveyed the old shack, the overgrown yard. El wouldn't welcome his coming.

Rapping on the worn door, he glanced across the open plains. What a desolate place. A man could die of loneliness out here.

The door opened a crack, and a pair of faded blue eyes focused. "Yeah?"

Johnson's greeting was less than cordial, but at least the hermit didn't shoot on sight.

"El Johnson?"

"Who wants to know?"

"Adam Baldwin. P.K.'s son."

"What d'ya want?"

"I'd want to talk to you."

"Said all I needed to say thirty-three years ago."

"Could I come inside?"

El looked as if he wasn't going to cooperate, but finally he stepped back and motioned for Adam to come inside.

Adam focused on the small, dirty room. Dust coated every surface, and the stack of unwashed dishes said that El didn't have a woman.

"Sit if it suits you," he said, pulling a shabby wooden chair forward.

Adam sat. "You remember my father?" he asked.

El nodded. "I remember him."

"But the two of you haven't kept in touch over the years?"

"No."

"Can you tell me why?"

"No reason to keep in touch."

"That's true, unless it affects me. And it's affecting me."

Johnson studiously avoided Adam's gaze. His eyes burned with such intensity that Adam wondered if the man was entirely sane.

"Whatever happened between the two of you has cost me the woman I love."

El sat, staring reflectively at the soiled tablecloth. "Your papa ever tell you about the war?"

"Some," Adam admitted. "He doesn't speak of it often."

"Didn't think so," El said, digging at a dried-egg splatter with a broken fingernail.

"Most men don't like talking about the war."

"Yeah, some don't."

"You and my father, Teague Taylor and Franz Schuyler were friends at one time, right?"

Johnson's eyes shifted warily. "We fought together."

"You rode in the same company."

"We did," El confirmed.

"And you all came back to Amarillo after the war."

There was no immediate answer, and Adam took that to be a fact.

"Why was it that only Teague and Franz remained friends? Why did my father hate Teague so bitterly, and why did you choose to move to another county and not associate with P.K., Teague or Franz?"

El's hackles rose. "Why should I tell you?"

"You keep your distance from my father, and the others. Why?"

"Things change."

Adam studied the man for a long moment, wondering what kind of man, what kind of soldier, he'd been. Lean, tall as P.K., a firm jaw, scruffy with a week-old beard. El Johnson was the oldest of the group.

"What things changed?" Adam asked.

"Just things. Now go along and leave an old man his peace."

"I can't. This feud won't let up or die out. I want to know what happened. What changed and caused some of you to become bitter enemies?"

"I came out here to be left alone. You got no right to come here nosing around."

"Someone I love is in danger. I don't know why, but I think it has something to do with what happened among you four men."

Lifting his eyes, El stared at him. "A woman?"

There was a long, brittle silence. "Vonnie Taylor. Teague's daughter."

"Teague's baby girl?"

"She's not little anymore," Adam admitted. "You know Teague is dead."

His eyes clouded. "No, I didn't. He was a good man."

When El didn't elaborate, Adam pressed harder. "If he was such a good man, why didn't you remain friends?"

"Old memories. Things best forgotten," the old man said softly.

"The four of you went through the war together. As a rule that strengthens friendships. The four of you built lives, some had families, but only Teague and P.K. acknowledged each other through necessity. They only spoke if they were forced to. I want to know what happened."

The old man squinted, momentarily lost in his own reverie.

"El, help me. Tell me what happened to cause the hate and animosity."

"Nothing we're proud of," he said. "We was comin' home," the hermit began, so softly Adam had to strain to hear. "Just young bucks, full of havin' survived. Sick of war." He rubbed his hand down his face. His beard against the callused hand sounded like sandpaper against wood. "We…come upon the farmer…his wife, and kids."

Tears filled his eyes as the story unfolded. It was the same story P.K. had told. Hurt, remorse, shame colored his voice.

"Teague wouldn't have no part of it. Said them jewels wasn't ours to take. Said we was thieves, but I was young…foolish…without a brain in my head. I threw the pouch to Teague and told him to take it and shut up.

"He had a young wife waiting for him when he got back.

I knew the money would keep them going until they could get a new start."

He hitched himself up straighter in the chair. "Teague was hardheaded. Said he'd sooner starve than take the jewels."

P.K. knew Teague had taken the jewels, but the feud went deeper.

"He took the pouch, but not because he wanted to. I left him holding them. What happened after that I couldn't say, but I suspect P.K. figured Teague used the jewels for his own gain."

"Teague wouldn't do that."

"A man never knows what he'll do until he's faced with a choice."

Adam's mind raced. There had to be more to the story. Did El know or was he not saying? Without the answer he could never free Vonnie.

"How's your pa?" Real interest showed in the old man's face and voice.

"Slowing down. He's got a knee that gives him trouble. A horse fell on him a few years back."

"One fell on him during the war. His right leg as I remember."

Adam nodded. "He favors the right knee."

Johnson nodded. "He had bad luck with animals."

Adam rose, extending his hand. El got up slowly, feebly accepting the shake.

"Thank you."

"I hope it helps," he said. "It's been a terrible load to bear.

If I could live that day over…" His eyes misted. "Well, things would have been different for all of us."

It occurred to Adam that all four men had paid a heavy price for whatever had happened that day…and the weeks and months afterward. The atrocity had eaten Teague alive; P.K. had become a bitter old man; the knowledge of his part in the crime was so intense for El that he had withdrawn from life and become a hermit. Franz was the only one untouched by that day.

"It's those jewels," El said. "They were a curse to the family that owned them, and the men who took them. The curse goes on."

"Yes," Adam admitted. "The curse goes on."

The last time Adam saw El Johnson, he was a broken man, thin as a shadow, standing on his porch, waiting for death.

Vonnie stopped at the mercantile to order glass for the parlor window before heading to the post office to wire Cammy's sisters that they would be leaving Amarillo at the end of the week. She'd left Eugenia packing. She ran into the pastor's wife on the way to the mercantile.

"Oh, Vonnie, I was just on my way out to the ranch."

Noting Pearl's red-rimmed eyes, Vonnie guessed it was bad news. "What's happened?"

"It's Audrey—"

"Oh, no."

"She's gone to be with the Lord."

"When?" Vonnie whispered.

"About an hour ago. I knew you would want to know right away."

Vonnie thought about how she hadn't been to see Audrey in several days.

"I'll go to Franz immediately."

"The poor man is beside himself with grief. Pastor is with him, but he'll need our support."

Vonnie hurried to her buggy, forgetting the earlier chore.

She arrived at the Schuylers' minutes later. Hurrying up the walk, she registered surprise when the door opened before she reached it. Adele Wilson and Shirlene Majors, both deacons' wives, visibly upset, lace handkerchiefs to their noses, came toward her.

"Oh, Vonnie, thank you for coming so quickly. Poor Franz. I don't know if he can endure this. Go on in."

The front door was ajar. Pushing it open, she stepped inside the foyer. She found Franz in the kitchen, sitting at the kitchen table with his face buried in his hands, sobbing.

At the sound of her footsteps, he looked up with glazed eyes.

"Franz, I'm so sorry."

Shaking his head, his face crumpled. "She's gone…Audrey is gone."

Coming to kneel by his chair, Vonnie tried to comfort him. "It's so hard, Franz. I know how I felt when Daddy passed."

Her own wounds were still very tender.

Looking up, Franz's eyes suddenly hardened. "It's your fault."

Vonnie drew back. "Franz…"

"You killed her. If Audrey had had her piano, she would have stayed with me longer." He suddenly turned wild. "If

I'd only had more time, I could have found the jewels, bought the Steinway back. Carolyn would eventually sell. I'd make her…"

He was rambling, Vonnie realized. His grief was so intense that he wasn't thinking coherently.

"She would have played, like before, lost herself in her music. I would have had more time with her."

"Time wouldn't have helped, Franz," Vonnie comforted.

Tears rolled down his weathered cheeks. "My Audrey loved to play, the music flowed from her. You saw it, how she made the keyboard come alive."

Vonnie reached out to him, but he jerked back. She understood the rejection. He had loved Audrey so deeply it was impossible to imagine life without her.

"You did everything you could, Franz. Audrey loved you."

"She didn't know," he said. "No one knew where I hid them. Just me. Now it's too late. Too late to help her. Oh, why can't I find them? Why can't I remember?"

Vonnie heard the despair in his voice and her heart ached. If only she had the words to lighten his grief. Later, he would realize that he'd done everything that could be done.

People started arriving, the church women to help lay out Audrey's body, the Women's Missionary Circle with food, neighbors, close friends. The small house filled, and Vonnie, knowing her immediate help wasn't needed, went home to break the news to Cammy and Eugenia.

When Eugenia heard the news she broke into tears.

"Oh, the poor, poor soul. 'Tis a far better place she is now."

"Franz is beside himself. He feels he's not done enough for her."

"Everyone feels that way at times like this. There's so little anyone can do."

"He was rambling. He kept saying he wished he could have gotten her piano back for her. If she could have played her piano she'd have lived longer. How odd he would think the piano would have made the difference."

"Grief does strange things to a body. I remember when my John passed on, I kept thinking of things I could have done, should have done. Silly things. Like, I didn't ask if he wanted a second cup of coffee that morning. And I'd thought to fix his favorite dinner the night before, but I hadn't because I'd been at a church meeting that afternoon and didn't want to take the time to catch a chicken, and clean and fry it. If only I'd done that, I thought, then he'd have known how much he meant to me." Eugenia dabbed her eyes with a handkerchief. "As if a scrawny chicken could have made a difference."

"Franz has always regretted selling that piano. Audrey didn't feel half as bad about it as Franz did," Vonnie mused. "And Carolyn has a bit of a selfish nature."

"Time will lessen his pain, child. Just as time will allow your mother to pull herself together."

"I hope so, Eugenia." Vonnie sighed. "I'm hoping this move to San Francisco will help."

"I hate to see you go," Eugenia gathered up her belongings. "But you must do what you think is right. Now, if you don't need me anymore, I'll go see what can be done at the Schuyler house before I go home."

"You go along. I'll go up and tell Mother."

"Oh, I let that foolish dog of yours in the house. Nearly chewed off the back door wanting in."

Vonnie smiled at Eugenia's description of Suki which wasn't exactly affectionate. She was a dear little dog in spite of her excess amount of energy.

"I was going to take Beth's dress off the form, but I didn't know what you wanted to do with it."

"I'll take care of the remains."

"It's a shame. A cryin' shame that somebody has to be that spiteful."

"You think that's what it was? Someone jealous of Beth?"

"Why, of course. Don't you think? I mean, why would someone do such an awful thing if it wasn't jealousy? She was planning to marry one of the most sought after men in the county."

"I'd never considered that." Pressing her fingertip to her lip, Vonnie considered the implications. She had assumed the vandalism had something to do with the birds, but maybe not. "But who would be jealous of Beth and Adam?"

Who, except her? And every other single woman in the county. But Adam was available again.

"I'm sure I don't know, but you have to admit, it's a drastic thing to do. Well, I'm off. You're sure you'll be all right here?"

"I'll be fine. I've got Suki, remember?"

"That fool dog," Eugenia chuckled, walking to the door. "You be careful, child. What with dead birds, ruined dresses, rocks through the windows," she muttered. "What will be next?"

Yes. What would be next? Vonnie didn't want to speculate. She'd had enough surprises for the year.

Chapter Twenty-Two

✤

It was nearing dark when Adam rode into the Taylor farmyard. Handing the reins to Genaro, he took the stairs two at a time.

Vonnie answered the door.

"Hi."

"I guess you know about Audrey?"

"Yes, I'm on my way to pay my respects." Adam looked past her shoulder. "How did your mother take the news?"

"Hard. Five minutes later she was saying she didn't know how to tell Daddy."

His features sobered. "Is it true what I hear?"

"I don't know. What do you hear?"

"You've decided to sell to Tanner."

Leaning against the door, she wiped her hands on her

apron. "Mother and I are going to San Francisco at the end of the week."

"Permanently?" His eyes locked on hers.

Vonnie tried to keep her heart cold and detached. "Permanently."

"Why?"

"Why not?"

"Is this about you and me, or about your mother?"

"All three."

"What about your business?"

"I'll start a new one in California."

His voice dropped, but his eyes never left hers. "Did your father ever talk about the jewels that started the feud?"

"Jewels?" She frowned. "Nothing other than that they were dirty money. Something he wanted nothing of."

"You're sure?"

"Of course I'm sure. Why?"

"We need to talk. Privately. Later. After I've paid my respects to Franz."

"All right. Is something wrong?"

He gave her a dubious look. Well, she supposed *everything* was wrong.

"Are you going to the Schuylers' later?" he asked.

"Yes, I have a cake in the oven. I'll bring it over. Momma will want to be with Franz."

Their eyes met again.

"Don't go to San Francisco." The startling request hung heavy between them.

"Give me one reason why I shouldn't."

"I can't do that. Not until I find out what started this feud."

"Does it really matter?"

Silence. Then.

"We need to talk about that, too."

"Will talking change anything?"

"No, but it will get a lot off my conscience."

"You want me to purge your soul?" She laughed.

"I'm sorry, Vonnie. I'm doing the best I can. I took your rejection that morning to mean you had second thoughts, that you didn't love me. I was young too."

His eyes met hers and she saw the old Adam.

"I wouldn't let you go that easily today."

She had been too young and easily intimidated, afraid to tell the truth, fearing the look of betrayal in Teague's face.

Adam's eyes searched hers for an answer. She had none. Not one.

He shifted, looking away. "That afternoon I felt less of a man. To this day I blame myself for not standing up for us. Even more, I blame myself for not honoring sacred vows we spoke before the Lord. I let you down and I disappointed my Maker. We might have married in the middle of a road with a judge frying bacon for supper, but I loved you and I meant every vow I spoke—and I know you did too. I can't change the past. I can only hope to change the future." His gaze softened. "If you leave, that won't be possible. I'm trying my best to get to the bottom of this senseless feud and destroy it before it destroys other lives."

She sighed. "What good will it do to identify the source? We know that our fathers were involved in a heinous crime, one that changed their lives forever. Daddy took his sin to his grave. I believe God forgave him, but Teague never forgave himself. Nor do I believe that your father has forgiven himself. But if they refuse to tell us what happened, or happened when they rode away that day, how can we defuse this insane hatred? It's not possible. And now Daddy's dead."

"I spoke to El Johnson yesterday."

"And?"

"He told me the same vague generalities. A family was killed, jewels taken. El forced the pouch off on Teague, but then the pouch disappeared. I think Teague buried it, disposed of it—did something to it and it made P.K. even madder, but I can't prove it."

She shrugged, frustration building. They could talk about it until they were in their graves and nothing would change. She loved him too much to stay in Amarillo and fight this mess until there wasn't a breath of life left in her. She would not subject her children to the same heartbreak she'd endured. A new start. She had to concentrate on a new start, away from Potter County and the endless feud.

Closing the door a moment later, she sagged against the heavy wood, allowing tears to fall. Suddenly she flung the door open and shouted at Adam's retreating back.

"It wasn't entirely your fault! I allowed my father's feelings to sway me from honoring our vows. If I was old enough to know that I loved you with all my heart and soul—and I knew that clearly—I was old enough to leave Father and Mother and cling to my husband!"

Shifting, Adam turned in his saddle. A slow grin spread across his features. "So what are you going to do about it?"

She quickly slammed the door before she blurted out her true wishes. The future was set. She was moving to San Francisco.

Clearing the table later, she carried the empty frosting bowl to the sink. A fresh chocolate-fudge nut cake sat waiting to be delivered to the Schuylers'. Cammy was upstairs dressing. Vonnie could hear Suki barking as her mother moved around her room.

She wasn't sure if Cammy understood the significance of the visit they were about to make. It was hard to tell these days what she retained and what was lost in her confused state.

As she turned from the sink, a movement in the doorway caught her eye.

"Franz? Wha— My goodness!"

Franz stood there, viewing her paternally. "Why, Puddin'? Why didn't you leave?" Vonnie carefully laid the dish towel aside.

Tears trickled down the old man's cheeks. "You were always here, always coming to the cellar to see how I was doing, always checking on me. If you'd left me alone, I could have found them. Then, I could have bought Audrey's piano back and everything would have been good again."

"I don't understand." A cold chill raced through her. When he'd confronted her earlier, she'd supposed grief was causing him to be so distraught. Now, it seemed to be even more serious. She suddenly wanted him to leave.

"The jewels. I couldn't remember where I buried them." He held his head in both hands. "I've tried to remember where I buried them—even drew a map, but I can't find them. So many years have passed—my memory—I can't remember like I once did. Teague wanted no part of those jewels. He threw them away, but I saw where they landed. I got them later. I didn't want them, either, little one. They were blood money, but I took them because your daddy was so upset. Later, I thought, when the grief passed, we might feel differently, might need the money they'd bring. Times were hard. We had families to rear. So one day I buried the bag of jewels in Teague's cellar, knowing nobody would ever think to look there. But then…" He looked up, tears rolling from the corners of his eyes. "Then P.K. started to have financial troubles, and my Audrey's time was growing close. I decided to dig them up and sell them. I wanted Carolyn to sell me Audrey's old piano. She isn't a mean-spirited girl, and I knew she would eventually give over and sell if I offered enough. When I told P.K. what I wanted to do he agreed. He was surprised that I had the money, but so many years had passed… Said he could put the money to good use. What was done was done. We couldn't change a thing. And the money from the jewels could give Audrey a measure of happiness. She was innocent to the whole matter."

"P.K. agreed to let you dig up the jewels?"

Franz nodded. "Said the money could be put to good cause."

"But daddy never knew the jewels were buried in his cellar."

"No, he never knew. He'd have made me dispose of them, like he had."

"And the other men involved?"

Franz turned, confused, distant. "Other men? We didn't discuss…I can't find the jewels. I have to remember…"

Vonnie's stomach churned. P.K. would take blood money? To what avail, and for what good?

Adam. He would be hurt by this knowledge.

Franz's eyes glinted with madness. "All I needed was a little more time. They're here someplace. But Audrey left me, and now you've sold the ranch. Oh yes, I know about that. Tanner let it slip. Now it's too late. I'll never find them. I have to find them, don't you understand—" His head dropped. "It's too late. Audrey's gone."

"There are no jewels here, Franz." Adam's earlier visit raced through her mind. Jewels. Where were these mysterious jewels? In the cellar? Impossible.

"They're here. I buried them," Franz shouted.

He was ranting now. "Buried the jewels somewhere down there." He looked up plaintively.

Grief had driven him out of his mind, Vonnie realized, just as it had her mother. She searched her brain for a way to distract him and go for help.

"Franz, you're not thinking straight. Come sit down and—"

What was he talking about? His ramblings didn't make sense, but she had the awful feeling that his words were somehow connected with the strange things that had happened at the ranch recently.

"It was so long ago. No one will know, and Audrey can play again. She can play again."

His thoughts changed in a breath. Vonnie knew his mental state was becoming even more unstable.

"Audrey needs her piano. If she has her music, she'll get better. You'll see. She'll be her old self again. I need that piano. I must find the jewels."

Lunging forward, he caught Vonnie by the arm. Her cry was smothered by his free hand as he twisted her arm behind her back and propelled her out of the kitchen, toward the attic stairs. He was much stronger than Vonnie had imagined.

Forcing her up the stairway, he jerked her when she stumbled and pushed her past the second-floor bedrooms toward the attic workroom.

"Franz, no, let me go. You're not thinking straight. You don't know what you're doing!"

"I have no time. Audrey's waiting for me."

Pushing open the attic door, he shoved Vonnie inside. She stumbled to her knees, catching her hand on the edge of the sewing machine.

"Franz—"

"Hush," he hissed. "I must look for the jewels."

"Please," she tried again. "You don't know what you're doing. Please."

Softening, he reached out, briefly touching her hair. "My lovely baby girl. I would never, never hurt you. You'll be safe here. Franz will let no one hurt you."

He whirled and disappeared through the doorway before Vonnie could struggle to her feet. Reaching the door just as it slammed shut, she heard the ominous thunk of the heavy wooden bar dropping into place on the other side.

"Oh, please!" she whispered, resting her face against the rough wood. "Don't do this."

Only one window in a dormer across the east wall

allowed light in, and with the fast-approaching twilight it would be dark soon. And the window was painted shut. There was no way out. She shivered with apprehension. What did Franz intend to do? What if Cammy wandered downstairs? Would Franz hurt her?

Were there really gems hidden somewhere in the cellar?

If what Franz said was true, then the trouble between P.K. and Teague was a tragic misunderstanding. Adam's father believed Teague had willingly taken and used the jewels. Why were two close friends so stubborn they hadn't bothered to learn the truth?

Knowing she had to keep a clear head, she pulled herself to her feet and began to search for a way out.

"Got to search—" Franz mumbled as he made his way back down the narrow stairs. "Clive will sell the piano. I must hurry. I'm hurrying, Audrey, don't leave me."

Suki's bark startled him as he neared the bottom of the stairs.

"Go away. I have to look—"

Suki leaped up, greeting him enthusiastically. Franz lost his footing and slipped on the step, his feet flying out from beneath him.

Throwing out his arms to catch himself, he hit the burning oil lamp on the hall table, sending it crashing to the floor. Oil splashed out on the carpet and onto the drapes at the parlor window.

Suki obediently ran over to lick his face.

There was a crackling sound as flames reached the drapes, the tongues of fire licking up the patterned material and inching their way across the flowered wallpaper.

Franz struggled to his feet. Confused, he turned in a circle. "Cammy!" he cried softly. "Vonnie? Puddin'? Audrey...Audrey..."

The parlor, fully consumed by flames now, poured smoke into the foyer. Fire licked at the edge of the Aubusson carpet and at the foyer wall as Franz crawled toward the stairs.

Adam was returning from the Schuylers' when he passed the entrance to the Flying Feather. He glanced toward the house.

Suki's yapping caught his attention. He pulled his horse to a standstill when he saw the dog loping toward him. It was unusual for her to be so far from the house. She was clearly agitated, barking with high-pitched yips.

"What's wrong, girl?"

The little dog danced up and down excitedly, barking.

"Suki," he greeted, getting off the horse.

The little dog ran to him, yapping, then reversed her direction and ran back toward home a few paces, then back to Adam.

"What is it?" he asked, peering into the distance. A thick cloud of black smoke rolled across the darkening sky.

Remounting, he rode hard up the lane. The east side of the house was engulfed in flames. The farmhands had formed a bucket line to fight the fire.

"Where's Vonnie?" Adam shouted.

"Not here!" Roel shouted back.

"Where is she?"

Confusion drowned out the reply.

Spotting Franz's carriage, Adam ran to check on the nervous horses tied to a post near the barn. "Where's Franz?"

he yelled. No one had seen him. And he hadn't been at his house when Adam called to pay his respect.

"Anyone in there?" Adam asked, stepping from one to another. Neighbors had begun to arrive and passed buckets of water down the line. "Where's Cammy?"

No one seemed to know.

Turning, Adam ran back to Roel. "Are you sure there's no one in the house? Did anyone go in?"

"We do not know, Señor Baldwin. We only saw the smoke a few moments ago. We are trying to douse the fire."

Dashing to the back porch, Adam kicked in the door.

"Señor Baldwin!" Roel shouted.

Shielding his face from the heat, Adam dropped to his knees and felt his way through the dense smoke.

"Vonnie! Cammy!"

He tied a hanky across his nose and mouth, and bending low, he fought his way to the stairs. At the top of the first landing, he tripped over Franz's sprawled body.

Pressing his fingers to the old man's neck, he frowned. No pulse.

Adam fought his way to Vonnie's bedroom and kicked open the door. Finding it empty, he continued to the end of the hall, where he knew Teague and Cammy had shared a room. There, he found a confused Cammy huddled at the side of the bed. She cried out.

"Teague, I'm glad you're here. The smoke scares me," she whimpered.

"I'm going to carry you out," Adam said gently.

When she hesitated, he swung her into his arms and headed back to the stairs.

Upright now, smoke burned his eyes and his lungs nearly burst from lack of oxygen. He stumbled downstairs and out onto the porch with Cammy in his arms.

More neighbors had arrived in buggies to join the bucket brigade.

"Son!" P.K. yelled. Joey took Cammy from Adam's arms and Pat helped him off the porch.

P.K.'s expression tightened. "Have you lost your mind?"

"Franz—" Adam choked. "Franz is in there."

"Franz?" P.K. started into the burning house.

Gripping his father by the shoulder, Adam said. "He's gone, Dad. Leave him be."

Stunned, P.K. turned to look at him. A great sadness touched his eyes.

"There was nothing I could do. Smoke, or maybe even a heart attack from shock."

Squeezing P.K.'s shoulder, Adam headed to the side yard where several women were hovering over Cammy.

"Adam," Beth cried. She rushed to meet him. "You could have died in there—"

"Beth, what are you doing here?"

"We heard the Taylor house was on fire. Naturally, Daddy wanted to help—"

Adam turned back to Cammy. "Where's Vonnie? Was she in the house?"

"Why, I don't know. Maybe she went to Audrey's. She was baking a cake."

Panic filled Adam's voice. "Think, Cammy, where was she when you last saw her? She was getting ready to take you to Franz Schuyler's. Was she downstairs?"

Suki nipped at Adam's boot, jumping up and down, up and down. It was unnatural, even for her, to be so aggressive.

Darting toward the burning house, she darted back again, yipping a high-pitched bark.

"Get back, Suki!" Pat shouted.

"Suki!" Joey yelled when the dog tangled in his feet. She darted back to the burning house.

"The dog's nuts!"

"No, she's not." Adam's eyes suddenly glimpsed movement at the attic window. He realized what the dog was trying to tell him.

"Vonnie's in there."

Those close by turned at his words, and before he could be stopped, he charged back into the house.

The flames licked high, the heat too intense now to enter the back. He raced around the house and, with the help of four men, broke down the front door. Fire had not reached the kitchen or front hall. Pulling the handkerchief back across his face, he squinted against the gray, choking smoke and crept on his knees until he reached the stairs.

Leaping quickly, he grabbed the railing and pulled himself up and over it, swinging onto the second-floor landing.

He raced up the attic stairs and threw his shoulder against the door.

"Vonnie!" he shouted. The fire's roar engulfed his words.

Kicking the door, he fought to gain entrance. He groped the bar and finally dislodged the barrier. The door gave way.

"Vonnie?" he thundered. The room was a roaring inferno. Rolls of tulle, yards of colorful ribbon, bolts of elegant lace, spools of delicate thread blazed out of control.

In the far corner, a sewing form draped with pieces of fabric, the pattern still pinned in place, hoisted hot flames to the low ceiling.

Above the flaming holocaust he heard a weak cry.

"Vonnie!"

"I'm here," a faint cry answered.

Dropping to his stomach, Adam crawled across the floor, groping for her. His hand finally found hers. Grasping her tightly, he held on to the hand that he had taken a vow to "love until death do us part."

"Adam," she choked, wrapping her arms around his neck.

Lifting her into his arms, he carried her to the door but was forced back by orange flames licking halfway up the steps.

"I'm going to try the window," he yelled.

Her arms tightened. "It's stuck…won't open."

Backing into the workroom, he fought his way along the back wall through the billowing smoke.

He used a chair to break the window; the flames multiplied, turning the room into a fiery cavern.

He pushed her through to the eaves and shouted for her to hold on as he crawled out beside her.

A roar went up from the crowd that had gathered below to watch and wait, anxiety written on every face.

Pulling Vonnie into his arms, he held her. Burying his hands in her hair, he looked down into her smoke-smudged face. He whispered in a husky, choked voice, "Little one, you make me nervous."

Laying her hand gently across his cheek, she turned her head and coughed. "It seems I'll do anything to get your attention."

Chapter Twenty-Three

❧

Friends and neighbors hovered close as Adam carried Vonnie to the backyard. He laid her on the ground and knelt beside her until she gradually oriented her senses.

"I…I'm all right," she said. "Momma—?"

"She's safe. Neighbors are looking after her."

"Franz?"

Adam shook his head.

"Adam, it was Franz. Franz was behind all the ugly things that have been happening," she whispered. "Apparently Audrey's illness was slowly driving him insane. He thought he'd hid jewels in the cellar. In his troubled mind, he thought that if he could find the jewels he could buy Audrey's piano back. That's why he was constantly down in the cellar. He wasn't cleaning. He was searching.

"It goes deeper than that. Daddy threw the jewels away,

but later Franz came back for them. Franz says he buried them in our cellar thinking no one would think to look there. But poor Franz forgot where he buried them. He's dug and searched for weeks, and can't find them."

"Why would he want them now?"

"Because, in his confused state he thought he could buy back Audrey's piano. Carolyn won't ever sell, but Franz thought that it was just a matter of offering more money." Vonnie broke off. "And P.K.—"

"My father what?"

"Franz told P.K. what he planned to do, and that he wanted to split the money between the two of them. He thought so many years had passed that P.K. might now accept the money. Your father agreed, said he could put it to good use."

Adam shook his head, pain flooding his features. "I can't believe P.K. would take blood money."

"Maybe he needed it badly. There's rumor he's having financial problems." She looked away, unwilling to pry into his business.

"The rumors are true, but P.K. would never take blood money. Never."

"Unless he thought his reasons were valid."

"I can't imagine him taking it for any reason."

Vonnie turned to stare at the licking flames. The Flying Feather, her home, was no more. "Well, the jewels are supposedly buried deep in the cellar."

"And that's where they'll stay. No one but you, me, Franz and P.K. know about the jewels. Franz is gone and P.K. will never tell anyone about them. I can promise you that."

Someday he might tell her the lengths he'd gone to to

learn the story behind the endless feud, to make it possible for there to be a Vonnie and Adam, but not tonight. "I don't know many things, but I do know my father and his ethics. He's stubborn and has his share of faults, but he deals fairly."

A low rumble turned all heads to the flames. A great roar suddenly went up, bringing a stunned cry from the spectators.

The house collapsed in a shower of sparks. Smoke billowed and debris shot upward, then dropped. Neighbors scurried to stomp tiny wildfires, leaving small black circles dotting the yard.

"The birds!" she cried suddenly.

"They're taken care of," Adam said. "Genaro and Roel moved them to safety."

Vonnie put her face in her hands. "Oh, Adam," she sobbed. "Andrew threw a rock through my window."

"Andrew? You saw him?"

Andrew stepped from the shadows. "She's right, I did, but I can explain." He glanced at Adam, then back at Vonnie's questioning look.

"I saw you and Adam when he was mending fence by the pond. He was leading you on, playing you for a fool. I knew about the strange things happening here, and I didn't want you to get hurt. I was afraid you wouldn't leave the ranch."

"So you broke my window?"

"I threw that rock through the window to scare you into leaving. I thought it would be best for everyone if you were away from here…away from Adam."

"Andrew." She reached for his hand.

"I'm sorry. It wasn't the best way. I see that now." His eyes switched to Adam. "I guess I've been wrong about a lot of things."

He stopped when they saw P.K. approaching.

Sparing Vonnie a glance, P.K. inquired gruffly. "Are you all right?"

"Shaken, but greatly indebted to Adam," she said. It was the first time in her life P.K. Baldwin had ever addressed her personally.

Drawing Vonnie to his side, Adam said quietly. "You're coming home with me."

"Adam, I can't." She watched P.K., walking away looking old and beaten.

"Don't argue." Taking her arm, Adam turned to his brother. "Andrew, will you see that Cammy is taken to the house immediately?"

Adam caught up with P.K. as he crossed the foyer and headed for the study. "Dad, can I have a word with you?"

P.K. grunted. "Save it until morning."

Adam stepped in front of the double-paneled door. His eyes met his father's. "It can't wait until morning."

Grumbling, P.K. pushed past him and entered the room. Adam followed, closing the door behind him. P.K. moved to stoke the low-burning fire, refusing to look up.

"Is it true that Franz buried the jewels in the Taylor cellar."

"What jewels?" P.K. stirred the fire.

"No more games, Dad."

Jabbing a log, P.K. kept silent. Tension was so thick Adam felt he could slice it. But he was not leaving the room until P.K. admitted the missing ingredient in the longstanding feud. If he didn't, the grudge would never cease.

"Dad," he repeated.

"All right!" P.K. flung the poker into the embers. His anger dissipated as quickly as it had flared. "Franz buried the jewels in Teague's basement. I didn't know about it until recently."

"But you were willing to accept a share of the profit. Why? Why now, when you refused thirty-three years ago?"

"I didn't want that money, never wanted that money." He turned tired eyes on him. "I never wanted that money. Will that day never fade? Will I take that hour to the grave with me?"

"Teague and Franz did."

Adam couldn't remember his father ever looking so beaten. P.K. moved to a chair and sat down, burying his face in his hands. "What do you want to know?"

Adam crossed the floor, kneeling beside his father. "You've taught me to honor, love and respect God. You shaped me into a man, yet all I can remember of my childhood is the hatred you had for Teague Taylor. I know the story behind the jewels, and how they were acquired. I want to know the real reason you hated Teague so bitterly and he you. You don't bear the same hatred toward El Johnson or Franz."

"He disappointed me. I thought he was a better man than that."

"Than what? To take something that was forced on him?"

"I wouldn't have taken them."

"You did take them. By association. The four of you rode away with those jewels that day. Four of you, Dad. Does it matter if you did or did not want them? Teague may have carried them, but you were all guilty."

"No." P.K. shook his head. "I'm a man of God. I would not have done that."

"Teague was a man of God, too, and Franz loved the Lord. El was the one who ransacked the wagon, why not hate El?"

"El Johnson meant nothing to me—never saw him more than a couple of times on the battlefield. He moved on. I am not responsible for El Johnson."

"But you were responsible for Teague." Slowly light dawned. Teague was different, even from Franz. P.K. had loved Teague.

Openly weeping, P.K. admitted Adam's thoughts. "Teague was like a brother. I loved…that man. When he took those jewels it did something to me—filled me with a hot rage. He was a better man than that. I expected more from him."

"And apparently he expected more from you. You didn't trust his intentions." Over the years, the two men had allowed bitterness, pride and misunderstanding to destroy a once-sterling friendship. Both men had been too proud to back down. "Why didn't you go to Teague and ask why he did what he did?"

"I did—once. He told me to get off his property and never come back. I granted him his wish."

Adam rose and moved to the desk. "Teague was a proud

man. You knew that. If you accused him of being less than honorable, you wounded his pride. His reputation. His soul. If he had accused you of the same, would you have felt any differently?"

P.K. sat for a very long time, staring into the fire. Finally, he said, "No. I would have felt the same."

"So all along, the hatred has grown and spilled over into your children's lives and the feud amounts to little more than one man's expectations of another man." Adam shook his head. "Aren't you the one who taught me that man will let you down every time? Man is an imperfect creature. Did you forget your own lessons?"

"Apparently so."

"Well, it's over. Teague is dead, his wife and daughter burned out of their home. You know Vonnie and Cammy are moving to San Francisco?"

"I know."

Adam turned to face him. "How do you know?"

"I…heard."

"Then you know Vonnie's sold out to Tanner."

"So I understand."

Something wasn't right. Adam knew when P.K. was hedging, and right now that was exactly what he was doing. So he added casually, "I heard she got fleeced."

"Fleeced!" P.K. glanced up. "She did not get fleeced. She got a lot more for that land and those birds than they're worth!"

"How would you know?"

"I know because…" He snapped his mouth shut.

Adam lifted a brow. "Yes?" For a moment Adam thought

he was about to confess to buying the Flying Feather, but he couldn't have. P.K. was in deep financial trouble. Or was he? Would the money from those jewels accomplish what P.K. and Teague couldn't in life? A truce.

Suddenly it was as clear as a running spring: P.K. had agreed to accept Franz's offer of the money for no other reason than to save Teague's birds. A man like P.K. would accept such money for no other reason. He turned accusing eyes on his father. P.K. stiffened. "Oh all right! I'd hoped I'd never have to tell you, but I'm buying those stupid feathered nuisances!"

"Through Tanner?"

"Through Tanner. I was supposed to have the money to him by the end of the week and nobody would know I was the buyer." Defeat bent the old man's shoulders. "Now I can't buy the land or the birds. The jewels will never be found."

Adam tried to digest this news. P.K. had planned to buy the Flying Feather—to accept blood money, to save a dear friend and sworn enemy. He shook his head to clear the thought. Man was crazy. How did God deal with idiotic humans? Yet every man had his weakness; every family had its secret.

"What will happen to Teague's family now?" P.K. asked.

Clearing his throat, Adam sat down behind the desk. He picked up a pencil and tapped the end on the polished wood, took a deep breath and said, "While we're on the subject, there's something I should have told you years ago."

"Oh?" P.K. lifted his head.

* * *

Alma turned down the wick on the hall lamp, jumping as if she'd been shot when she heard P.K. boom, "You what?"

Shaking her head, the housekeeper scurried up the stairway.

Alma fussed over the two women, ordering bathwater heated, providing warm gowns for Cammy and Vonnie, and supplying a light supper for them all. She was a whirlwind of activity, accepting nothing but complete compliance with her mothering.

Vonnie stood at her bedroom window and stared out at the darkness. How strange it felt to be under the Baldwins' roof. It seemed it had been her due all along. The lamplight reflected her silhouette, and she smiled. The robe Alma loaned her was so large it fell off her shoulders.

She was working a tangle out of her freshly washed hair when Adam knocked and then entered.

"Has Alma taken good care of you?"

"She has been the proverbial mother hen."

His hair was still wet from his bath. He was wearing a blue shirt and matching trousers. A large white bandage covered the back of one hand.

Vonnie was acutely aware, when he came to stand behind her, of the smell of soap clinging pleasantly to his skin.

"What about you?" he asked softly.

"I'm wondering why your father allowed us to be here, considering his feelings toward all Taylors."

Removing the comb from her fingers, he drew it gently through the tangles in her hair. She closed her eyes, drinking in the moment.

"Perhaps he saw the truth today. What happened all those years ago is no longer relevant. It was a tragic mistake, but it should not have stood between four friends. P.K. realizes that now."

He pulled the comb through her hair, creating an ebony curtain down her back.

"What about the jewels?"

"They're gone. They don't exist anymore as far as I'm concerned."

"I'm glad."

He laid the comb aside, smoothing the hair from her face with gentle hands. Weariness overtook her, and she leaned against him.

"Tired?"

"Very tired."

Adam suddenly turned her into his arms, holding her tightly. Years fell away. He was seventeen; she was fifteen. And they were in love.

"I was scared, so scared, when I saw the house on fire," he whispered into her hair. "I thought I had lost you again."

Stepping back, his gaze searched hers. Then he slowly lowered his head, his mouth inches from hers.

"Forgive me. I've wanted to do this for so long."

His hands cupped her face gently as she responded to his kiss with long-denied emotion. He abruptly broke the embrace, turned and left the room, closing the door behind him.

Sinking onto the bed, Vonnie touched her fingertips to her lips, where his taste remained. She would have cried but she was too empty to cry anymore.

Chapter Twenty-Four

❧

After breakfast, Vonnie wandered out to the veranda early the next morning. The air was brisk but hinted of spring. She noticed P.K. wrapped warmly, basking in the sunshine.

"Sit down," he said, indicating a wicker chair.

"I don't want to disturb you. I'm waiting for Mother to get dressed. We're going out to the Flying Feather to see what we might salvage."

White teeth flashed in a rare smile. "Sit down. You know me well enough to know that I am never polite."

She acquiesced. The two sat in shared silence, watching the sun creep across the frozen countryside. She was struck by the strong resemblance between father and son. In another thirty years Adam would look like this, still ruggedly masculine and in command.

"Your father was a good man."

"He was," she agreed, relaxing for the first time. "I'm sorry you harbored such deep distrust for each other. You are both good men."

His focus grew distant. "The past no longer matters. Don't know what happened to Franz. Must have gone out of his mind when Audrey passed."

"He wanted so desperately to return her piano."

Silence, then.

"Do you love my boy?"

The question took her by surprise. She searched for an answer. Which one of his boys? But then he was a wise old owl. He knew perfectly well she would know to which son he referred. Did she dare speak her heart? Of course she did. She was tired of games. "With all my heart."

Silence settled over the veranda once more. A peacefulness surrounded them, like a lull after a horrific storm.

"Don't think that I'm too old to remember what it was like to be young and in love."

"You were able to marry the woman you loved," she gently reminded him.

"Yes. I was. Wind's picking up, child," he said after a while. "You're going to catch a chill. Go inside and have Alma fix you breakfast."

Rising, Vonnie prepared to do as he said. "Forgive yourself, P.K." She smiled. "I have forgiven you."

He nodded. "I'm working on it."

She left him sitting on the porch, rubbing the right leg stretched out in front of him. She had once thought of him as evil. Now she saw him as a tired old man.

"Did you know about the jewels, Momma?" Vonnie stood

looking at the smoldering house remains, wondering how life had so quickly gotten out of hand. Nothing much was left of Teague Taylor's homestead, or his earthly life. A wife who could no longer function, a daughter who had no idea where to turn except to the Lord. And a smoking pile of worthless rubble. It was true what they said: you enter the world with nothing but your soul, and you leave it the same way.

The birds appeared unaffected by the previous night's turbulent events. They wandered around the pens, thrusting their necks high above the wire as if searching for a reason for the destruction.

Cammy huddled against the chilly wind, her eyes red and swollen from crying. The past months had taken an irreversible toll on her mother. Vonnie knew she would never again be the rosy-cheeked, bright-eyed woman of years past.

"I didn't want to know."

Vonnie turned to look directly at her. "But you did know the jewels were in the cellar?"

Her mother nodded. "I suspected—no, I knew Franz buried the jewels in the cellar. I came upon him quite unexpectedly that day. It wasn't often I went down there, but you were gone and Teague was with the birds. I needed a jar of tomatoes for the stew. I found Franz digging a hole and I asked why."

"And he told you?"

"No, not the truth, but I saw the pouch. Teague had awakened many a night sweating, shouting. He'd described the pouch to me before. I recognized it immediately. I didn't know why Franz would have it, but I didn't ask."

"And you didn't confront Franz?"

"His behavior worried me, so I pretended I believed his explanation that he was burying old coins for safe keeping."

Poor Momma. She had carried the secret as long as the men.

Cammy's tone dropped to a whisper. "Teague never suspected—that's the important thing to remember. Your father never knew those jewels were mere feet from where he slept every night. Had he known…"

The women turned at the sound of hoofbeats. Sheriff Tanner rode up, his heavy bulk a familiar sight.

"Miz Cammy. Miss Vonnie."

"Sheriff," Vonnie acknowledged.

"Right sorry about the fire." He removed his hat, fingering it. "I'm even more regretful to bring more bad news."

"More?" Her heart sank. How could there possibly be more?

"Seems your buyer's gotten cold feet. He's backing out of the deal."

Oddly enough, the news did little to disconcert her. Rather it brought a rush of sweet relief, though she was solely dependent upon God for where she and her mother would sleep that night. Giving up the ranch and the birds was hard; at the moment, she wasn't sure she could have given them to a complete stranger.

"Know you must be upset," Tanner mumbled.

"Everything happens for a reason." She turned, her eyes meeting his straightforwardly. "Thank you for riding out."

The sheriff nodded. "You and your mother going to be okay?"

Vonnie reached for Cammy's hand. "We're going to make it—through the grace of God. We're survivors."

And she knew they would make it. God had seen her through losing Adam, then watching the only man she would ever love announce his engagement to another woman, watching that man battle with pride—right and wrong—and ultimately break the engagement. Family death, vile pranks to run her off her land, fire and now this. She was back to square one. But He wouldn't abandon her now, or ever.

Still an onerous duty lay before her. She didn't want to leave for San Francisco without a buyer, someone who would love the land as much as she and her father had. She had to humble herself, go to Adam and accept his earlier offer to purchase the Flying Feather shortly after Teague's death. She bit her lower lip, dreading the prospect. The house was gone, but a Baldwin would be more interested in the land. The birds were an asset, a worrisome one to be disposed of quickly.

Adam glanced up when a tap sounded at the door. "Yes."

"Adam?"

A devious smile shaped the corners of his mouth. He checked his pocket watch. By his calculations, she was nearly on time. Tanner would have made his announcement and she was now running back here with singed tail feathers to invite him to buy the Flying Feather. It would be a good many years before he told her the name of the former buyer, P.K. Baldwin, and why he had mysteriously backed out of the deal. Adam had been surprised how easily P.K. had agreed to back out, to let Adam have his way for once. Unfortunately for Vonnie, he planned to let her stew in her own juice for a while. He grinned.

"May I come in? I need to speak to you."

He got up and went to the door to greet her. Her cheeks were wind kissed, her hair blown from her cold and blustery ride. She spared him a brief glance when she brushed past him.

"I'm sorry to bother you, but something unfortunate has come up."

"More unfortunate than your house burning to the ground?"

She shook her head, unbuttoning her cloak. "It seems like bad luck has struck again."

"Oh?" He motioned for her to take a seat, debating on how much rope to allow her to hang herself.

Adam, be merciful, as God is merciful to you. An old saying of Alma's rang in his head.

Vonnie sat down. "My buyer has backed out."

Seating himself behind the desk, Adam reached for the coffee carafe. He glanced up, silently inviting her to join him. She declined.

"Backed out, huh? That has got to be upsetting." She would never want for anything. He, through God's grace, would personally see to that. Dad had been unpredictably calm about the news of his brief marriage—after the initial outburst. He'd come around. When Adam asked him to withdraw his offer to buy the Flying Feather, so that he, Adam, could propose to Vonnie a second time, P.K. had accepted the news with awkwardness but no restrictions. It would take some getting used to, but P.K. would eventually accept the idea of Baldwin/Taylor blood running through his grandbabies' veins.

"Yes." She interrupted his musings. "I was wondering…I mean Momma and I are leaving shortly and I was—" She sprang out of the chair and started to pace in front of the desk.

He leaned back, crossing his hands across his trim middle. *Tell her, Baldwin*…just not yet. She'd put him through a lot the past seven years. What's a little humble pie compared to seven years of pain?

"Wondering?" he inquired.

She whirled and faced him, planting her hands on the edge of the desk. "You can have my land and birds if you still want them."

He pretended to be floored. He dropped his jaw, widened his eyes. "Really?"

She nodded. "It's yours if you still want it—you did offer to buy it," she reminded.

His right hand came to his temple. "Did I? Wasn't that months ago?"

"Yes, but it's still the same land and birds."

"Oh, birds, I remember those birds quite well."

She drew a deep breath and held it. "Then you'll buy?"

"Hmm." He cupped his chin. "Buy the Flying Feather? Well, I guess I might be interested."

She visibly wilted. "Thank you. I don't want to leave until I'm sure the land is in good hands."

"You think Taylor land going to a Baldwin will rest your mind?"

"I know that you love this land, this county, as much as I do. Yes, I will feel better knowing you have it, Adam."

He shrugged. "Okay. When are you leaving?"

"Saturday."

"Three days. That doesn't allow much time."

She turned and ran her hand along the low row of books lining the shelves. The books had always fascinated her, even as a young woman. Adam grinned. They would be hers now.

"You'll have the money by then?"

"Of course." He leaned back in the chair. "Do you want cash?"

"Cash is preferable."

"All right. I'll have twenty thousand cash—"

She turned abruptly. "Twenty thousand?"

He frowned. "You had another price in mind?"

"Thirty thousand! That's what Tanner's buyer was offering."

"Well, now, I'm not Tanner's buyer, am I?" He grinned and reached for his coffee. "And unless I miss my guess, it's a buyer's market."

Her upper lip formed a stubborn pout. "Then I'm not selling."

The smugness in his tone was clearly getting to her. *Baldwin, you're going to pay dearly for this.* But right now, the temptation to tease her was worth whatever price she'd inflict.

"Then I'm not buying." He took a sip from the cup.

She spun back around to face the books, and he knew that she was about to blow. *How dare he?* she must be thinking. Just because he had her over a barrel he thought he could steal her blind?

He approached her from behind, leaning in, his mouth close to her ear. Her unique scent, fresh air, a hint of lemon, teased his senses and he closed his eyes and silently praised God. She was where she ought to be—here with him, soon to be in his arms and in his heart forever.

"Think about it, sweetheart. Why should I buy your land when I'm going to get it for free?"

Her breath caught and her body tensed. For the briefest of moments, she struggled against his embrace and then gave in. She nestled more deeply in the warmth of his arms. "What makes you think I would *give* you my land, Adam Baldwin?"

"I believe it's called community property?"

He slowly turned her to face him, allowing a moment for the meaning of his words to sink in. She lifted her eyes to meet his. Could she see his love—his absolute devotion and surrender? Her eyes clouded with uncertainty.

"Do I need to make myself clearer?"

"Yes," she whispered. "I'd like that very much, since Momma and I planned to leave in three short...very short days."

He shook his head, sobering. "You're not going anywhere in three days or three years. Cammy can visit her sisters—or you can go too for a couple of weeks, but then you're coming home."

"Home being...?" she prodded softly.

He kissed her then, leaving no doubt as to his intent. Lifting his head a good long moment later, he prompted, "Doesn't Ecclesiastes say there is a time for every season? A time to love, a time to laugh..."

She nodded, echoing the familiar verse:

A time for birth and a time for death,
A time to plant and another to reap,
A time to kill and a time to heal,
A time to destroy and a time to build,
A time to laugh and a time to cry—

Their lips met, lingered. Moments later he whispered, "It's finally our time to love, Miss Taylor." He tilted her face upward, looking deep into the depths of her tear-filled eyes. "Nothing on this earth will ever separate us again. Will you marry me, again, Vonnie? This time I promise it will be forever."

She nodded through a veil of mist.

"Till death do us part?"

"In sickness and in health," she vowed.

He drew her closer, holding her tightly. "Forsaking all others?"

"Oh, Adam." She wound her arms around his neck and held him so forcefully he knew he would never slip her grasp. "Yes! Yes."

Forsaking all others—that was a given this time.

"There is one thing," she murmured, between snatches of adoring kisses.

"Vonnie, please, no more problems. We've had enough of those—"

She laid a finger across his lips to still him. "No problems, but I'd like us both to go to Beth and tell her what's happened—why there is and always will be an irreversible bond between us."

Smiling, he kissed the tip of her finger. "That would be a good place to start our new life."

She grinned and kissed him again. "How do you feel about Friday?"

"To talk to Beth? What's wrong with today?"

"No, you goose." She looped her arms more tightly around his neck. "To get married."

QUESTIONS FOR DISCUSSION

1. What made you want to read this book? Did it live up to your expectations? Why or why not?

2. Discuss the book's structure. Does the author weave an intricate trail? How does this affect the story and your appreciation of the book? How do you think it might have been different if another character were telling the story?

3. Have each member read his or her favorite passage out loud. How does this particular passage relate to the story as a whole? What does it reveal about the characters?

4. Talk about the time period in which the story is set. How well does the author convey the era? Do you have a sense of whether or not the author remains true to the events, social structures and political events of the time period?

5. What new details about the time period did you learn from the book—what aspects of the time period were a surprise? How do people today use stories from the past to guide them?

6. Is it difficult to keep our own, modern-day experiences from influencing the reading of a historical tale? What tools do you use to put yourself in the place of the historical characters?

7. Forgiveness posed a problem for Vonnie, particularly since she couldn't discuss her trials with her friends. What advice would you have given someone in her situation?

8. The memory of a person's first romance is a lasting one—how can an early romance affect one's life today?

9. How would you have resolved the misunderstanding between Vonnie and Adam? How did their youth affect the outcome?

10. The family feud in this story had far-reaching effects for everyone. What Bible verses would you suggest to give comfort to a family in such a crisis?

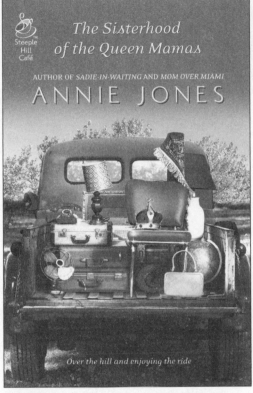

It was a story to put Hideaway, Missouri,
in the national headlines...

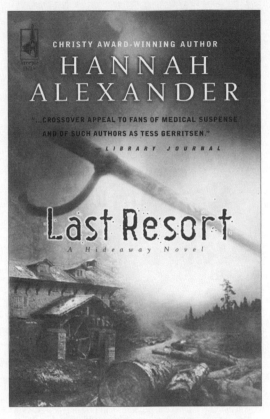

A missing child...
A woman in crisis...
A man of faith...

Don't miss this next exciting
novel in the Hideaway series.

In stores now.
Visit your local bookseller.

From *USA TODAY* bestselling author Deborah Bedford comes BLESSING

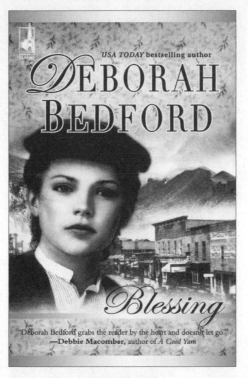

The secret beneath Uley Kirkland's cap and mining togs is unsuspected in 1880s Tin Cup, Colorado. She longs to hide the clothing of deception and be honest about her feelings for handsome stranger Aaron Brown. But while Uley dreams of being fitted for a wedding gown, the man she loves is being fitted for a hangman's noose, and she is the inadvertent cause of his troubles.

The truth will set them free, and Uley will do whatever it takes to save Aaron's life—even risk her own.

Steeple Hill®

"I'm going to have a baby.
Me. Ann.
My dad is not gonna understand."

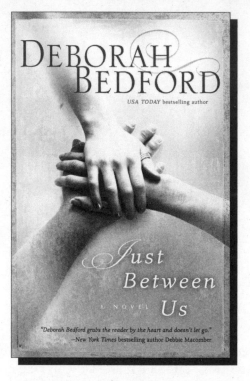

Fourteen-year-old Ann was right. Richard Small didn't understand.
Nor did he know how he and his daughter could have grown so far
apart. Missing his late wife more than ever, he arranged for a Big Sister
to offer Ann the support he felt incapable of giving himself.

What he didn't count on was falling in love with
the wonderful woman he brought into Ann's life
or that the very person who brought them together
could ultimately keep them apart....

Visit your local bookseller.

Steeple
Hill®